MARY KING'S PLAGUE and OTHER TALES OF WOE

Brian Kaufman

DARK SILO PRESS

P.O. Box 1712
Fort Collins, Colorado
80522-1712

Mary King's Plague and Other Tales of Woe
A Dark Silo Press Book / July 2016
Copyright 2016 / Dark Silo Press / All rights
reserved

Cover Illustration: Jack Larson
Cover Design: Brent Hauseman
Cover Layout: Jessica Babb-Raymundo

To Harold Kaufman,
My North Star

Introduction: Dark Fiction and the Novella

My first encounter with the novella form was Stephen King's fine collection of novellas, *Different Seasons* (1990). Back then, the novella had no real place in the publishing world. In fact, King referred to the form as an "anarchy-ridden banana republic," having little or no opportunity for publication outside of pulp genre magazines.

Today, the advent of the eBook offers a new market for novella writers, allowing small, independent presses (and self-publishing authors) a chance to sell their work through Amazon and Barnes & Noble. In fact, two of the novellas presented here are available as stand-alone *Dark Silo* eBooks.

But there's nothing like a physical book, is there? (Feel free to bend the binding, dog-ear the pages or sniff the ink.) Because these stories are comparatively short, I could pack a trio of them into one volume.

My interest in novellas, though, goes beyond economy. I write dark fiction. Why does the novella serve my genre so effectively? I believe that question has two answers.

The first advantage involves familiarity with the form. The modern horror audience is more likely to watch a movie than read a book. Should the film enthusiast pick up a novella, they discover a form analogous to the movie script with its standard three-act structure. The scope and pacing are similar. Novellas give the reader what they expect in terms of storytelling.

Second, horror requires a suspension of disbelief. As a friend recently explained (with the straight-faced air of someone imparting great wisdom), "You know, zombies don't really exist." The same pronouncement might also apply to werewolves, vampires and Bigfoot.

Let's skirt the opportunities for debate offered by political zombies, corporate vampires and the elusive Sasquatch. Instead, suppose you've settled into a comfortable chair and, drink in hand, start to read a horror novel. The crafted atmosphere and mysterious plot conspire with the nightfall to give you a genuine chill.

Then, you put down the book.

A day has passed. In the interim, your car broke down on the morning drive to work. You could hear something wrong with the engine because your radio was off—no news is good news. At work, rumored layoffs have everyone on edge. Your son calls, wanting advice. His girlfriend is pregnant. Driving home, in a rental car you can't afford, you discover a mailbox full of bills, expected and otherwise. One of the neighborhood kids has dumped trash on your lawn. Your spouse isn't speaking to you. You are unable to muster the energy to discover why. Instead, you long to escape to that book you put down.

But you can't get back into the story. Vampires suddenly strike you as silly. And perhaps they are (especially the sparkly ones). When the real world interrupts (or bludgeons) you, the joys of a dark escape can be lost.

A novella, on the other hand, can be devoured in a single night—an uninterrupted dance with the macabre, with the attending chills and catharsis.

The three stories included here are each meant to be read in a single sitting. Think of this book as a three-night tour through some of my dark places. For those interested among you, I included some story notes to answer questions like, "Where do you get your ideas?" and "What the hell is wrong with you?"

One last note. If you're reading this, you're a throwback. Statistics say that 80 percent of American households will not buy a book this year. Yet here you are, book in hand. Thank you.

Brian Kaufman   July 2016

MARY KING'S PLAGUE

I grew up reading comic books. My favorite was Superman, but I also had a taste for the horror tales from EC Comics. Having completed a fairly serious project, I was in the mood for a palate-cleanser. I wanted to write a comic book story with nothing more ambitious in mind than excitement and mayhem.

A coworker of mine asked if I'd ever heard of Mary King's Close, which he claimed to be genuinely haunted. Google verified that Mary King's was a real place. In the 17th century, Edinburgh had been built around a single street running east and west, bracketed on either side by a series of neighborhoods called "wynds" or "closes," each consisting of branching lanes and alleyways.

In 1644, a plague rocked the city. Stories of ghosts and hauntings began almost immediately after. Some of these accounts were chronicled in Satan's Invisible World Discovered (1685), *a contemporary account of the supernatural.*

The modern Mary King's Close offers tours, complete with actors playing historical roles. Supernatural sightings persist. Over the past decade, a number of paranormal investigators have studied the Close. Yvette Fielding of the BBC stated that Mary King's was "one of the most terrifying places" she'd ever examined.

Fine setting for a horror tale. I began my comic book.

But a story can be hijacked by its characters. As I wrote, I found myself exploring serious themes like betrayal, redemption and forgiveness. I strayed into theological concerns, like the resurrection of the flesh and the promise of eternal life, and a zombie plague seemed an apt metaphor for the kind of betrayal I envisioned. Scene by scene, my characters began to weigh in on the subject, offering argument and counterargument, and suddenly, my comic book became serious business.

I

Sheriff John MacThomas walked the narrow
streets without fear, arms swinging, his beloved
Claymore broadsword tapping against the side of his
leg. He splashed through the raw sewage, sending
rats scurrying to darker corners. Such was his
reputation for courage and virtue that the residents
above would avoid dumping their piss pots when he
passed, waiting for more opportune targets. Ahead,
one poor rascal shrank as a sudden rain of urine hit
him, accompanied by the call, "*Gardy Loo.*" But none
dared dash their sewage on Sheriff John.

He paused at the west entrance to the
Close—a stack of tenements on the south side of
Edinburgh. The rabble called it Mary King's Close
after the matron of the place. And it was Mary King
he'd come to see this morning.

A particularly loathsome rat barred his way.
The thing appeared to have been abused by a cat or
dog. Bite marks left the fur coated in brown scabs.
The rat trembled but did not retreat when John
stamped his foot, splattering piss. Instead, the rat
wobbled forward, teeth gnashing, as if to take a bite
from John's leather boots.

He gave the rat a tentative kick, hoping to send it scurrying. It lurched forward, locking onto the toe leather.

John bent down, curious. The rat's eyes were clouded over with pus-yellow rheum. He kicked again, harder this time. The rat held on like a washerwoman with a shilling in her grip.

John scowled and pulled his sword free. He was loath to coat the blade in the foul creature's blood, but he wanted the rat off his boot. He stabbed forward, skewering the rat. It shuddered, but did not let go. Using the sword as a lever, he pried it loose, and pitched it against the foundation stones. The rat landed with a thud and lay still.

The sword was coated in brown mucous. John lifted his leg and wiped the blade clean on the sole of his boot. "Filthy vermin."

He squared his shoulders and took a deep breath. Once he stepped through the door to the Close, he would not care to breathe. The potent mix of human commerce, waste and spoiled food made a perfume for the devil—not fit for a freeman's nose.

Mary King's small apartment lay a short distance to the left. Mud and rat excrement lined the dark alley. An ale vendor gave a single wave with his noxious wares before realizing he was in the presence of the sheriff. He lowered the offered bottle and his head, silent and shamed.

A crowd had gathered in front of Mary King's door to watch two men battle. They pushed each other in turn, shouting curses. The dispute seemed to be over a shirt—a poor rag not worth the trouble of a fight. One of the men was heftier, but he was much older as well. The younger man seemed to be getting the better of the sad battle.

"There now, what's this all about?" Onlookers gasped, realizing who addressed them. The two combatants took the gasp as a warning and turned to face the sheriff.

"He cannae ha' ma shirt," the older one said in a thick brogue, wiping a bare arm across his bloodied nose. He seemed ancient, perhaps fifty.

"It's mine then," the younger lad answered, lip trembling. Both men stood still, arms folded, gazes down in deference.

Mary King's door opened, slowly at first, then thrown wide at the sight of Sheriff John. Mary herself stepped into the muck, pointing at the two men. "Have you come to take these two reprobates away?"

"I'm no criminal," the old man protested. "I was a craftsman!"

"A craftsman no more," said the lad. "A thief now."

"It's nae stealin' to take your own shirt!"

"Your own shirt is on your back! Or did ye take that as well?"

The crowd began to offer opinions, pressing forward. John held up a hand to silence them. Better they should stand still. Four years earlier, a crowd like this had suddenly turned on a magistrate, dragging him through the streets. Soldiers seized several of the instigators, but the court would not find them guilty.

John cleared his throat to seal the silence. Then, in a voice that welled up from his ankles and burst out like a bugle horn, he addressed the crowd. "These two would destroy the peace over this rag of a shirt? Where is the crime? Is it the theft of scrap cloth, or is it the filthie sin of disturbance?"

The crowd murmured its approval. Having been eager for the diversion of a fight, they seemed equally eager for harsh judgement.

The older man appeared to be weeping, though it was difficult to know for sure in the dim light. The Close was stacked high—seven stories tall—as if to press the alleys into the earth like underground caverns. "But it's ma shirt, sir!"

John drew his sword. "If I hear another word about the shirt, I'll run you both through with the same thrust and let you die on the blade, cod-to-bum." The old man shivered and stepped to the side, away from his younger antagonist.

Mary King folded her arms, a look of triumph on her face. "I'll not have your brawl at my doorstep." She turned to the crowd. "And this is no meeting place. Go on now! Be about your business!"

Slowly, like a snake uncoiling, the crowd began to disperse. John felt a brief moment of dissatisfaction—it was his place to dismiss the mob, not Mary King's. But he had need of her assistance, so he let her play the Burgess without comment. The two men who'd fought left, the younger man having tucked the shirt of contention under his arm; no further complaint from either, apparently well satisfied to still be breathing.

When the crowd had receded into the tenement, John turned to Mary. "I'll have a word with your servant girl," he said. "Send her out here and be about your own business."

Mary King bowed gracelessly and slipped behind her door. In a few moments she returned, dragging her servant girl by the arm. The girl was not bone-thin as the other girls in the Close. She had a fair shape with the hips and bosom of a grown woman, despite her lack of years. Her hair was dark, shoulder length with curls and only a hint of red. Her large eyes were her most striking feature. Even in the dim light, hints of brown and green did battle, the signs of a secret storm, or so John imagined. She was only seventeen years of age. This he knew, because he had been a friend of her family for more than a decade.

"Have you come for me at last?" she asked, nearly breathless with anticipation.

"No Lass, not yet." He closed in on her, but in her disappointment, she turned away. He stepped back, no expression on his face.

After long moments of silence, she met his gaze. "I'm sorry," she said, her voice hushed with regret. "I had hopes that we would be together."

"And we will," he promised, his voice cold with impatience. "But your situation is delicate."

"Perhaps I should just go home."

He shrugged. "If that's what you want, you're sure to be disappointed. Your family will not have you now."

Her shoulders fell, and he thought that perhaps her sigh would become a sob if he didn't comfort her. Still, she needed to understand her situation. "It's a hard truth you face. There's no forgiveness when a girl leaves her home unmarried."

"But you told me—"

He held up his sword hand. "If you've grown tired of waiting for me, so be it. But the position you've secured here is the best that you can hope for outside of an advantageous marriage. And without the blessing and assistance of your family, you will have no such marriage."

"But it's taking so long!"

"Perhaps your patience is gone." His voice was no different now than it had been when he'd addressed the crowd and the two brawlers.

A look of horror crossed her face. "Are you dismissing me?"

Her trembling voice touched him, and he allowed his anger to recede. "Come then, Lainie. Don't be stupid." He held his arms out, and she pitched herself into his embrace.

"Do you still love me, then?"

"Of course I do," he promised, petting her dark hair. "We were meant to be together. Even your name foretells our union. But you must not press me. I will wait until the time is right. Then and then only will we be together."

She nodded, face pressed against his leather vest.

"Until then," he said, easing her hand downward. "I've missed you."

"We are in the street, sir."

Her alarmed whisper did not dissuade him. "I am John MacThomas, Sheriff of Edinburgh. None will dare say a word against me. You are safe." He bent down and kissed her neck. She drew a sharp breath and closed her eyes, almost purring.

When he'd been placated, he hustled the girl back into Mary King's room with promises of love and an early return. Then he strode out of the stinking tenement, refreshed. The bright sunlight gave him pause. He glanced down and away, eyes watering, surprised to find that the rat he'd skewered was gone. *Some cat has itself a filthie meal,* he decided.

* * * * *

When her sheriff was gone, Lainie let herself back into Mary King's home. The landlord was a hard woman, wanting the work of two servants for the trouble of one. Lainie did not care to draw her attention, having been with John for nearly half an hour, her chores unfinished.

Lainie crept along the wall and knelt by the scrub bucket and brush. Her knees screamed at the rough touch of the stone floor. It was the finest floor in the Close, but she was not accustomed to hard work. She'd been born to privilege.

As she scrubbed, her raw fingertips scraping against the flagstones, she cursed her stupidity. She'd traded her virtue for a promise. "We can't be together if you stay in your father's house," the sheriff had told her. "I will find a place for you where we can be together. And when the time is right, I will come for you and make you my wife."

But John's idea of a "place" was a servant's position in a tenement, and he'd not come for her. Instead, he'd come for his own comfort.

"I see you've returned, your highness," Mary King said. Her voice was like a rasp on a blade.

"I'm sorry," Lainie said. "The sheriff wanted—"

"I know what he wanted. Now I'll tell ye what I want. I will have this place clean. You sleep here well enough, do ye not? Ye can keep cleaning after supper, if ye get supper at all."

Lainie nodded.

"I cannae hear a nod."

"Yes, ma'am."

How had it come to this? She scrubbed harder. The bristles of the brush were worn to the quick, and the wooden handle scraped the floor, as did her knuckles. The stench of lye soap stung her eyes. *It's my fault,* she thought. *Men are hollow vessels full of piss and promises. If he hadn't kissed me, hadn't touched me, I'd be in my father's house, in my own room.*

Then she remembered the sheriff's touch, his kiss, and her body went limp at the thought. Were all men so skilled at love? She felt a tingling at the thought of his body, and she stopped scrubbing altogether.

Mary King clapped her hands together. "Have you lost your senses?" the landlady demanded. "Are you bewitched?"

Lainie bent to the task again, pursing her lips to keep them from trembling. *Am I?* she wondered. *Am I bewitched?*

* * * * *

The winter sun set early, bringing on the cold wet air, freezing everything in the Close. The old man, bloodied and without his outer shirt, sat in a corner, his back pressed against the clapboard wall. *A fitting end for a shitepipe,* he sobbed, arms wrapped around his own shivering torso. He hoped the thief who'd taken his shirt would enjoy the lice.

As the evening turned to night, the man's melancholy deepened. Though he hadn't eaten in two days, he'd gladly have traded a meal for a bottle. An ale vendor passed by, selling his piss, but the old man didn't have a single coin to his name, and the ale sold in the Close might kill.

Then again, even death might be a blessing.

The moon rose through the stink and vapor, into the crystal night. The old man could see a sliver of light between the support slats that kept the tenement from tumbling in on itself. Morning would not come for many hours. The old man's damp legs were numb.

Curse the night, he whispered. As if in answer, a wet, black rat the size of a kitten crawled toward his ankle, visible in the thin moonbeams. "Go on then," he growled, kicking at the thing.

The rat stopped and fell over on its side. Matted blood on the rat's torso spoke of a terrible bite or piercing wound. The damage was surely mortal. *Lucky beast. The Lord looks after the rats and leaves men to suffer.*

The old man nudged the rat with the toe of his boot. The beast snapped, sinking its teeth through the poor leather, drawing blood. The old man howled, more from the indignity than from pain. He tried to rise, to stomp the thing to pulp, but his legs were stiff and bloodless. He fell back into the muck. The rat released the boot and scurried up his leg—slow for vermin, but faster than the old man by solid measure. He cried out in surprise and disgust as the thing bit the inside of his thigh. He thrashed, pulling at the rat's body, but the vermin sank its teeth deep into his flesh, and he couldn't bear to tear the thing free.

As the pain rose to a hot pitch, he jerked the rat free. In shock, the old man realized that the thing had severed a chunk of his flesh, and lay in the frozen mud chewing its prize.

He tried to stand again, hindered by the pain and the hole in his thigh. He pulled himself upright, bracing himself with one hand against the tenement wall. The rat's jaw worked furiously. The old man raised one leg and came down hard on the rat's back. The spine gave way with a satisfying crunch. The old man stood, huffing clouds of vapor into the night air.

Serves the damned thing well, he thought. He bent forward, staring at the dead vermin by the light of the winter moon. The hole in his thigh poured blood down his pant leg and into his boot. Feeling faint, he closed his eyes for just a moment, and when he opened them, he was on his side in the muck. He'd fallen. In front of his face, the rat lay pasted to the ice, a pile of pulp and fur. Only the head was intact, jaw opening and closing in steady rhythm, still chewing its meal.

* * * * *

McCarty scowled at the entrance to the tenement. "I cannae see the sense in it," he repeated. "They should wall the place shut and let the vermin take it."

Balfour Gunn, deputy to the sheriff, put a hand on McCarty's shoulder. "Ye find good and bad here. Some of the vendors are honest. And this won't take long. We make ourselves known and then we leave."

"The stank will stick tae our boots for days."

Gunn laughed. "We were here yesterday, and you smell like a baby."

McCarty shook his shaggy head, his brown hair tossed with the violence of the motion. "There's no reason for it. Ye cannae explain it."

"Of course I could explain. But I will not." Gunn tightened his grip on the dirk strapped to his right side. The sheriff carried a baskethilt Claymore—a beautiful weapon given to him in England. A simple dirk was good enough for Gunn. He could carve a scoundrel with the one-sided blade as easily as cutting a meat pie. The thought cheered him, and he stepped through the entrance to Mary King's Close.

The sheriff sent his deputies into the Close nearly every day. To most he said, "I'll not let the cutpurses and ale-sellers settle in as if they were farmers. You will walk the Close, and you will roust those vermin. The Close belongs to the city, not to the unfreedmen."

But to Balfour Gunn, his most trusted deputy, the sheriff said, "I'll not have those ne'er-do-wells touching my Lainie. You watch over her. And watch what she does as well. If someone thinks to have a way with her, dissuade them. And then report to me."

Gunn knew McCarty was right. They'd been assigned a fool's errand. But it was the sheriff that had tasked them with the duty, and he would do the sheriff's bidding without question.

Lainie seldom left Mary King's residence. That tough old raven got every possible moment's work from her charge. He'd only seen the girl a few times—once when the matron of the tenement sent her to fetch a bottle from the winery to the north of the Close. He'd followed her, at a safe distance, making a show of staring at everything around him, as if inspecting every road stone in Edinburgh, ready to disapprove. Secretly, his gaze locked on the girl. She had a round bottom that rocked from side to side when she walked, tossing the hem of her dress in a most pleasant way. Her dark hair flared in the sun, casting bits of red and orange like a sputtering flame. The sheriff was a lucky man.

But this time, there was no girl to be seen. There was only the Close, a cluster of plasterboard buildings, stacked six and seven stories tall, jammed together so the window ledge of one led to a bedroom in another. Timbers groaned and floors sagged, braced by a meager patchwork of logs and scrap iron, threatening to tumble inward with each gust of wind.

McCarty covered his mouth with the top of his tunic. "Crivens, the stink!"

"Breathe through your mouth," Gunn said, staring at the door that led to Mary King's apartment.

McCarty looked at Gunn, and then looked at the door. "That's where the cow lives then?"

Gunn turned to stare at his companion, a look of anger searing his features, as if McCarty committed blasphemy. "John MacThomas is the sheriff. He's your benefactor. And he's my friend."

"And I'm yours."

"So ye are. But friend or no, I'll not listen to your insults."

"I said nothing against the sheriff. He's a good man."

"You spoke against the girl," Balfour said, standing taller, his hand straying to the side, dangerously close to the hilt of the dirk.

"Are you taken with her too then?" McCarty asked, his voice so soft that Gunn was placated. The two men stared into each other's eyes, long enough for an understanding to pass.

McCarty broke the gaze first. "Let's show these numpties a glimpse of Scottish steel." He tapped the hilt of his dirk for emphasis.

Gunn snorted. "A waste that would be. I'd sooner clean a fish than run one of these bastards." McCarty laughed, and it did Balfour good to see his friend so genial, since McCarty had been so recently close to visiting his ancestors. Gunn would not allow an insult to Lainie. The thought of her name made him tremble. The thought of her figure made him weak.

As McCarty rhapsodized about his aversion to the tenement residents, Gunn turned with a sudden lurch and marched into the Close, leaving his friend to scramble at his heels, still yapping.

They wandered the dark alleys, past chimney stones and plastered walls, bits of broken wares and the discarded souls that peopled the Close. Men pressed back into the shadows as the two deputies passed. Women stepped into the feeble beams of light that filtered down to the muddy ground, bosoms thrust forward, dirty faces and teeth fixed in the rictus of the whoring poor, selling one hunger for another. Gunn felt cheapened by their presence. They would eat him alive if they could—he was certain of it.

"By the by," McCarty said at length. "I was nae calling the girl a cow. I meant the woman. Mary King. The old hag has cud stains on her chin."

Gunn nodded. The old woman was indeed ugly.

After rousting the ale salesman, poor old baw bag, they doubled back to the entrance, sliding down another alley. At first, Gunn led the way with certainty, but when the alley jogged left, he stopped. For a moment, they were lost. "We're goosed," McCarty moaned.

"This place is larger than it looks from the outside." Gunn scratched his chin and then pointed. "There. That way." Twenty steps down the path, he stopped again. "Bloody hell, I think we're going the wrong way."

"Let's keep going. We'll either run into a wall or a door."

Gunn shook his head. "No, I'm sure we're going the wrong way. He turned back, hand on the hilt of his dirk. They passed several residents along the way, but did not ask for directions. Gunn's gait was strong and purposeful, and the residents stepped aside so the two could pass. Having given the appearance of someone who knew his destination, the west entrance appeared to Gunn as if by magic.

Task accomplished, they stepped to the exit when the sound of shouts and screams pulled them back in. The afternoon sun hung overhead, sending a single shaft of light between the buildings like a shuttered lantern. The beam fell on a scene of great horror, and they found themselves stopped, weapons drawn, wondering just what sort of people lived and died in the Close.

An old man, crusted with scabs, stood over a screaming young boy who'd fallen into the mud. The old man had the boy's arm pressed to his lips. A coat of red covered the man's face and the boy's arm.

A crowd had gathered nearby, but no one seemed willing to help the boy. One old woman darted forward and then scurried away again, as if to draw the old man's attention. She squealed like a butchered hog as she splashed back and forth in the mud. Two men tugged at a crossbeam, trying to dislodge it. Gunn realized they wanted the wood for a weapon. The thought spurred him into action.

He drew his dirk and strode forward, point extended. "Let the lad go." The old man ignored the order, fixing his teeth into the boy's wrist. The young victim, limbs as thin as wheel spokes, thrashed and screamed for his mother.

The boy partially shielded the old sot, but Gunn thrust forward anyway, the blade of the dirk sinking into the old man's face just below the nose. Instead of letting go, the man ground down harder, teeth to bone, and the boy's cries reached a new pitch.

"What's this?" Gunn grunted, pulling at the dirk. The blade came free with a sucking sound. The old man staggered for a moment, then lunged at him, mouth open. Gunn backed away, dirk extended. Why didn't the scabby bastard fall? He took two, then four steps back. The old man followed, arms extended.

McCarty leapt forward, screaming, swinging his cudgel, bashing the short club into the old man's chest. Gunn could hear the crack of broken ribs. The scoundrel stumbled back, nearly falling. Then, righting himself, the man came on again. McCarty stared in disbelief, club dropping to his side. The old man's stagger-steps ended in a sudden lunge, face-first into McCarty.

Gunn jumped into the fray again, stabbing forward with the dirk. This time his thrust caught the old man in the forehead, sinking six inches into the skull. Close in, Gunn could smell rot and clay on the man's skin. The creature stopped, shuddered once and then dropped.

The boy's wailing pierced a brief moment of silence. The woman scurried forward, kissing his little wounded arm, mumbling words of small comfort.

Gunn stepped forward and kicked the old man's corpse. It didn't move. He kicked again, harder.

"He bit me," McCarty said. His voice was flat as soda bread.

Gunn's hand shook as he tried to push the dirk back into its scabbard. After a sideways glance at McCarty, Gunn stooped down and addressed the young boy directly. "You have a bite. Let your Mother dress the wound. And stop crying."

The boy sobbed.

"Boy! Stop it now!"

The boy swallowed his cry, leaving only a sniffle. He nudged at his wound—a bite on his right arm that exposed raw muscle and a small patch of bone.

"Let your mother clean the wound," Balfour repeated, standing up again. The old woman pressed close, covering the boy with her arms.

"I've been bit." McCarty touched his fingertips to his left cheek. A tiny flap of skin ran thick with dark blood.

"I know," Gunn said. "We'll report to the sheriff. Then we'll see tae your wound."

* * * * *

Balfour Gunn ran his hand across the apothecary's shelf. Dust. The glass vials staged in a row at the window were covered in candle grime and dirt, obscuring the contents. Gunn shook his head. How does he know which bottle is which? The old man stood hunched over McCarty, a disc of glass at his fingertips, staring at the injured deputy.

Sheriff MacThomas stood over the old apothecary, his arms folded, a sour frown on his face. He tapped his boot impatiently while the examination continued.

McCarty sat slumped to the side, a sick, open-mouthed expression on his face, as if he were about to spill his lunch on the floor of the shop. His skin, naturally pale, had gone bone white. His lips seemed nearly gray in the waning light. By contrast, the bite on his cheek had festered, flaring with reds and purples. The apothecary, leaning just inches from McCarty's face, moved in even closer, touching the wound with a fingertip. McCarty flinched.

"Aye." The apothecary placed the glass disc against the wound.

"Tha' hurts!" McCarty moaned.

"It's necessary. The glass enlarges the wound, allowing me to see secrets I might otherwise fail to see." He peered through the lens. "Clearly a bite."

"I said so!" McCarty said. "A bite from a dead man!"

The apothecary scowled. "If unfreedmen were easy to kill, Edinburgh wouldn't be overrun. Rats and unfreedmen. They'll outlive us all."

"He was dead. I bashed him in the chest with a cudgel."

Sheriff MacThomas turned to Balfour. "What happened to this dead man?"

Gunn shrugged. "I ran my dirk through his forehead."

"And did he die then?"

Gunn nodded.

"Well then." Sheriff John turned back to the apothecary. "The old shite had enough left to bite my man. What do you think of the wound?"

"Difficult to say."

"You've been staring at it for half an hour!"

The apothecary tapped the wound again, sending McCarty into a spasm. "Highly unusual. Inflamed in so short a time. If your man didn't tell me otherwise, I'd say this wound happened yesterday or the day before, and that the lack of care caused it to rankle." He pointed, his finger close enough to elicit a flinch from McCarty. "Look at the edges of the tear," the apothecary continued. "Swelling and pus. The wound looks flyblown."

McCarty moaned, slumping to the side. Before anyone could catch him, he pitched from the chair and struck his head on the apothecary's stone floor.

The sheriff shouted at the old man while Balfour Gunn bent to grab the fallen man by the shoulders and right him. After struggling for a moment, he stopped and leaned in closer.

"Cold cocked?" MacThomas asked.

Gunn held a hand to McCarty's lips for a moment. "Maybe worse."

The apothecary darted in, putting two fingers to the fallen deputy's neck. He moved his fingertips twice, searching, then shook his head. "Your friend is dead."

"What?" Sheriff MacThomas pushed the apothecary aside and put his hand over McCarty's mouth. Gunn sat back, flat on the floor, furrows creasing his brow.

"Are you certain the wound occurred as you said?" The apothecary's face betrayed his disbelief. "If so, then some poison is the likely cause—"

"You said the wound showed *lack of care*," MacThomas growled. "Yet you kept us waiting for an hour. Then you spent another hour staring at the hole in his cheek."

"I have other patients, and some of them are men of great substance."

MacThomas snorted and stood up, hand on the hilt of his broadsword. "Yes, and I know all of them. They defer to me in matters of safety—"

"Could the man's teeth be poisoned?" Gunn asked.

The apothecary pointed at McCarty's corpse. "His teeth are rough, but no worse than most."

"No, you bastart! I mean the old man in the Close. Could his teeth have been poisoned?"

The apothecary studied his shelves for a moment, his gaze racing over the rows of bottles. "The poison would have to be applied to the teeth, and that would result in ingestion—"

"The death of one of my men is a matter of safety." The sheriff rattled his sword in the scabbard for emphasis.

Balfour Gunn and the apothecary looked at each other, and then looked at the sheriff.

McCarty stirred suddenly, his foot lashing out, kicking the apothecary in the ankle. The deputy sat up, stiff and pale, a dazed expression on his face. The angry tear on his cheek wept a cloudy yellow fluid, giving his face its only color.

"What idiocy is this?" the sheriff demanded. "Can you not tell a living man from a dead one?"

Gunn knelt to comfort his friend, but McCarty brushed him away, his mouth opening and closing like a fish on a river bank. Balfour grabbed McCarty's shoulders. McCarty bowed his head and began biting the air, just inches from Gunn's grip.

"The man would injure me!" Gunn cried. "McCarty! McCarty!"

Sheriff MacThomas knocked McCarty back to the floor, pinning him with a boot. He pointed at the apothecary. "We need to tie him up. Have you any rope?"

"Rope?"

"Yes, rope. What do you tie off splints with, man? Rope."

"Twine." The apothecary shuffled to a back room while MacThomas and Gunn struggled with the thrashing form beneath them.

"What's in that room?" MacThomas called.

The apothecary reappeared with twine in hand. "Supplies. A bed."

"Good," the sheriff said. "We're putting McCarty back there. If we tie him up, he'll be less likely to hurt himself."

"The room is not for patients—"

"It is now." The sheriff's lips pressed together; set firm like bricks. The apothecary did not argue.

Moving McCarty and tying him down took several long minutes. The injured deputy managed to catch the sleeve of the sheriff's blouse with his teeth, tearing material. "The loon would eat my arm if he had the chance!"

"Be careful," the apothecary called from the doorway. "His bite may have caused his present state. A bite from him may do the same to you."

MacThomas finished tying off McCarty's hands and scowled at the apothecary.

"Quite the kerfuffle," the apothecary said, a hopeful smile on his face.

McCarty's legs tied, Gunn sat back flat on the floor and sighed. McCarty continued to thrash, though the twine knots kept him from moving much. A pink froth bubbled from his lips. Blood.

"You'll watch over him," the sheriff ordered. "I'll be back to check on him." The apothecary started to speak, but MacThomas cut him off. "Just do it."

"Aye." The apothecary's expression crumpled.

As Gunn stood, a disheveled boy, covered in grime—an oobit—stepped into the shop, calling for the sheriff.

"What do you want, boy?" The sheriff signaled the boy to come no closer. "What's your message?"

"Dunnachie wants to see you. At your convenience." The boy breathed hard, as if he'd been running.

"The good merchant sent you?"

"Aye."

"Does he know how casually you use his name?"

The boy blanched and looked down, stammering. "I were running hard, sir."

"Walk then, and use your head," the sheriff advised.

* * * * *

MacThomas gripped Dunnachie's hand and held it for a moment. The sheriff bowed to no man but the King, but Dunnachie was the closest thing to a father MacThomas had ever known.

Aengus Dunnachie was a textile merchant, one of the wealthiest men in Edinburgh. The sheriff owed his position to Dunnachie's kind patronage. In fact, the merchant had shepherded MacThomas through much of the sheriff's career, financing two years in London as the capstone to the best education a Scotsman could obtain. In return, MacThomas looked after family interests, a task the sheriff took more seriously than the merchant knew.

Despite the merchant's wealth and prestige, MacThomas felt at ease in his presence, certain of the older man's affections. For a decade, he'd been a guest in the great man's cottage and shared meals with the family. If the old man blathered on, MacThomas kept his tongue in his teeth. Like a son who chaffed to be his own man, MacThomas had differences with Dunnachie, but he kept them to himself. And because he seemed nothing if not dutiful, he was certain of his place in the great man's heart.

But upon being ushered into the great room of the Dunnachie cottage, a sudden fear gripped the sheriff. Dunnachie was not alone. Mary King sat to the side, her hands folded in her lap like a gentlewoman. Her face bore lines of concern, an expression that changed to sly amusement when she saw the sheriff's face.

"What's this, then?" MacThomas asked, certain that he knew the answer. The old cow had spilled the milk.

"Most troubling news," Dunnachie said, his voice soft and trembling. Something had shaken the man to his core.

MacThomas looked away. A blue pitcher rested on a stand against the far wall. While he stood still, his gaze fixed on the pitcher, his mind raced like a cat across a rooftop. What could he say? What excuse could he offer? Mary King shifted in her chair. Was she smiling? Did she not understand that her own situation would suffer immeasurably if the sheriff were to lose his position?

Dunnachie's wife entered the room, locking the others in temporary silence with her presence. She wore a floor-length dress, all lace and bright colors. Her hair was gray, but full and soft with curls. She stopped as she passed Dunnachie, reaching out to brush his hand with hers. He closed his eyes. A flicker of a smile passed his lips.

When she was gone, Dunnachie sat down heavily, exhaling in a sudden rush as if someone had punched him. He ran a hand across his age-spotted forehead, disturbing the gray strands that strayed from beneath his night cap. "I must ask you something."

MacThomas started to speak, but waited for the question instead. There was no use in serving a gallon when a pint would suffice.

Dunnachie closed his eyes. "I am mindful of all your efforts on your behalf."

MacThomas bit his lip.

"Now, I face the challenge of our time. Edinburgh dangles in the balance." He gestured to the matron of the Close. "Mary King has informed me of a most disturbing plague. I would scarcely give her account a moment's notice. But members of my guild have confirmed her story. No, they have enhanced, embellished the account until I wonder—do we face the end times? Tell me now, my son. What news of your deputy?"

MacThomas glanced at Mary King. She looked away. Then he turned back to Dunnachie. "The man was bitten. He is beset by some sort of madness."

"As if possessed?"

MacThomas nodded. The sheriff sat taller in his chair, ignoring Mary King as if she were not even in the room.

Dunnachie slumped further, thin limbs exposed beneath his dressing gown—legs as thin as the spindles of his chair. "I cannot allow the plague to spread."

"Agreed," MacThomas said. He made an effort to appear grave, but cheery relief spread to the corners of his mouth. The cow had kept her milk. So far.

"We cannae afford to be merciful." Brogue thickened Dunnachie's whisper.

MacThomas turned and pointed at Mary King. "It is time for men to make plans."

Dunnachie dismissed her with a wave.

Mary King stood, and then hesitated, as if she needed to say more. MacThomas silenced her with a glance. Face reddened with fluster, she followed a servant girl to the cottage door. When she was gone, MacThomas straightened his shoulders and held his head erect. "What would you have me do, Father?

* * * * *

Sheriff MacThomas was able to assemble his six remaining deputies, as well as a stonecutter, two masons, a blacksmith and twelve freemen; the latter dozen recruited from local taverns. By the time the necessary materials were commissioned, paid for by writs from Dunnachie himself, the sun was long down.

The great merchant had decided, against his better judgement, not to send for soldiers. MacThomas spoke eloquently for carrying out the plan quickly, without interference. Soldiers came with strings, and Dunnachie was not accustomed to being tethered. Nonetheless, the merchant might have sent for help if MacThomas had not convinced him that the Dunnachie's response to unusual occurrences demanded some degree of secrecy.

Balfour Gunn arrived with a cart full of stone, pulled a step at a time by a swaybacked horse that looked ready for the spit. Gunn went on foot, urging the rig forward. When he saw the sheriff, he hurried forward, dirk slapping against his thigh. "I came as quickly as this old beast would allow."

"What word on McCarty?"

Gunn shook his head. "He is past sense. He foams and snaps like a rabid dog."

MacThomas looked skyward. But for a few stars poking holes in the clouds, the night was an upended cauldron. "We must bend our backs. I'd hoped to have this settled before dusk."

"What is our charge?"

MacThomas pointed at the entrance to the Close. "We're to wall it up."

Gunn tilted his head.

"It's plague, man. It cannot be allowed to spread."

"Who will run food and water to the plague victims?" Gunn asked.

MacThomas shook his head. "The few must be sacrificed for the many."

Gunn's face twisted with apparent dismay. "That cannae be! We have always cared for the sick. The infected tie a handkerchief to their doors, and we bring them food and water! That is the way it's always been done!"

MacThomas glared at him, his voice dropping down to a low growl. "This is no ordinary plague. As you well know, having watched your friend McCarty descend into possession." He cleared his throat, and his voice returned to a kinder register. "I can only be grateful you weren't the one who was bitten."

Gunn shuddered, while MacThomas thought, *It's cold. Let this work be done quickly.*

Gunn stepped closer, in order to whisper. "What about Lainie?"

MacThomas nodded. "I would fetch her, but her father would have no exceptions."

"But he doesn't know his daughter is in there!"

MacThomas glared.

"You must rescue her!" Gunn's voice rose with the wind.

"I must attend to Dunnachie's whims," MacThomas snapped. "If the great man comes by to survey his handiwork, I must be here to greet him. That is my burden."

"Then let me fetch the girl."

MacThomas stared. Gunn had never spoken to him this way before. Gunn was a good man—a willing horse that would be worked to death. But the plague had surely unnerved him. "That was my intention. I did not expect you to take every back alley with your load of stone. Our time is short."

Gunn stood erect as if in salute. "Dismiss me now, then. And I will have her back here in moments."

MacThomas nodded. "Hurry then. The wall is already underway." Indeed, the freemen had formed a crude human chain, moving stones from hand-to-hand, stacking them near the Close's entrance. Masons with trowels set the first row of stone. The blacksmith worked at a brace of iron rods meant to shore up the wall from behind. The cutter and several of the deputies stood to the side, encouraging and berating the men, adding to their grunts and curses.

MacThomas watched as Gunn scurried to the entrance. The deputy pushed a mason aside and stepped over the row of stones. The mason bowed and backed away, his long white beard swaying as he moved.

* * * * *

Balfour Gunn took a dozen steps into the Close and stopped. A trick of the wind kept sound from penetrating from the outside. Instead, he heard the shrill chatter of a woman somewhere in front, unseen in the dark. Mary King's door was ahead and to the left. With light, he'd have had no difficulty finding his way. But he'd plunged headlong into the

Close without a torch to show the way. And he was loath to return without the girl.

Another few steps made matters seem worse. He could not see his hand in front of his face. He would have to creep, arm outstretched, reaching for the door that should be nearby. He turned back to reassure himself that the entrance was not yet blocked. Torches from outside the Close, burning behind the new masonry, shone like an arch-shaped beacon. He would be able to find his way back. Once he had the girl.

Cold air hung like wet fog. He inched forward, shivering. As his eyes adjusted, a sliver of moon revealed shadows. Soft gray shapes drifted past, soundlessly. In the daylight, Balfour Gunn did not believe in ghosts or daemons. He shivered again. Surely, the door was just ahead. Gunn forced his feet to move, each step a victory over his trembling heart.

His fingers brushed a wall. *Well, then,* he thought. The door would be either to the left or the right. And once he found the door, he'd have the girl. He moved to the left, his fingertips never leaving the rough wood. He counted his steps. *Nine. Ten.* He stopped. He retraced his steps to the right, and began counting again. When he reached six, he found the doorframe.

He pushed. A latch barred his way. He shouldered the door until the sound of splintering wood brought a brief smile. One last shove and he was inside. "Lainie?" he shouted. "Lainie?"

A clammy silence answered him. He called again, louder still. Somewhere in the Close, a man called back, "I'm here, ye spunkfarter." Laughter. Balfour Gunn growled. Why had he plunged into this stink hole without a torch? He called out one last time, spawning more laughter. No hint of movement from within the room.

The girl wasn't there. Which meant she was lost in the Close.

He would have to go back. He would get a torch, and return. He would find her. His resolve had not wavered. He would return for the sheriff, his friend. And for the girl, who must be frightened witless.

The entrance was a tiny gray arch in the distance. He took a few tentative steps, his hand out in front again.

Something warm and wet closed around the fingers of his outstretched hand. He stood frozen in place. He felt pressure, soft tissue clamping his fingers in place. The clouds that blocked the moon slipped past, letting dim light into the alley. His stomach dropped into his loins.

His fingers rested in the mouth of an old woman. She stood, toothless, gumming him.

Crying out, Gunn shoved her away with his free hand. She pitched back, dropping to the frozen mud like a bundle of kindling. Then the clouds crossed the moon's path again, leaving him blind.

II

The Close was a collection of buildings surrounded by a shared wall. The tenement had two entrances—one east and one west. "Seal the Close," Dunnachie had told him. "The plague cannae be allowed into the rest of the city." Containment was a simple matter. Two doors walled up with stone and mortar, and the danger would end.

Sheriff John MacThomas stood frowning.

Mulled wine and a fire, he thought. If the scuppered clods building the new masonry would hurry, he could be home, out of the cold. His deputies could guard the outer wall while he slept. But when he saw Dunnachie and the priest approach, MacThomas steeled himself for a long, cold night.

He stared at the priest with respect and no small amount of fear. Torchlight from behind the priest sparked and jumped like a fiery halo. His thin body swayed, a frailty belied by the stern black strength in his eyes. No torch could burn as hot as the priest's gaze. He saw everything. MacThomas scarcely dared to stand in front of the man.

MacThomas believed in God. What man did not? But he did not necessarily believe in priests. The pretense and hypocrisy, from the granting of indulgences to the opulent mode of living, left MacThomas feeling sardonic admiration.

But this priest was different. As rail thin as the poorest onlooker, a cruel judge of wealthy men and beggars alike. Powerful. Angry. He was as MacThomas imagined God to be—old, unyielding and unapproachable. And in the priest's eyes, MacThomas saw the futility of forgiveness and redemption. In short, the priest frightened him.

Stopping before the entrance, Dunnachie hovered near the priest, his arm extended in support. The priest touched the merchant's elbow every few moments, and then released his hold, as if anchoring himself to the merchant would be an unacceptable admission of weakness. Dunnachie stood at the ready, elbow stiff, his face expressionless.

"Your Eminence?" MacThomas asked at last.

The priest shifted his glance from the rows of stone that rose to seal the entrance to the Close to the sheriff. His mouth was a thin gash, turned down at the corners, trembling. He muttered softly. A prayer? A curse? MacThomas couldn't tell.

A crowd of onlookers had gathered. They were silent in the priest's presence.

"Can you tell me why we are walling up the poor of Edinburgh instead of tending to them?" The question was directed at MacThomas.

"That was the Dunnachie's decision." An easy answer.

The priest's eyes widened. "Do you disagree then?"

MacThomas bowed slightly. "That would not be my place. I am the right arm of the town elders. I am the sword of the church."

"But why are you erecting a wall? Who will run food and water for the afflicted? Who will offer them comfort for the soul?" The priest's voice showed no trace of brogue. Until a year ago, he'd served the Holy One in the northern part of Italy, a station that scoured all traces of his Edinburgh childhood from his voice. Instead, he spoke with the lilt and cadence of the Old World.

"Shall I leave a portal for supplies?" MacThomas asked. Dunnachie closed his eyes.

"No you shall not!" The priest's voice cut through the night air like a scythe.

MacThomas bowed again.

"Are you mindless, then?" The priest's voice had dropped, more menacing still.

"What would you have me say?" MacThomas glanced away, trying to avoid the priest's gaze, and was horrified to see Mary King sliding their way, one small step at a time. If the woman slithered any closer, she would be able to strike. MacThomas put a hand on the hilt of his Claymore. He could feel blood pounding in his temples.

"I would have you explain the necessity of that masonry."

MacThomas stepped back, panicking.

The priest held up a hand as if to stop the world. He closed his black eyes for just a moment, and then opened them, letting the darkness spill in. MacThomas shivered. Mary King took another step.

"I will tell you why." He took a breath, ready to speak.

One of the masons let out a shout. "It cannae be! It cannae be!" The other workers began to shout as well, and the sounds of panic seemed to infect the onlookers. A single figure spilled from the open space above the fresh stonework, striking the frozen ground headfirst. One of the workers hoisted a smaller piece of rock and pitched it into the void behind the wall. Another helped the prone figure to his feet. MacThomas could see the man in the flickering light. Gunn, his deputy.

MacThomas turned back. Mary King stood within an arm's reach of the priest.

MacThomas could not receive Gunn's report in the presence of Dunnachie and the priest. Nor could he leave the two men alone with Mary King. Yet he had to act.

He grabbed Mary King by the arm and dragged her away, shouting, "Do you see what you've done? This falls to you, wench. This falls to you!"

Dunnachie called out to him, but MacThomas was already halfway to the Close, dragging the old woman like a sack full of kittens. He continued to shout, grabbing Gunn with his free hand as he passed. "Where is she?" he hissed.

"I cannae find her!" Gunn's expression was stricken. He glanced past the sheriff. Dunnachie and the priest were surely following.

"The fates are against us, then. Say no more." Mary King tried to twist free, so MacThomas squeezed her arm, causing her to cry out. He put his face inches from hers. "Not a word, cunt."

"She's in there." Gunn hissed. "But I need light to find her."

Seconds remained. MacThomas put as much steel in his voice as he could manage. "Grab a torch and go then. Keep her safe. Say nothing." He shoved Gunn in the direction of the entrance. Mary King tried to pull free again, and MacThomas gave her another rough squeeze before letting her go.

"What has happened?" the priest demanded. He stood directly behind MacThomas, clutching Dunnachie's arm.

MacThomas did not have to answer. The stonemason ran toward the priest, babbling, "Deid! Deid! It cannae be!"

MacThomas grabbed the worker. "What are you saying, man?"

Despite the cold night air, the stonemason's face was covered in sweat, rivulets cutting a path through the rock dust on his cheeks. He hunched down, shrinking in the sheriff's grasp. "It's nae possible! The woman was deid! An arm gone missing, I tell you! And her walkin' and such like there were nothin' wrong! The De'il's at play! The De'il's come to Edinburgh!"

MacThomas was of a mind to slap the mason back to sense, but the priest seemed calmed by the outburst. "*That*," he proclaimed, "is why we must wall up the Close. The depths of Hell hath bubbled up like a boil, and we must seal it off, lest it spread."

MacThomas nodded in understanding and let the stonemason loose. The priest wanted the Close walled up. Why hadn't he just said so? He glanced back at the gathering crowd. They'd crept closer in order to listen. Now they murmured amongst themselves, nodding and genuflecting.

At the entrance, Balfour Gunn climbed back into the Close through the narrow gap between the stone wall and the top of the doorframe. A worker passed a torch through the opening after Gunn was inside.

"Where is that man going?" Dunnachie asked.

"He's making certain no one of importance is still in the Close." MacThomas turned without a pause. "It's cold, Father." It was not clear to either Dunnachie or the priest to whom the sheriff was speaking. "There's nothing to be gained by freezing old bones. Please let me attend to this tragedy on your behalf."

The two men stood silent. Mary King hovered, her cheeks puffed with the need to speak, as if her mouth were full of nails. MacThomas glared at her.

"Just so," the priest said.

Dunnachie was not so quick to leave. "Who would trap themselves in the Close after dark? Do you have reasons to risk that deputy?"

"Reasons of diligence," MacThomas replied. "But I must insist. The cold is oppressive. Allow me to complete my task."

Dunnachie persisted, his eyes on the men at the entrance, endeavoring to seal the door with the last rows of stone. "How will your man get out?"

"The rear entrance is not yet sealed," MacThomas promised. "More, I'll be at the new wall myself, listening for a signal."

"Why seal the entrance if you'll simply tear it down?"

"Diligence," MacThomas repeated. He had run out of lies. Lainie was gone, that much was certain. A horrible tragedy, yes, but there would be many deaths in the Close tonight. As for Gunn, the man was a loyal deputy. But one who knew too much—a millstone around the sheriff's neck. When the last row of stone went up, the problem would disappear.

Save for Mary King.

Dunnachie shook his head. "This is an odd business," he muttered. He turned to leave, the priest at his elbow.

MacThomas hurried to the entrance. "Come on, then!" he growled. "Finish this wall!" He felt a tug at his sleeve, an unacceptable breach of manners. Mary King! "All right then," she said. "I kept shut. Enough of your jobby! Wha' about ma things? I cannae lose ma things! Ye blackheart! Claw me, and I'll claw thee!"

"Your belongings are sealed up. You have your health."

"No. Take some men and torches in tae get ma things. It will take minutes. Minutes! Ma humble belongings are just paces away."

MacThomas shook his head as the old woman talked. She was a shrill, harping witch. A punch to the gob would seal her mouth well enough.

"Donnae shake yer head at me, Sheriff MacThomas. We both kin the why of it. A fine time ye had, with the merchant's bairn, eh? That's over. I wonder, what will the good man say when he hears that his sheriff has been playin' hide-the-cheb with his daughter?"

MacThomas tilted his head. He stared at the woman's face, twisted in anguish over the loss of her few, piteous belongings. Words slithered out of her mouth, leaving a trail of spittle. His head and his ears hurt. The woman was too much trouble.

He sprang forward and grabbed her by the neck and thigh, hoisting her like a sack of grain. Turning, he jammed her, face-first into the open space above the stonework. With only a single row left unmortered, MacThomas had to struggle to stuff the woman through the opening. She thrashed, shoulders turned, grabbing for a hold to keep herself outside the Close. She managed to hook an arm across the top of the arch, but MacThomas was strong and Mary was old. "No! No!" she barked, her voice like a twa-penny on slate. Her grip loosened, and MacThomas pitched her forward, a flap of skin and a thin trail of blood on the stonework as she tumbled inside.

"Seal the opening," MacThomas said. He stepped back and took a deep breath. Done. And for the best! He turned, bumping into the priest who stood directly behind him, his hot, black eyes seeing all, seeing everything.

* * * * *

The light of the torch was scant comfort for Balfour Gunn. Was the wind wailing in the building tops, or was the sound he heard suffering made incarnate? A gust raced through the alley, twisting his poor flame, threatening to extinguish it and leave him lost in this icy hell. He made his way back to Mary King's door, still open. He listened for the sound of steps, his hand wrapped around the hilt of his dirk. He tried to call out for the girl, but his voice refused. His knees went soft as churned butter.

Gunn thought of McCarty. What sort of plague turned men into wildcats? He'd looked into his friend's face in the back room of the apothecary. There was no understanding there—only teeth.

Gunn searched the inside of Mary King's hovel, already gutted by looters and thieves and left to ruin. Perhaps Lainie had been frightened away by a cutpurse. Would she have left the Close? If so, he was on a fool's errand. He held the torch aloft where shreds of cloth told a story of a fight over spoils. Shadows jumped and fell away to the dance of the flame. No hint of the girl—broken plates and torn linens and nothing else. Gunn glanced back to the open door, but found he could not move.

I cannae stand here like a post, he thought. He drew his dirk and pointed it at the open doorway. A figure stumbled in as if summoned by the blade.

"What huvv we here?" Gunn whispered. The hunched shape shuffled forward, step by sliding step into the orange glow of the torch. The man wore a simple tunic and trousers. No shoes. Lice-riddled hair covered his forehead and eyes. Gunn leveled the dirk to the man's approach, point to chest. The man paused for only a moment, then moved forward. The blade punched through the man's tunic and buried itself in soft, yielding flesh. Two steps more and the man raised his face, teeth gnashing. Gunn pushed with the dirk, sinking the blade to the hilt, but the man kept coming, mouth open, stinking like rat dung.

Gunn dared not release his grip on the dirk, so he pulled. The blade slipped out momentarily, then sank back in with the man's inexorable step. The man's mouth snapped shut to the sound of teeth breaking. Then open again, broken shards just inches away. Gunn leaned back and laid the torch against the man's cheek. Flesh popped, and the man's hair caught on fire. Gunn let go of the dirk and backed away.

As if confused, the barefoot man stood still, flames leaping up to the low ceiling of Mary King's hovel as his hair burned. Gunn watched in dismay as flames swallowed the man's face. His eyes popped from his sockets in a sudden gush, teeth still snapping. Then, hair gone to stink and smoke, the flames died.

The man stood still as if listening.

Gunn drew a ragged breath, and the burned man turned, lips peeled back by the flames, exposing teeth and blackened gums. "The de'il, by God," Gunn whispered, and at the sound of his voice, the burned man came toward him, bare feet scuffling through the broken plates.

Gunn held the torch in front, afraid to use it as a weapon lest he blunt the flame. He tried to back away, but found himself in a corner with just two steps. The burned man pushed forward, his face weeping ash and pus, mouth open again. Gunn grabbed for the hilt of his dirk and pulled, spinning away to avoid snapping teeth. The blade pulled free from the man's chest without a sound. Gunn swung the free blade at the man's neck, burying the blade halfway, and then pulled, jerking the weapon loose. The burned man came on, mouth gaping.

Gunn swung again, and this time the blade stuck. The man's head hung to the side. No blood. Gunn pushed him against the wall and pinned him with his boot. He pulled at the dirk once, twice, finally pulling the blade free. The man started forward again. Gunn swung the blade with all of his strength, cutting through the neck, leaving a stump. The head struck the ground and rolled away.

The body stood quivering for a moment, then tumbled to the ground, thrashing. After long moments, the body lay still. Gunn held the torch out to examine the head.

The mouth still worked, broken teeth clicking.

Gunn lurched away, dropping the torch. The flame sputtered, throwing beams of moving light like a swinging lantern, creating the illusion that the head was crawling. Gunn took a single, rasping breath and reached for the torch, afraid that the head would leap at him. Shaking, he wrapped his fingers around the bottom of the torch and lifted it up. The flame flared back to life.

"God's wounds!" The head's gaze followed the light of the torch. Gunn waved the torch from side to side. The head moved with the flame. "I'll be a bampot then," he whispered, rubbing his temple with the hilt of his dirk.

He wanted out of the Close. But if he returned without Lainie, the girl would die. That much was certain. *I am Balfour Gunn*, he thought. *I will find her.*

But in the end, it was the dimming of the torch that sent him back into the Close. The fire would not last forever. He had to find the girl and get out. He moved to the door, step by trembling step, dirk raised for a quick thrust.

It was the dirk that gave him away. The tip danced in the black air, a shudder that he tried and failed to still. He braced his back against the outer wall of Mary King's apartment to steady his nerves. Distant screams punctured the foul night. Gunn stared at tiny puffs of vapor, visible by the light of the torch—his shallow, rapid breathing made visible by the cold. "I am not a coward," he whispered. Unable to control his shaking, he lowered the dirk.

As the blade point dropped, a blurred shape leapt forward with a shriek, slamming him back against the wall. He yelped, and his bladder let loose, sending a stream of piss down his leg.

* * * * *

The priest knelt at the foot of his bed, hands on the straw mattress, lowering his knees to stone. Washerwoman's knees, he thought. The swelling was unbearable at times. His flock did not mind an old man's shuffle. Each halting step gave him an air of solemn gravity. His walk added to his venerable image. How could they know that his damaged knees reminded him of the past? He had not always been old, and he had not always been a priest. He carried the memory of a girl in the barn—her soft skin, his knees pressed into the wooden planks of the loft, cushioned only by a thin layer of hay, the thrust, the smell of her hair. Or the evening when his father's cart stuck in the rain and he, just nine years old, knees churning in the mud, fighting the storm for a load of oats.

Age was a curse.

Flesh is weak, he thought. *Life is a process of corruption.*

But at the end of a life of service to the one true God lay the promise of life everlasting.

Until now.

The priest moaned, hands clasped in desperate prayer. He had seen the abominations at the Close with his own eyes. He alone understood the full import of the plague. This was the resurrection of the flesh. The prophecy and the promise, made whole. But instead of a blessing bestowed on the pious and chaste, the everlasting was a pestilence visited on the wretched.

Earlier in the day, the Dunnachie had summoned him to the apothecary. One of the sheriff's men had been bitten, and had become unhinged. The apothecary dithered on about daemons. Daemons were real enough, but in the priest's experience, they stayed clear of Edinburgh. Instead, the priest expected to find a fever victim. A man taken by fever could easily be mistaken for someone possessed.

But the man tied to the apothecary's bed was not a daemon.

He was a corpse.

The priest shuddered. He'd performed certain tests that made the verdict of death impossible to deny. He'd inserted a blade himself—not once, but repeatedly. The corpse thrashed, but not at the touch of the blade. Every time the priest leaned in, the corpse bit the air, teeth extended, neck straining with the effort to break free of its bindings.

Someone in the Close had bitten the dead man. Worse, the apothecary had been careless in his care of the corpse and picked up a bite of his own for the trouble. Ill, the apothecary sat down in the corner of his storage room, eyes closed. Just as the priest finished his examination of the corpse, the apothecary's eyes opened again. If the Dunnachie's servants had not been present, the priest would have been killed as well.

A single tear squeezed from the priest's old eyes and traveled the creases down the side of his face. Eternal life bestowed, not by covenant, but by a single bite. Blasphemy.

The priest shifted. Pain shot through his knees. The cauld stone floor was unforgiving. He tried to return to his prayer, but pain shot through him again. Age, he thought miserably. Age had whittled him like a branch, leaving him a trace of his former self. To what end? What meaning death? The deputy and the apothecary were chained in the Gaol. Under his direction, the gaolers tried to end the sacrilege with blades and hot irons. Nothing short of dismemberment seemed to work.

The priest had given his life over to God, and now, in the November of his days, a litany of promises was revealed as a monstrous deception. The betrayal was too much to bear.

A knock at the door startled him. He feared more news. Instead, he discovered that his evening wine had arrived. He waved the young servant boy away. No wine. Not tonight. Then, changing his mind, he called the boy back into his chamber.

The thin young lad was a local, embarked on a life of service to the church. The priest knew he frightened the boy. That was proper. Young boys should have a healthy fear of the Lord and of his Church. But now, he wanted to ask the boy something, and the little rabbit wouldn't meet his gaze.

"What's your name?" he demanded. His voice was too stern by half, and the boy jumped.

"Alban, your Grace."

"Alban. A fitting name. Do you know what it means?"

The boy shook his head.

"It means 'rock.' Your name recalls Peter—the rock on which the church is built. Did you know that?" The boy did not. "Tell me, Alban. Why do you want to serve the Church?"

The boy shrugged.

Stupid boy, the priest thought, his dark eyes narrowing. "What is your purpose, boy?"

The boy finally met his gaze. "Tae serve the Church."

"Why?"

The boy blinked. "That's wha' God wants."

"Serving God is a difficult life. The ways of the world are cruel."

"Because a' sin," the boy said.

For a moment, the priest felt an unreasonable surge of anger. He'd hoped for an easy epiphany. Now he noticed a grease spot on the boy's tunic. Pointing a bony, curved finger at the spot, his frown deepened to a scowl. The boy looked away, ashamed.

And this, the priest thought, *is the wisdom of the innocents? God's will? Sin?* The boy's clothes were dirty. His hair was a nest. What on earth had prompted the priest to ask the boy anything?

Then the priest's gaze fell on the crucifix hanging over his bed.

"That's right," the priest whispered. "Yes." He stood, and took a step toward the boy. Startled, the boy nearly fell, backing into the chamber door. The priest shuffled over to him and tousled his dirty hair. "Good boy," he whispered. "Now go to bed."

I have duties to perform this night, the priest thought as he washed his hands. He would speak to the Dunnachie, and tell him of his daughter. Dunnachie had been a loyal patron of the church. But all men sin, and all men seek grace. Like most, the Dunnachie was his own most persistent foe, the architect of his own misery. He had, after all, sponsored the sheriff.

Having performed that unpleasant duty, he would return to the Close. He would do God's bidding. Surely, the plague was a judgement on a wicked city. If so, his task was clear. His flock must know their part in the dire events. They must understand their culpability. The sin was theirs. The fault was theirs.

If there were to be any hope for Edinburgh, it would come through God's grace. Redemption through forgiveness was an urgent message worth delivering.

Filled with resolve, the priest gathered himself to face the cold night. When he heard renewed sobbing, as if from a great distance, he was surprised. He touched his wrinkled cheeks. Tears. He was crying again. The sobs he heard were his own.

* * * * *

When the woman struck him, Balfour Gunn dropped his sword and torch. The woman pressed forward, moaning, clutching at him. He grabbed her shoulders and tried to throw her back, but she slipped from his grasp and wrapped her arms around his waist. *I cannae let her bite me!* he thought, trying to twist free from her grip. His boot slipped, and he fell into the crusty mud. The woman pushed her way into his lap, arms snaking around his neck, pulling him close.

Undone by a woman. He waited for the teeth.

Shivering, he came to two realizations. First, the woman was not possessed. She was frightened out of her wits. She'd latched onto him for protection. Arms locked him up so tight he could barely move. Her face buried in his shoulder, she sobbed against his shirt.

The second realization came when he retrieved the sputtering torch. He'd found Lainie.

"Is it you, then?" she whispered.

"Aye." He held the torch up. The flame restored itself, sending a feeble glow into the night air. Were any more of the wretched creatures coming? "Get up," he said, trying to sound brave. Lainie didn't move.

"Get up, Lass!" he repeated. She unwrapped herself and pulled away an inch at a time, whimpering as she went.

The initial shock gone, he found he was grateful for the mud. She'd frightened the piss out of him, but none would know it. She knelt in order to stand, her bosom directly in front of him, and despite the soft, flickering light, the sight stirred something in him. She'd been pressed up against him. Perhaps he'd been hasty. He could have comforted her a moment longer.

No. No! Even the thought of such was a betrayal of his friend. MacThomas did not deserve to be ill-used. And Balfour Gunn was a loyal friend. Gunn stood and returned his sword to his belt. Then he grabbed the girl's arm, pulling her down the alley. "The exit is over here," he said.

She mumbled something, trying not to fall as he pulled her along. Gunn reached the entrance and stood—stupefied. He reached out, fingertips to stone. Walled in! The masons had finished closing the entrance. He pushed at the rock near the top of the arch, but it didn't budge. "Hello!" he called.

"Hello," came the reply, followed by laughter. Someone down the alley found Gunn's predicament funny.

"Didn't I tell you?"

Gunn scowled. "Tell me what?"

"It's sealed up. We cannae stay here," she continued. "There are daemons here."

He shook his head.

"I'm not daft. You'll see."

Gunn grabbed her arm. "There's an entrance in back. I think they kept it open." He pulled without waiting for an answer. Heading back through the alley, he glanced down at her. Despite the cold, a sheen of sweat covered her face. Her hair was disheveled—one strand had pasted itself to her cheek. She looked wonderful in the torchlight. She glanced at him, her expression one of total despair. He stopped and turned her around to face him. "You're safe now," he said. "I'll look after you and get you outside."

She didn't answer.

A scream pierced the momentary silence. The shrill cry—a man's voice—rose to an impossibly high pitch and then stopped abruptly. Gunn and Lainie waited, pausing in the dark, his hands brushing hers. The silence gave way to the scuttle of rats. Gunn relaxed for a moment, but then the screaming began again, only to be cut off again.

"Shite," Gunn whispered. "Come on!" They moved through the maze, pausing every so often to stare up at the stars, as if they had secrets to yield. Crossbeams and bracing hung like black lace. The moon, peering from the corner of the sky, was a solitary eye, cold and rheumy.

At one point, Gunn tried to turn left down a gap between hovels. Lainie grabbed his arm and dragged him the opposite way. "Here," she insisted. "This way." He followed without question. He couldn't negotiate the alleys in the daylight. She lived here. He would trust her.

They'd gone no more than fifty feet when she stopped, a moan of hopelessness escaping her lips.

"What is it, Lass?" he asked.

She pointed. "That's the exit," she said, her voice as cold as the wet night air.

By the light of the torch, he could see the newly erected masonry. They were walled in.

He only paused for a moment. "All right then. We go up."

* * * * *

Dunnachie sat in the great room of his cottage. The priest had come and gone, leaving him to his thoughts. He slumped forward, his hands on his knees. He drew short, shallow breaths. He looked down, and when his wife entered the room, he stared even harder, fixing his gaze on a single slat of the wood floor.

"Husband?" Her voice was thin and timorous.

He ignored her.

After a time, he realized she had not moved, and that her initial query stood unanswered. He glanced up. Her wrinkled face could not diminish the beauty that had captured him when they'd first met. He stared at her cheekbones, her proud nose, her teeth, still straight and lovely, her green eyes, flecked with the color of straw. She wore a dressing gown of the same green and gold, cinched under her breasts. He thought perhaps he'd never loved her so much as he did at this moment.

At the very moment he'd failed her.

"I had to wall up Mary King's Close," he started. It was the right way to tell the tale. If he blurted out the worst of it first, she'd never hear the answers to the questions that she was certain to ask, to cry, to scream. "There's a plague."

"Who will carry them food and water?"

"No one. It could not be helped."

His wife crossed the room and sat in the adjoining chair, her hands placed in her lap. Old hands, wrinkled by time—not labor. He'd given her that much.

"The plague is not a normal plague," he continued. If it gets out into the city, everyone will be affected."

"The plague never takes everyone. Some are blessed."

"The blessed will be cursed. Those spared the disease will have the worst of it."

"Why, husband?" Her concerned expression cut him to the quick. She was, in the end, sincere in her love for everyone.

"The plague victims don't take to bed. They become feral. They bite. And those they bite are taken by the plague."

His wife's face went pale. "I've ne'er heard of such things. Can it be true?"

"I've seen it. The sheriff's own man tried to bite me at the apothecary."

The mention of Sheriff MacThomas brought a frown to her lips. His wife had never liked the man. "You must beware that one," she'd warned more than once. "There's no honesty in him."

"Some in the village call him Honest John MacThomas."

"A jest, I think."

Dunnachie started to protest. His wife had a sharp tongue, and her words were like a rasp to a burr. Then he remembered the news with which he would burden her and he was chastened.

She shrank in her chair, as if rebuked by his silence. "I have spoken out of turn."

"No," he said, shaking his head.

She stared at him.

"There is more. When the plague victims die, their bodies seem to—" He stopped and shook his head. "They continue moving for a time. Still walking. Still biting."

His wife put her hands over her mouth, her eyes startled wide. "That cannae be! Is it witchcraft, then?"

He nodded. "It seems so. But the plague renders them immune to the cross."

"What about burning?"

"The flesh burns, but does not rest."

"The sheriff's man?"

Dunnachie nodded. "I must do everything in my power to stop the spread. You see that, don't you Lass?" A pleading tone crept into his voice, and his wife stared and stared.

"If one got out and bit two others, and those two bit two others—"

"Yes!" he cried, seizing on her sudden understanding. "I had to wall them in. A harsh decision, and not without personal cost."

"Were you fond of the sheriff's man, then?"

He sat back, limp, like a scare-the-crow with its stuffing pulled out and scattered. In the end, he said it outright. "Lainie's in the Close."

"Lainie? Lainie? But how?"

He couldn't say the rest. He couldn't tell her that Sheriff MacThomas had secreted their daughter away and stashed her in the Close like a servant girl or a whore. He squeezed his eyes shut, as if he could keep the very idea at bay.

"You walled our daughter in the Close?"

He nodded, his eyes still shut.

"You knew she was there, and you walled her in?"

"*Ah didne kin it!*" The words burst from his lips. He took a deep breath, waiting until he could control his voice before continuing. "I just learned the news from the priest. He heard it from Mary King's own lips."

"You must open the Close! You must find her!" She stood, panic in her voice. "You must! You must!"

He sighed, a look of resignation on his face. She saw his expression and she stopped speaking, uttering instead a shrill moan.

"I cannae do it, and I have already told you why." His voice was low now, with all the iron he could muster. Her face twisted for a moment, shifting from rage to anguish and settling finally on utter misery.

Then came the tears. She fell to the floor, her dress pooled around her like tree skirting. He let her weep. He would do enough weeping of his own later.

At length, she raised her head and held his gaze. He felt his resolve crumble, and for a moment, he felt guilt crush him like a stone. He'd chased his own daughter from their home. Yes, she was willful, but he'd raised her to be so. When she left, he'd cut her from his life like mold from a cheese. He'd left her to the sheriff, a boy he'd loved more than his own child. He'd turned a blind eye to his daughter's shame and degradation.

` And his sins would continue. He would allow the sheriff to stand before him as if no crime had been committed. Because confronting the sheriff would make a lie of his patronage and call into question his decision to wall the entrances. *Seal the Close? Not if my daughter is inside.* He was trapped.

When he looked into his wife's eyes, he saw all of it. He saw his shame and guilt in the red-rimmed eyes, the tears, and the unblinking gaze. "I've betrayed you," he whispered.

She nodded.

"I've betrayed you. You whom I loved most of all."

She took a deep, ragged breath, and touched his face. "That is as it must be."

"No—"

"Yes." Her voice was grave and resigned, like the music of a requiem. "How could it be any other way, husband? If you were a stranger, you could not touch me. Only someone I love could hurt me. Only someone I trust could betray me. Were we all strangers, betrayal would cease to be." She turned and walked slowly into the bedroom, leaving him to the tears that would surely begin.

* * * * *

The tenements in Mary King's Close were stacked six and seven stories high—tottering piles of wood frame and plaster, braced on the outside by a lattice of crossbeams and wishes. A strong wind might shift the stack to the side, snapping a support beam, sending the entire edifice down, floor-by-floor, collapsed like a layer cake baked without soda. Balfour Gunn dragged the girl up the plank-steps that lined the side of the tallest of these buildings. Wooden steps, some less than three feet in length, jutted from the side of an inner wall. In the winter, snow and ice made the steps perilous. There was no handrail to support a misstep.

Lainie clung to the wall, face pressed against the plaster, her progress slowed with every step up until, two floors above the alley, she froze. Gunn pulled gently on her hand, whispering words of encouragement, then demands. When she still would not move, he pulled hard on her arm, nearly sending her into the abyss. She screamed. He waited a moment for her to settle, and then whispered, "We must go now."

"No. I'll stay here." She was crying now. She tried to pull her hand free, but he tightened his grip.

"Ye can move up the steps or ye can fall. But ye cannae stay here."

A scream came from below, just down the alley—like the high-pitched shriek of a rat caught in a tom's jaws. Lainie stared up at Gunn, her face a mask of horror. He nodded as if to say, "That's what waits below. That's why we *must* go up." She tried to move and failed. Then, with a shudder, she slid along the wall, inching up the step, her face scraping against the rough exterior.

Gunn waited, hand extended. Lainie climbed, moment by long moment. A snell wind buffeted the building, putting the steps to sway. Lainie moaned and pressed even closer to the wall. When the wind passed, she took a huge, sobbing breath and moved up another step.

They continued up, three, then four stories. The moon's waxy light made a pale torch. More screams came from below.

He urged her on with a gentle pull. "Nearly there, Lass." Above the crossbeams, far above the mud and ice at the alley floor, he could see her face in the moonlight. Her eyes pressed shut. "Move your feet." She nodded, and took another step.

He backed up the stairs, leading her on, nearly tripping and plunging into the yawning space between the buildings. And then, with a suddenness that surprised them both, they reached the roof. She stared, half laughing, half crying, then threw her arms around him. "I cannae believe it!"

"Feartie-cat," he chided.

She backed away, slapping at him playfully. Then she turned to look at their surroundings. The thatch-and-reed rooftop sagged and sloped in turns, rising up like a tent where support beams held up the ceiling from below. The cold, cutting wind blew again, and she pressed closer to Gunn. "I hope ye have a scheme."

He pointed to the opposite side of the roof. Together, they crept to the edge. Below, the streets of Edinburgh. The nearest building, just to the west, six stories tall, outside the quarantine. A running jump and they'd be safe and away from Mary King's Close. "One last adventure, Lass, and I'll have you home with your mother."

She looked at him in horror. "I'll not spangy with you!"

"Rooftop to rooftop," he insisted. "That rooftop is lower. Take a run and jump. Close your eyes if you like. Don't worry. It's not that far."

"You first."

Gunn considered the idea. "Good. I can stand at the edge. When you jump, I can pull you in." He needed to get her off the roof. He stepped away from the edge and made ready. Two deep breaths. A quick smile for Lainie to give her comfort.

She looked away. She seemed so frail in the moonlight, swaying with the wind. And suddenly he knew.

"You don't intend to jump."

"No, I will! I will! I will try, I swear it."

He pointed. "That roof is lower than this one. You can make it."

She nodded.

"The roof is lower," he repeated. "If I go first, I won't be able to jump back. You'll have to try. Or you'll be trapped."

She tried to smile. The twitch at the corner of her mouth, the black, melancholy gaze and the shivering lip gave her away. She walked to him and laid her head on his chest. "You go. You can get help for me. I'll go down the steps. I'll go to the west entrance. You can make the soldiers tear down the wall."

He considered this for a moment. "No. You'll jump. Or I'll stay."

She sank into his arms and wept. "I can't jump!"

"You must. You cannae get down the steps alone. Think, Lass!" He felt her shiver.

"Down the steps, then," he sighed. "I'll lead you."

Each tentative step was a battle. Going up to the roof, they had the sky to draw their hopes, their attention. Now they descended into darkness, and each faltering move left them swaying over the lip of the pit—cold and frightened. Gunn kept up a steady stream of encouragement—anything to keep her feet moving into the dark hole below them.

Near the bottom, they came face-to-face with one of the creatures.

The man appeared on the stair steps as if he'd formed from the frost. He was full-grown—twenty years old if he was a day. His face was bathed in blood from the lips down, icy strands of red spilling across his tunic. The moon reflected in his dead eyes. Lainie let out a startled cry. Gunn pressed her close to the wall so that he could move past and defend her from the assault that was sure to come.

The apparition took a single step, and then another. The wind whistled through the support timbers. Gunn drew his weapon, but did not get the chance to strike.

Swayed by the wind, the apparition stumbled sideways and fell from the steps, striking the frozen mud below.

Gunn took Lainie's hand and pulled her down the last level of steps. "Come on," he begged. "We're nearly there." Soon, they reached the ground floor. "Safe," he whispered. And then the apparition, the one that had pitched down the stairs just minutes before, reached out from the darkness—bent and broken. The creature leered forward, mouth open, snarling like a dog. Lainie screamed, and Gunn almost dropped his sword with surprise. He flailed wildly, pushing the thing away and buying himself a moment to gather his wits. When the thing came at him again, he was ready. He buried the blade in the socket of its right eye. The stain of some dark liquid spilled across its cheek. The apparition shuddered and then dropped down—dead weight pulling free of the blade like a cloth sack full of potatoes. Gunn hacked at the thing's neck again and again until the head detached.

"Will it get up again?" The girl's voice was a tremor in the wind.

"No," Gunn said. "Take the head and it's goosed for sure." He kicked the corpse with his foot. It did not move. "A wee rickle-a-bones, Lass." She pushed away from the wall she'd been hugging—a slow, faltering movement that exposed a soul in shock.

He held out a hand. When she didn't take it, he grabbed her by the elbow and led her down the alley. She followed, clinging to him like ivy to a wall. "I would get out of the Close now," she whispered.

"We will, Lass," he promised.

But when they rounded the corner, they ran into a crowd of a dozen and more, silent as the grave. The only sound was the scrape of shoe leather on ice.

* * * * *

Dunnachie wandered in the general direction of the Close, negotiating the cobbled streets with gingered steps. The people of Edinburgh were asleep—nestled into down and straw. He shivered in his clothes and wondered, "Is it the cold or my choices that cause me to quake?" The evening was cold enough, that was certain. But the thought of his daughter, trapped in the Close, made him physically ill. And when he recalled his wife's words, he had to stop and take a breath, a frail hand at a shopkeeper's door for support. He looked up. The winter sky was so clear the stars scarcely twinkled. They sat unblinking, like pox in the darkness. He felt bile creep up from the back of his throat, and with a sudden lurch, he vomited against the shop door.

"I am the Dunnachie," he whispered, wiping his mouth with a coat sleeve. "It is within my power to undo this. I will redeem myself." He took a deep, cold breath and began to walk again. "I will return to the Close and pull down the masonry. I will order this sheriff to have his men guard the entrance. I will send him in to find my daughter. If he hesitates, or if he returns alone, I will have him hung on the spot." Bolstered, he quickened his steps. He would unplug the Close.

But what if the plague spilled into the streets? Would the sheriff's men be able to contain the monsters of the Close? The creature at the apothecary had tolerated a dozen deathblows. How would a few armed men handle dozens of daemon creatures? And what if his daughter had already succumbed to the plague? Would MacThomas even look for the girl? Or would he find a hidey-hole until the danger had passed?

And what of his responsibility to the city? His daughter's situation was in doubt, as was the fate of the residents of the Close. But the consequence to the city should the plague spread was a certainty!

Dunnachie stopped still. Torchlight from the Close lit the sky ahead. They would look to his lead. He must take control. He must arrive, answers in hand. And so he waited, his arms wrapped around his chest, his head against the alley wall, praying for the answers to come to him.

* * * * *

"The daemons cannae be stopped!" the beggar cried, clutching his wrap around his neck. "We tried! They will nae die!" The others voiced their agreement—a dozen or more, shouting in the dark, clamoring doom.

Gunn folded his arms and waited for the others to be still. They'd run blind into this frightened group—men, women and a single child, pushed from their hovels into the cold streets of the Close, squealing like pork at a butchering. And, in fact, were they not all so much food? The sheriff and the Dunnachie had sealed them like grain in a silo.

Gunn was a deputy. Could he help them? Could he save them? The clamor finally stilled as the crowd waited for his verdict.

"They can be stopped." Gunn's voice was firm.

A stupefied silence followed his pronouncement.

Gunn cleared his throat. Lainie pressed closer, her hand across his chest.

"How?" The beggar's voice was a blend of disbelief and hope.

"The creatures die when you sever their heads."

"I took an arm, and the daemon could nae grab me," shouted one man in the back of the crowd, a bloodstained short sword extended skyward.

"Take off a leg, and they'll not follow you!" agreed another. Suddenly, the alley was filled with shouts and boasts. Gunn smiled.

The child stepped forward, arms pinned to her side. She leaned forward and laid her forehead against his hip.

A small, shriveled grandmother came forward as well. Her teeth were gone, and her lips sank over her gums. Her spine had curled in on itself, leaving her hunched. A sprig of gray hair spilled from under the rag she'd wrapped around her head. Her fingers were stiff and bent as she pointed them like the bill of a duck. "This is our home," she said. "Help us take it back."

Gunn nodded to a dozen cheers. He drew his sword and held it aloft. A great shout echoed down the alley. At that moment, Gunn felt a swell of regard for the free people of Edinburgh. And within that feeling—a warmth that transcended the winter night. He was Balfour Gunn, the sheriff's best man. And he would lead these people to safety.

And, as if on cue, the living dead arrived from behind the group—a surging crowd of silent, stumbling corpses, mouths open, teeth working furiously. Gunn pushed his way through his new friends and struck out at the first of the attackers. He buried his blade two-thirds of the way through an old man's neck, eliciting little more than a grunt. Gunn pulled free, backing away as he fought. The crowd behind him shrank from the attack, so he did not trip. A second swing severed the old man's head. The torso dropped and the head rolled under the step of a dead woman. She wore no expression of surprise as her leg pitched out from under her, sending her tumbling into the frozen mud.

The shriveled grandmother scuttled forward into the mass of daemons brandishing a knife. She swung the blade once, a slow arc that failed to connect with flesh. The pile of creatures pushed forward, toppling her, pressing the old woman into the ice. She struggled for a moment, and then began to scream as the plucking and biting began. Gunn tried to cut his way to her, but the rush of bodies thwarted his efforts. He fell back again amid the old woman's desperate screams.

"Come on!" Gunn shouted, trying to rally his faltering allies. They ignored him, retreating— weapons forward, frightened. Then a second group of the dead came stumbling into the alley from the other direction, shambling mindlessly into the crowd. In an instant, the alley became a maelstrom of chaos. Bodies stumbled and fell, screaming, grunting and thrashing on the cold ground. Dim moonbeams lit patches of ice and blood. Gunn couldn't tell the living from the dead. He felt a mouth clamp on his forearm, teeth pulling at the cloth of his shirt. He lashed out, elbow to face, and then struck again with his sword. Then he remembered—

Lainie.

He whirled in place, desperately trying to spot the girl. There—pressed against the wall. Was that her? Dark bedlam left him uncertain. He fought his way to her. An older man blocked his path. He thrust the blade forward, driving into the base of the man's neck. He screamed and gurgled. Gunn's heart sank—he'd stabbed a living man. The moving dead ones fell on the stabbed man, desperate to bite and tear.

Gunn circled the feeding, sword extended. *Guid God!* he thought. *They're eatin' him!*

He'd lost sight of the girl. There—moving up the stairs! Lainie! He raced to join her. The dead ones were too unsteady to follow—he was sure of it. He pulled her back up the steps. A single story above the alley, he stopped to look behind him. No one had followed, living or dead. Though the muffled sound of chewing had begun to replace the din of battle, it was too dark to be certain what had become of the free people of whom he'd recently become so fond.

Standing still, Lainie clung to him, pressing herself between Gunn and the wall. She shook like a child. He put an arm around her and stared into the darkness. Would the dead ones follow them? If they did, he would move up to the roof. And if they followed them there, he would pitch them into the streets and dash their bodies on the cobblestones.

A cold wind slipped through the alley, but the girl had wrapped herself around him, keeping him warm. He could feel her heart hammering through her blouse. She pressed her face into the crook of his arm. "Don't let them," she groaned.

He put both arms around her now. "You're safe."

"It seems not," she said, stifling a sorrowful laugh.

He smiled. Despite the nightmare, she'd tried a small joke. He held her tighter. He felt her body pressed against him and felt his body's response. He tried to pull away, but she held on. What was she doing?

He couldn't see her face, buried in his tunic, but he could smell her hair.

Sheriff John! he thought, even as his hands betrayed him. He felt her shudder. She looked up at him in surprise—surely a false note. He was as stiff as timber and had been for long moments. Did she not know what she was doing to him? His hands began to move of their own accord. He caressed her, pinching her nipples and tugging at her hair. Their balance threatened, they melted into each other. He sat down on the steps, pulling her into his lap. She fumbled with his trousers while he pulled at her skirt.

This is wrong, he thought. She pulled his boaby from his trousers, and then sank down on it. She began to move, slowly at first, afraid to spill them both down the steps or off into the abyss. He pulled at her top, but she pressed forward, shrugging him off. "I'll freeze," she whispered. He fondled her instead. Even with the cold, the sensation was overwhelming. He began to drive into her, and she thrashed in his lap with a violence that surprised him. He shuddered and filled her in a sudden rush.

She continued to squirm in his lap, even when he shriveled back down into the cold. At first, he sat still, his head thrown back against the steps. Then he remembered why he was in the Close. He'd come to do a favor. And now he'd betrayed his friend.

The girl stopped moving. She looked down at him in dismay. "Balfour?" she whispered. She knew his name! He tried to stand—a comedy. She stepped back, pulling down her skirt, nearly tripping with the effort. He pulled at his pants, tucking himself back in.

"I was so frightened—"

"Shut up." He fumbled for his sword, dangerously near the stair's edge.

She came closer again, whispering. "I thought you wanted me. Was I wrong? I know I wasn't wrong! Did I do something wrong?"

Wrong? He tried to think. He couldn't do it. His head hurt.

"Balfour?"

He stared into her eyes. They were little more than black sockets. Suddenly, he realized that he saw her more clearly in the dark. A rush of anger washed over his remorse, drowning his regret. This moment hadn't been his fault! He'd been tricked.

He'd betrayed no one. The girl was daemon. Women were temptresses.

"Stay here," he commanded.

"Balfour! What did I do wrong?"

He backed up a step. He thought of Sheriff John—his friend—and he thought of the brief moment he'd had with Lainie. He felt sick to his stomach.

"Balfour?"

He turned and climbed the stairs, leaving her clinging to the wall.

III

Lainie Dunnachie stood rooted to the stairs. Dread crept past the shock, past the cold that seeped into her marrow, past the bewilderment and betrayal. She shuddered, and pressed herself back against the rough wall, scratching the skin through her blouse. Gunn would come back for her. He would not leave her to the monsters below. He was angry, and that was all.

She waited. Each second crawled.

What had she done wrong? She'd given him what he wanted—what the sheriff wanted—what all men wanted! Gunn had no reason to be angry. She was his charge. He was the sheriff's man. She was obliged to do as he wished.

Could a girl sin if she had no choice? The path that led her to a cold stairway in the Close did not branch, but seemed instead to plummet down in a single narrow course, destination obscured. She could only follow where the path led.

An inner voice reminded her she'd wanted him to take her.

She cursed herself. She was wicked. His seed ran down her thighs. She swabbed at the dampness with her skirt, rubbing until her sex was raw. "Serves me well," she whispered. "Serves me quite well."

What to do now? She could scarcely muster the courage to stand still, let along wander the dark alone. She couldn't go up. The heights frightened her. And if she went down, she was surely doomed.

"I will wait for you," she whispered, perhaps to Gunn, perhaps to MacThomas. Her father as well? Her heart sank with the thought of the old man. She could be home now, deep in feathers, fast asleep.

Then she thought of her mother, and she began to weep. The tears came slowly at first, turning to huge, wracking sobs. "I am so wicked!" she cried. "I must be; else this should never happen!"

When she realized others could hear her lament, she tried to stop. Panic took her breath. She reclaimed it, gasping. Had she not finally quieted, she'd never have noticed the dead man.

The footsteps came from above. She turned and saw the silhouette of a figure, visible against the night sky. "*Balfour?*" No answer. The shape took a tottering step forward, arms dangling at its sides. One hand bent inward at an odd angle, as if twisted at the wrist and broken free. The sight frightened her. She backed away, scraping her shoulders as she moved. The man followed, two steps above her. A low, gurgling sound issued from his throat.

Lainie gave up ground a step at a time. Fear bubbled up in her throat, and she began to cluck. She tried to stop the sounds, clamping her fingers over her mouth. But she continued to cluck.

Worse, she knew what the sound meant.

Once, her father had taken her to the clan games. A bright sun lit the morning meadow, and there was food and music. Men dressed in their coats, weapons displayed. Everyone competed in the games. The strongest threw stones and tossed the caber. Boys wrestled pigs. Even the younger girls tried their hands at fetching a chicken. The winner could take home a hen of her own. Lainie tried her best, but though she was quick for a six year-old, the chicken had no trouble evading her. The girl who caught the chicken didn't move as fast, but she cut the chicken off in the pen, step-by-step, calmly backing the bird into the corner of the pen, where she pounced on it. Her family ate the hen that evening.

Lainie realized she was being herded down the steps. The thought turned her spine to ice.

When she reached the ice and mud of the alley, she ran.

* * * * *

Sheriff John MacThomas stood, torch in hand, staring at the fresh masonry that sealed the entrance to the Close. Muffled screams from the other side subsided. There had been two long periods of silence, interrupted with shouts and the dim hammering of whatever tool or stone the residents of the Close brought against the stone barrier. It was long past midnight now, and the silence would not last. For that reason, the stillness was nearly unbearable.

A crowd had gathered in vigil. A handful of torches lit the street. MacThomas could see the crowd, poor souls, wrapped in thin clothing, blankets and skins, trembling in the night air. They were silent, too.

Why were they watching? If they lived in the Close but had been trapped outside, they should count themselves lucky. And if they lived outside the Close, his work was none of their business. And so many of them! Like moths, they'd been drawn to the street by torchlight. They made him nervous. Crowds were dangerous—he recalled the magistrate they'd killed just four years earlier. Beat him to death and then dragged his body through the alleyways. A grim business.

From behind MacThomas came the shuffle of footsteps. A man approached, hunched in deference, cap in hand. Stringy gray hair dangled forward, covering his eyes. With every other step, he walked the blade of his right foot, shoulder dipping with the effort. MacThomas frowned. Instead of evoking a sense of suffering, the man's limp gave him a comic air that had no place in the night's events. The Close had become a living grave, and the peasant clown before him was an unwelcome interruption.

"Sheriff." The man's voice was a soft hiss accompanied by a bow. A family followed in the man's wake—a woman and her five children. The woman was the puffy sort who proved the common belief that the poor are poor because every spare coin goes to food. Her thick, stupid-looking brood looked like their father. Two boys stood, caps removed, disheveled hair tumbling over their brows. Three girls curtsied, dipping the hems of their shapeless dresses in the mud. Each girl was uglier than the other.

From the corner of his eye, MacThomas saw Aengus Dunnachie emerge from between two buildings. He swayed in place, shaking. MacThomas turned back to the man in front of him and gave the peasant his full attention. "Speak." The sheriff's voice was clear and forceful, but not entirely unkind.

"Sheriff, ah woods ask a boon of ye." The man continued to whisper as if his full voice might offend. The mother pressed closer, shushing her children.

MacThomas waited, finally realizing that the man waited for his leave to continue. "Go on," he said, then cursed himself inwardly. His words might be taken as encouragement.

"I dornt care tae bortha ye sairr, but hits mah wee daughter. A bonnie lassie, trapped like a moggie in the Close."

MacThomas glanced back at the man's other daughters—not one worth bedding. *A bonnie lassie indeed*, he thought. He cleared his throat and let his voice carry. "The Close has been walled up. If your daughter is inside, she's in God's hands." The crowd had begun to stir. The spectacle of a family daring to approach the sheriff was good theater, and they were a willing audience. Good. Let them all hear his answer.

Then MacThomas glanced to the side, and was horror-struck to discover that the priest had joined Dunnachie at the edge of the crowd.

"Ye dornt kin—"

"Shut yer gob," the sheriff demanded. His voice carried the hint of a tremor.

"Yoo'll nae dyke Katie up!" the man said, stepping back. He produced a small knife, waving it in the air. "Either open the Close or meet yer end." The woman and her children shrank back, but the crowd hovered, growing bolder with each passing moment.

Sheriff MacThomas stared in disbelief. His Claymore dwarfed the knife. But the man had the stones to challenge him in front of a crowd. And the crowd scared him. "You'd come at me with that wee thing?"

"A smaa' leak will sink a great ship." The man stood his ground. MacThomas could see his eyes now—black as a peat bog. The tiny knife danced like a candle flame in his poor, shaking hands. He could not hope to win. The woman turned away and the children began to weep, expecting the little drama to end in blood, their father lying dead in the winter mud.

Not the crowd. Angry faces waited, and for a moment, MacThomas wondered incredulously if they would rush him to defend the old fool. His deputies had gone to secure the rear entrance of the Close. The sheriff was alone. One of the onlookers, a beefy man of years with forearms like mutton legs, edged in, his fists clenched.

The priest and Dunnachie seemed paralyzed by the quick turn of events. Both men looked old beyond their years, as if the cold night and the sight of the unruly mob had drained them of their remaining time, reducing them to pale, shuddering ghosts.

The beefy man from the crowd was near enough to smell. His little pig eyes were set too close together, giving him the thick, slow look of a gimp— a look belied by the sly, knowing grin that had begun to creep across his face. He seemed to pull the crowd forward, as if they were tethered to him. Despite the cold, sweat began to trickle down between the sheriff's shoulder blades. He had lost control of the situation in just moments. He needed to act.

MacThomas drew his sword and held it aloft. He was taking a chance, he knew, but the crowd had no love for him. Only a show of force would save him. "I think you did not come for your bairn, fool. You came for this." As he feared, the crowd pressed closer still. Only the scream stopped them from rushing him.

* * * * *

Balfour Gunn retraced his steps to the top of the Close. On the rooftop, he saw a man stand in silhouette, slumped at the building's edge. One arm hung much lower than the other, as if the arm of a much taller man had been stitched in place of his own. Gunn called out to him. The man did not respond at first. Then he began to move forward, step by hesitant step. The longer arm dangled, swinging with each step. Halfway to Gunn, the man's leg broke through the roof. He dropped through the wood to his knee, pitching forward with the force of his fall. He made no sound beyond the splintering of wood.

Gunn turned away. It was time to leave this Hell. He returned to the lip of the roof to find the right place from which to jump. He would need a running start. Should he untie his dirk? He gave consideration to pitching it across in advance of his leap, but the thought of the man wedged in the hole of the roof gave him pause. He glanced back. The man had not yet broken free. Still, Gunn decided to keep the dirk.

Standing at the edge, a moment's fear gripped him. He was no stranger to climbs. He'd been born in the highlands. But there was a difference between God's heights and man's. Men stacked buildings in straight, vertical lines. It was unnatural—the peak too high, the drop too severe. When he'd been on the roof with Lainie, earlier in the evening, the prospect of jumping had not bothered him. Now, alone, he was afraid.

"I'm Balfour Gunn," he boasted, but the words were empty now.

When given the time or the place to consider the thought, in church or on a hike in the hills, Gunn believed he was a good man. He did the right thing without requiring another justification. He protected the peace. He was a good friend.

That Gunn, he realized sadly, was gone.

All men sin, he thought, glancing back at the dead man struggling to pull free from the hole in the roof. *But I'll not pule and whine, nor ask for forgiveness. I'll redeem myself. I'll double my efforts. I will serve the sheriff in any way he asks.*

He lifted his arms to the night sky. "I am Balfour Gunn," he repeated, this time with some of his former enthusiasm.

Bolstered, he backed away from the wall eight, then ten steps. He gave a last thought to the girl he'd left below, but to think of her was to remember what had happened, and he would not dwell on that. MacThomas would never know. No one would know except Balfour Gunn. And he would not think of it again.

Now. No time to think or doubt. *Run.*

He began to sprint—a quick burst of speed across the thatch-covered roof. The edge rushed to meet him. He planted hard to launch himself out, but the wood gave way, tripping him, and he pitched forward just as he reached the lip of the roof. He had no more than two seconds to realize he was falling before he struck the street below, face-first.

* * * * *

The priest stared in horror, his mouth quivering. Had the promised Revelations begun? With all else that had happened, this was the thing he could not believe. The crowd had become threatening. Threatening!

One huge ox of a man moved step-by-step towards the sheriff, fists like beef roasts hanging at his sides. Others pushed in behind him. The old man who'd started the rebellion still brandished his knife. The sheriff stood, sword aloft, a serene expression on his face. The crowd could close the gap and be on him in a single moment, yet he stood fast. Perhaps he was every bit the stalwart of his reputation. Or perhaps he, like the priest, could not believe that the accepted order of things could shatter in a single moment.

I should speak out, he thought. But—

What if they turn on me as well? He glanced at Dunnachie. The man's mouth hung open like a fruit basket. More onlookers had come up behind them. The priest quaked as if naked to the wind. He began to pray. If the sheriff fell, Dunnachie and the priest would surely be taken next. Chaos! And would the mob destroy the masonry and let the daemons free as well? Nothing was unthinkable. Only the sheriff's sword stood in the way of apocalypse.

Then, as if in answer to the priest's prayers, the heavens opened up. A man struck the mud face-first, his neck and spine snapping with the force of his fall. The priest looked upward, but could see nothing in the dark skies beyond the top of the Close. The wife of the knife wielder screamed—a single shrill note that lasted forever—pulling her children back from the quivering mess. Her husband retreated as well, his knife now at his side. The sheriff stared at the pile of bone, tissue and cloth. He tilted his head and whispered to himself. Then he looked to the heavens. Finally, he returned his gaze to the crowd.

"You see?" The sheriff's voice echoed down the streets, silencing the crowd. "Men pitch themselves from the rooftops to escape Mary King's Close. And you would have me open the door and invite Hell into our streets?"

Silence. Even the screaming woman shut her mouth.

Sheriff MacThomas leveled his sword in the direction of the man and his family. "And you think to threaten me? Even as I save you and your fat, stupid children?"

The old man looked down in shame.

"I ought to run you through, you old fud." The man with the knife winced at the vulgar insult and dropped his weapon. MacThomas motioned with the sword. "Go to your homes." The command was almost a whisper—just loud enough to carry. The crowd began to disperse immediately.

The priest stared in disbelief. Even the huge man with the big fists had turned to leave. There would be no mayhem. How had so great a danger been averted in just moments?

The priest almost wept with relief. The plague had been contained. The crowd had been dispersed. The city would be safe. But what did it mean?

A merciful God had intervened. A miracle!

The sheriff stood alone at the entrance to the Close, his righteous sword in hand.

* * * * *

MacThomas shook his head at the shattered body of Balfour Gunn. With his deputy dead, the chances for Lainie's survival slipped to nothing. He would miss her. She was a fine lass.

Then he thought, *Just as well.* First Mary King, and now Balfour. The mess was nearly tidied, and just in time. But the real threat approached. The priest and Dunnachie crossed the street, somber and imperial.

Then came the surprise.

"That was magnificent, Sheriff MacThomas!" The priest gushed, his wet mouth working like a fish. He grabbed the sleeve of the Sheriff's tunic as he spoke. Relief had clearly overcome decorum. "Surely God himself was at your side."

MacThomas turned to Dunnachie—the bravest thing he'd done all evening—and bowed. Dunnachie paused for an uncomfortable moment, then grabbed him in a clumsy, tepid embrace. "Well done. The work of a diplomat," he mumbled.

"A wise man wavers. A fool is fixed."

* * * * *

Where could she hide? Was there no safe place in the Close? She had a sudden urge to try the roof again. Balfour was there. She would force herself to jump the rooftop. Just shut her eyes and fly. But that way had been blocked. She didn't dare try! Where else could she go? There must be an answer.

Mary King's! She knew every inch of the woman's home. She'd cleaned it on her hands and knees. She could find a cupboard in the dark and hide until someone came to save her. MacThomas would find her.

Unless Balfour told the sheriff what she'd done.

She could not bear the thought. Someone would come for her. Her father?

No.

Her father let her leave home without so much as a word. Many nights she'd lain awake, exhausted by a day filled with buckets and brushes, listening for a knock at the door. But he never came for her.

She sobbed, and then clamped a hand over her mouth. She had to get to Mary King's. She would hide there.

She rounded one corner, then another, before running into a hellish scene. A pitched battle raged between a dozen figures in the dark. Some carried makeshift weapons. She heard grunts, the crunch of bone shattered with blunt force, heavy breathing and the scuffle of shoe leather on the frozen ground. But there were no curses, no screams. The men grappling in the dark were beyond words.

The man closest to her, a burly sort with a full beard, hoisted an axe and brought it down on a squirming body, prone in the mud beneath. One sure blow separated an arm, sending it spinning off to the side. A second blow bit into a leg at mid-thigh, but it took a second and third blow to cut the leg free.

Lainie clamped her hand over her mouth and forced herself to slide along the edge of the melee. She had to move past in order to reach Mary King's. She wanted nothing more than to stop where she was—taking not a step further—and curl into a ball. But there would be no rescue. She had to move on her own.

One man backed into her, pinning her to the wall, then shoved forward, slashing with a kitchen knife. The blade opened a woman's face, spilling her jaw onto her chest so she could not bite. She scratched instead, hands arched like claws. Lainie pushed on, moaning through her fingers.

And then she was at Mary King's open door. She only hesitated a moment. There was no light, but she knew where the cupboards were. She moved inside, whispering a desperate prayer. She knew she'd sinned. She would sin no more. She would be a good girl. But as each word passed her lips, a wicked thought leapt to mind *(It wasn't my fault! I had no choice!),* and she wasn't sure that God would care to listen.

Then she stopped. Which was true? Had she sinned, or was she a victim? Can a person truly sin when no choice is involved? She shuddered. Was it a sin to ask such a question?

Then she tripped on something large and soft, falling forward, catching herself on a table. The cry that she'd tried to suppress finally slipped out. She spread her hands on the tabletop in front of her, sobbing openly. Hot, bitter tears coursed down her cheeks. She struggled for long moments to control herself, but anguish racked her with convulsions.

In the end, only the sound of footsteps silenced her.

She turned. Three silhouettes stood in the dim light from the alley through the open door. Thin, like sticks with clothing, the shapes wavered, unsteady and soundless. One last sob slipped from her lips, and they began to shamble forward, tentative steps in the darkness. "No," she whispered. The lead figure reached out for her. She tried to slip to the side, but they were on her, pushing her back on the tabletop. She felt a mouth on her cheek, broken teeth brushing the skin. Another mouth on her breast, biting through the cloth, not yet piercing the skin. Fear took the breath from her lungs, so she could not scream. She shut her eyes, even as they forced her legs apart.

"Help!" she cried.

"Now then," a voice said. "We'll 'elp ye. An 'elp ourselves as well."

* * * * *

The first rays of morning found Dunnachie in his great room, still and unmoving like the stone doors that sealed the entrance of Mary King's Close. He had lived many years, but had never felt the crush of time as he did now. Carts belonging to peasants and merchants had begun rolling at dawn, wheels tapping on cobblestones to the melody of birds. The night had lasted forever, and yet the people of Edinburgh were taking to the streets as if nothing had happened. They did not know they'd been a single misstep from catastrophe. Would they be grateful if they knew? Perhaps. They'd certainly have felt betrayed had he not done his best to contain the plague.

He was thirsty. He glanced at the wine glass to his left, well within his grasp, but he did not reach out.

Was the madness really over? What would he do if a report came from another part of the city—news of death and chaos? He would leave. He would pack up a cart, and his dear wife, and he would leave. He would go to the highlands and hide in the hills. The English could not find a Scot in the crags. Neither would the plague.

His wife. The thought of the old woman gave his heart a nasty pull. How could they survive the loss of their daughter? Would she not blame him for her child's death? Damn the sheriff. Damn his lying eyes! He'd taken the whelp in, raised him, sent him to be educated and given him a position. In thanks, MacThomas had plotted with the King woman to keep his daughter from him. Dunnachie clenched his fist, and for a moment, he gave thought to taking his sword from the wall where it had rested on display, never once used in anger. Then his hand went limp, resting again on his thigh. The sheriff would kill him. MacThomas was quick enough and ruthless enough. Good thing, too, given what Dunnachie had asked of him!

Yes, Dunnachie had demanded a hard thing, walling up the Close, consigning those inside to a horrible death. And MacThomas had done his job. He had earned some small measure of forgiveness, hadn't he?

His wife groaned in the bedroom. No pump handle ever sounded so low, so despairing! Dunnachie hadn't gone to her. He'd sat alone in the darkness. He wanted her touch, but the pain and shame were too great.

But—

If he could forgive the sheriff his betrayal, then might not his wife forgive him as well? The thought startled him. His hand stirred in his lap. She was a fine and true soul. She would give him the healing touch he needed to get past this tragedy. Bolstered, he would find the strength to forgive the sheriff. All men sin, he recalled. All men stumble. All men need forgiveness, the sheriff most of all.

And in forgiveness, redemption.

He tried to smile. His face would not cooperate. He took a deep breath and pushed himself from the chair. His joints screamed, and he tottered in place. He had suffered. Like a merchant, he would go to her now and collect his forgiveness. And she would make him whole again.

* * * * *

Morning found the priest with the one true Book open in his lap. Revelations had never been so ripe with meaning as on this morning. Had not the city been blessed with a glimpse of the end times? Had they not all gaped, stupid and unworthy, into the open mouth of Hell itself?

The priest's breakfast sat on a tiny table, uneaten. He was hungry, but it pleased him to ignore the demands of the flesh when there was so much of a spiritual nature to consider.

He cast his glaze around his small room. Bed, nightstand and a single ornament—the cross, with a depiction of the Lord, rendered in plaster and painted the color of a salmon. He'd brought the cross with him to Edinburgh when he came from the coast. Finer renditions of the passion were available in the city. He kept this old cross out of remembrance for his past. He was not without earthly vanities.

The plague had been a warning. The priest worried that the citizens of Edinburgh might not heed that warning. He must do everything in his power to ensure the lesson was not lost. The people lived their selfish lives, concerned only for themselves. Clearly, God was not pleased. They must attend to each other and to the church. They must give over their lives and serve.

Next time, God would not be so merciful. This time, he'd sent—in his compassionate wisdom—Sheriff MacThomas.

Strange, the priest thought. He'd not given the sheriff much credence. All the more reason to see the hand of Providence in what had happened. The priest had witnessed the sheriff with the unruly crowd—a certain miracle.

Absently, the priest grabbed a biscuit from his breakfast platter, about to take a bite. No, he thought. There will be no food today. He placed the food back on the tray. Today was a day for thanks and contemplation. The biscuit would keep.

After

Three months later to the day, the sheriff tore down the stone entry to Mary King's Close. He directed soldiers, sent from neighboring garrisons, into the tenement. The sheriff stayed behind, commanding a small reserve to ensure no escape through the open door.

The buildings of Edinburgh were packed like chickens in a tiny coup. Had it not been so, the sheriff might have burned the Close to the ground. Instead, soldiers retrieved the fallen residents and piled them into carts bound for the edge of town, where they were thrown into a pit to be burned. The stench lasted for weeks.

Not every corpse inside the Close had the grace to lie still. Soldiers reported that decaying bodies still moved, still attacked, though most had rotted past the point of imminent danger. The garrison dismembered the remaining plague victims, taking their cue from what they found inside.

MacThomas watched as soldiers, pale and shaken, deposited their burdens in carts. Piles of arms, legs, heads and torsos testified to how the long night of the plague had ended. The sheriff did not stare at the squirming body parts for too long. He feared the sight of a familiar bit of cloth.

Fire would solve the problem once and for all. The poor, dead deputy and the apothecary, sequestered in the goal, had stubbornly refused to rest, though their souls had long since fled. Under the direction of the priest, the sheriff's men took the shuddering corpses to the meadow, just yards from where the body pit would eventually be dug. There, they bound the unfortunates to a single stake, dabbed them with pig fat and stacked firewood to their knees. The corpses thrashed against their chains long after their flesh burned to ash—finally still when all that remained were blackened bones.

Sheriff MacThomas stood with ready sword, but no one came stumbling from the Close. It took a full day to clear out the tenement. Later, an army of washerwomen would take buckets and brushes and lye, and the Close would be scrubbed of everything but the memory.

The Dunnachie stood at the far end of the street, watching the soldier's progress. He'd been polite to MacThomas over the past weeks, even deferential. In turn, Sheriff MacThomas was careful to include the merchant in any decision that pertained to the Close. It was clear neither man would mention Lainie to the other. MacThomas suspected Dunnachie was occupied with other sorrows—his wife had taken ill and passed away a month earlier. Not the plague, of course. Dunnachie looked worse for the ordeal. Never a hefty man, he'd lost too much weight, and his face wore a hard, closed look that spoke of resignation and despair. A waste of power and riches, MacThomas decided.

For a week after the outbreak of the plague, MacThomas had walked the streets, worrying over another outbreak. When none occurred, he realized he was far better off for the event. Within days, everyone in town had heard the story of how he stood off a crowd with just a sword and a speech. He'd been feared and respected before. Now he was a legend. Women were his for the taking, and he took often, though he found that he most preferred the quiet company of Balfour Gunn's sister—a young redhead with whom he could share his grief over the loss of friends and family.

On the balance, he'd fared very well. The lesson was clear enough. Some men were born to ride history's stallion. And he, Sheriff John MacThomas, was one such man.

He did not know the plague of 1644 would also become legend—the plague outbreak that was walled up like Poe's Fortunato. Centuries would pass, but the stories would remain, aided by apparent hauntings. Ghosts inhabited the Close.

In modern times, a recreation of the Close will be erected on the site. Tourists will come from overseas to visit one of the most haunted places on earth. And each paranormal sighting will continue the legend, for the ghosts of Mary King's Close aren't shimmering apparitions walking the halls. *The ghosts of Mary King's Close are body parts—arms, legs and heads, floating down hallways.*

Why would a ghost appear as an appendage? No other place on earth is haunted by pieces, rather than the whole. Those who believe in the supernatural explain ghosts as lost souls, tied to a specific location by some terrible tragedy. What of floating arms and legs? Are they the reflection of fragmented souls, forever shattered, searching for continuity?

And so the stories live on. But every story must have an end.

* * * * *

It is two days after the Close is walled up. Sheriff John MacThomas paces, red-eyed and sword drawn, circling the Close. Darkness is coming, but the sheriff will not sleep tonight. He must be certain the plague is contained. He is not the best of men. He knows this in his bones. He does what he wants, when he wants, and he cares little for those in his care. But he is becoming a good sheriff. He's heard the whispers. He notices the look of awe in the people's faces as he passes. Men bow. Women blush and curtsy. Children smile and salute. When they look at him, they see something he is not, and he must not fall short.

The stone doors are solid, of course. The sheriff is worried someone might tunnel out like a rat. He listens as he walks, hoping to hear a telltale scrape or tap. If the plague dead try to burrow free, he will cut them as they crawl. Because he is concentrating, he hears the cat long before he sees it.

The growl is low, from the back of the throat. The cat has trapped a rat against the outside of the Close. The rodent barely moves, makes no sound, but the cat is crouched and wary. As MacThomas approaches, neither the cat nor the rat takes notice of him.

Even in the waning light, MacThomas can see that the rat has been ill-used. Scabby and blackened, the thing looks long past dead. But the cat is in no hurry to dispatch its prey. And the rat can't or won't escape.

MacThomas stops to watch.

Suddenly, the cat leaps. The rat seems to welcome the slashing claws. A chunk of the rodent's ear tears loose. The rat doesn't run. It bites, barely missing the cat's throat with sharp, yellow teeth. The cat shifts its attack, snatching the rat by the back of the neck, shaking it.

Then the cat drops the rat. And the rat, torn nearly in two, starts to crawl away. The cat howls and leaps again. A last, slashing attack shreds the rat into bloody, black pieces.

Suddenly aware of the sheriff's presence, the cat shrinks back into the shadows and runs away, leaving its tattered prize behind. MacThomas laughs, and remembers an old saying:

"None so vicious as an Edinburgh cat."

THE WRETCHED WALLS

I don't believe in ghosts. I also don't believe in walking into old, decaying houses alone, particularly at night. The first belief is a result of intellectual reflection. The second belief operates on a different level. My aversion to the dark and creepy settings runs marrow deep. I suppose these two beliefs ought not coexist, since one appears to contradict the other.

I don't believe in open-ended stories, either. I like nice, tight little bundles that don't stray or discomfit. But a serious exploration of my opposing opinions about ghosts cries out for a story in which both beliefs are true. Given such a story, one's peace of mind becomes collateral damage.

I

Garrett waited until the day he signed the mortgage to buy the sledgehammer. He'd shopped the local hardware store weeks earlier, mulling the differences between brands, but he'd waited until the bank had the papers ready before buying the hammer and placing it on the front seat of his truck.

At the bank, the blonde mortgage officer peppered him with small talk while he waded through the paper stack. She had a pretty face and a nice figure, but her voice was on the sharp side of cheerful, which made it hard to focus on the legal language in front of him.

"That's the life insurance form. It covers the mortgage in case anything happens to you."

He nodded and tried to reread the page.

"You got a hell of a price on that house."

He looked up. Her pink blouse was open at the collar.

"I understand the property was on the market for more than a year."

"I think the owner was sick of showing it. She took my first offer."

"Not surprised," she said, one eyebrow raised.

He returned to the form. He could feel the woman's eyes on him. He forced himself to focus on what he was doing. He remembered the sledgehammer. Taking a deep breath, he signed the bottom of the page.

When the pile of papers had been cleared, the woman stood up. She held out a gift basket wrapped in yellow cellophane. "It's mostly fruit. There are some bath products, too." Her voice was almost apologetic.

"You give a lot of loans to couples," he guessed.

"Yes." She tilted her head. "Is there a Mrs. in your future?"

"No." Then, "Yes. Sort of." He realized that he was hedging, and he didn't want the woman to get the wrong impression. "I have a girlfriend, and we've talked a little about the future."

The woman set the basket down on the table. "Perhaps she'll like the bath salts." She glanced at her watch, suddenly impatient. "Well! It seems that you're the proud owner of a house, Mr. Jenkins. Congratulations! What's the first thing you're going to do when you get home?"

Garrett chuckled.

"Oh, you have something in mind! You must tell me." Her voice had gone sly, as if they were about to share a wicked secret.

"Yes," Garrett said. "I'm going to take down a wall."

* * * * *

He drove to the house, parked his pickup in front and headed for the door, sledgehammer in hand. This was the moment he'd dreamed of. With a single swing of the sledge, he'd blast the past into splinters and plaster dust. Goodbye college, goodbye teaching. Hello future.

He went through the entryway, closing the door behind him. The home was an old Victorian, built in the early twenties, part of the post-war boom in Denver. To the left, the great room, a brooding chamber full of dark wood, faded floral wallpaper, and chipped wainscoting. A modern chandelier hung from the center of the ceiling—part of the realtor's efforts to stage the house for sale.

To the right, a stairway. Lathe-turned wooden balusters supported the heavy, polished mahogany handrail that curved up to the second floor in an S-shape. The wood's deep, glossy finish resembled a "French polish"—a painstaking application of thin layers of Shellac cut with alcohol. The stairway had been carefully maintained for nearly a century. Though Garrett planned to divide the house—the upstairs would be a separate residence—he couldn't bear to change the stairway. The entrance would have to be a shared space for both residences.

Garrett paused for a moment, eyes closed. The house creaked and shifted. The sounds were comforting in some odd way. The house was old, settling. Anything he did on the house's behalf would be welcomed. And he would make his changes with the proper respect for tradition and restoration. He had studied the old crafts and intended no modern shortcuts.

Straight ahead, a hallway led to the kitchen, a tiny room that needed to be opened up. The back wall bordered a closet at the rear of the house. He would take out the rear wall and open the closet, creating space for new appliances. And the wall between the kitchen and the great room would go too, opening a huge space for entertaining.

The kitchen smelled of grease, and Garrett wondered if he might find a nasty surprise behind the wall. Rodents didn't scare him, but he didn't care much for them either.

He stopped in front of the rear wall and shouldered the sledge. He thought again about how he probably should have invited Molly. She knew what this moment meant to him. They'd talked about it often over the last few weeks. She was, in fact, part of his fresh start. When he left the university, he'd made a clean break, parting ways with Pamela. Molly was just what he needed— sweet, clever, and patient. And as patient as she was, she would understand that this was something he had to do alone.

He tapped the wall with the head of the hammer, listening for the hollow spot. The gas lines for the stove were in the wall to the right. This wall was clear. There was likely to be some wiring, but that would be no problem.

He took a deep breath. This was his moment.

The kitchen ceiling was high enough to enable a full, overhead strike. He smiled and swung. The sledgehammer was heavy, and he pulled out at the last moment, like a golfer shifting his hips. The head of the hammer struck the interior frame to the left of his target, connecting with sturdy framework, shredding plaster and little else. The interior 2 x 4 absorbed most of the blow.

He shook his head and laughed. So much for ritual.

Standing, sledgehammer in hand, he found himself unaccountably sad. The walls were decorated with faded blue wallpaper. The color matched his mood. He ran a hand across the wall, fingers running along the indentations he'd just made.

He shouldered the hammer again and gave the wall a second shot. This time, the sledgehammer punched a hole the size of a frying pan in the wall. Dust filled the air. Garrett stepped back and took another deep breath. The air behind the wall was musty, but the stench of decay or feces that he'd feared wasn't there. Good.

He swung again, tearing the wall to the floor. The head of the sledgehammer caught, and he tore plaster loose tugging it free. One more swing and the wall opened up.

Inside the walls, he found an old-fashioned, wooden strong box. A handle rode the front face. Leather reinforced the corners. A keyhole sat on top—the box was locked. The wooden surface was pocked and scarred. Garrett lifted it up, looking for a key underneath. No luck.

What might be inside? He'd read recently of a remodeler who found a Superman comic worth $175,000 stuffed in the wall as insulation. What a nice surprise if the find paid him an unexpected dividend.

Opening the box would be no trouble. One strike with a hammer and chisel would reveal the contents. But Garrett had seen antique boxes selling on eBay. Contents aside, the box itself might be valuable. Surely he could get a locksmith to open it for him.

He moved the box into the great room, tempted for a moment to fiddle with the lock. But the wall was waiting for him. He returned to the sledgehammer, but only for a few moments. Curiosity, he thought. Cat-killer for sure.

* * * * *

He found a locksmith shop nearby, in the old part of Denver. Garrett wondered how the shop stayed in business. Foot traffic was all but nonexistent. The proprietor stood behind the counter, slumped to the side as if someone had stacked him in the corner. Garrett set the box by the cash register. "Can you open this?"

The locksmith stared at the box for a long time without speaking. Then he leaned under the counter and retrieved a small tool. He flipped the tool open, like pulling the blade from a Swiss Army knife, and began poking at the lock. A moment later, Garrett heard a click.

The locksmith started to lift the lid, but Garrett put his hand on top of the box, stopping him. The locksmith looked up in surprise. Garrett smiled. "Thanks. How much do I owe you?"

"Going to keep me in suspense?"

"Sorry."

The locksmith's dour face deepened. "Where'd you find this?"

"Believe it or not, it was walled up in an old home a few blocks from here."

"Intriguing." The locksmith ran his hand over the top of the box, an index finger tracing some of the gouges.

"How much do I owe you?"

The locksmith looked away, as if considering the question. "Four dollars?"

Garrett nodded and pulled out his wallet.

The locksmith took the money and pointed at the box. "My brother owns a pawn shop on Pennsylvania Avenue. If you find anything in there that's worth a damn, you might give him a shot at selling it for you. Okay?"

Garrett shrugged. "I think I want to sell the box. It's an antique."

The locksmith nodded. "You sure you don't want to open it now?"

"Nope." Garrett grabbed the box. "If what's inside is worth a damn, I'll bring it by your brother's place. Promise."

The locksmith pressed his lips together in what might have been a smile. "Great." He stepped back as if waiting. Garrett stood silent for a moment, then nodded. He wanted to say something else, but he had no idea what that might be. In the end, he bowed and headed for the door, box in hand.

* * * * *

Garrett abandoned the sledgehammer in a pile of plaster and wood. Bundles of building materials and equipment rested in the corner, untouched. He sat on the floor of the kitchen, sifting through the photos he'd found in the box. Molly had often commented on how animated his face was. "I can always tell what you're thinking. You can't hide a thing. Your eyes and mouth give you away." Now, alone, his expression was blank. The muscles of his face had gone slack.

Garrett shuffled the photos for a second time, careful not to scratch or bend them. They might well be worth something. Vintage pornography—didn't collectors pay a lot of money for that sort of thing?

The house had been built in the 1920s. Garrett was no expert in fashion, but the photo subject's headwear seemed to date back that far. A turban in one shot. A flapper hat in another. Feathers in a third. He imagined that the fashion choices in his own closet—tee-shirts and dress shirts, sweatpants and slacks—would probably not impress anyone in the future. But the hats in the photos were damn ugly.

He flipped past the largest photo—the one that had immediately caught his eye—and studied another instead. The camera work was grainy. Shadows, so important to black-and-white portraits, cut across the subject's face. She wore a black mask that covered her eyes. Odd, because her face was exposed in most of the other photos. The woman's hairstyle did not change, nor did the beauty mark on her left shoulder. Garrett was certain the same model had been photographed over a period of time. Perhaps the mask shot was an early effort.

Another photo. The woman wore a mask in this one as well. The camera work was better this time. The photographer had taken time to stage the shot, complete with a curtained backdrop and ornate loveseat. Had the elaborate setting been intended as art? If so, the pose destroyed the illusion. The woman's legs splayed open, her back arched against the loveseat and her arms pinned to her side. Her downturned mouth was set, lips pressed thin, as if anticipating a blow.

Garrett paused. He stared at the hole in the rear kitchen wall. Someone had placed the photos in a box and sealed them up. There was no sense in it. Why not simply burn them?

Had the woman in the pictures been the wife or the mistress of the man who built the house? Had he walled them up to keep them a secret? The woman had not been an entirely willing subject, as evidenced by the largest photo—the one that disturbed him most. A portrait, without hats or strands of jewelry or velvet curtains and decorative pillows—just a woman, naked, pinching her nipples for the camera. Her hair tumbled free, touching her shoulders. She had a lush body, not the rail-thin stick figure of a modern fashion model. And her face was beyond beautiful—lovely features, huge dark eyes and an expression of utter and complete despair.

She stared at him from the photo, as if pleading for his help.

* * * * *

This place is incredible, Molly thought. She brushed a strand of hair from her eyes and turned back to face him. Two steps further up the staircase than Garrett, she stood even with him, her dark blue eyes wide with excitement. "Your plan is going to work, isn't it?"

"Our plan," he said. "I'm going to need your help."

"Oh, I'll help, all right. I've got hammer skills, you know?" She began climbing again, her hand on the polished banister. She had never really noticed a banister before. Then again, she'd not seen this level of craftsmanship used in service of a stairway before. "Garrett, this is so smooth!"

"I didn't know you liked wood so much."

She glanced back over her shoulder.

"See what I did there?" he asked.

She shook her head and laughed. "We're going to christen this place later tonight."

"It's a big house. It will need extensive christening." He reached up and touched her skirt. She laughed again and hurried up to the top of the stairs, stopping suddenly.

"Is there a light switch?"

"Yes, but there are no light bulbs."

"How am I supposed to see?"

He joined her at the top of the stairs. A darkened hallway extended to the back of the house. She could see doors on either side of the hallway. Bedrooms? Garrett would have to turn one of them into a kitchen, she supposed.

Garrett put his arm around her shoulder and stood still, head cocked, as if to listen to the house. The last rays of the day were a dim, gray square in the window at the end of the hall. She took a deep breath. The house was a little musty, but it had been shut up for a very long time. She pressed next to him, side by side, and he felt warm and comfortable.

The loud thump scared them both. She jumped under his embrace, bumping him in the jaw with the top of her head. "What was that?"

He stared down the hall, but the darkness held no answers.

Removing his arm from her shoulders, he moved her behind him, gently. "This old place has a lot of noise to it," he said.

A chill passed through her and made her shiver. He had stepped forward to protect her. From what? She peered into the dark. Nothing. Then she glanced up at Garrett.

He was smiling.

She gave him a little shove. "I think your house might be haunted."

He turned and wrapped his arms around her, kissing her. She resisted for just one heartbeat, and then melted into him. He knew how to kiss. But when his hands began to work, she pulled away. "We can't. Not now. We're meeting your mother in an hour—"

He grimaced. "A miserable excuse not to make love."

"Excuse me, big fella. It takes you a half hour to shower and dress. We're a 15-minute drive from the restaurant if the traffic is light."

"That leaves 15 minutes."

She shoved him. "Whatever. A quickie's not going to do it for me. Besides, this is important. I'm meeting your mother. That means something."

He looked away. "You keep saying that. But you haven't met my mother. She may change your opinion."

"I don't think so."

He shrugged. "She's a sour woman, Molly."

"She's your mother. I'm sure I'll like her. I just hope she likes me."

"She might." He glanced down, suddenly focused on her face, as if he'd just awakened. He blinked, and then smiled. "How could she help but like you? You're pretty and you're smart. You're perfect."

"Seriously. What if she doesn't like me?"

"I couldn't care less."

She grabbed his arms and wrapped them around her. "I care, though."

Garrett frowned. "You worry too much about what people think. And if you're going to worry about someone's opinion, don't let it be my mother's. She's not worth it." He cleared his throat and looked down at his shoes. "Well. That sounded terrible, didn't it?"

She nodded. His words *were* a bit callous—not like him at all. One of the things that attracted her to him was his kind nature. She wondered just how bad Garrett's relationship with his mother could be.

But later, sitting in a lower downtown restaurant, he seemed to get along with his mother very well indeed. He held the chair for her, focused his attention on her (almost to the exclusion of Molly) and laughed appreciatively at her terse jokes.

Paige Jenkins was a sturdy woman in appearance, with a short, no-nonsense hairstyle, a beige pants suit, glasses with thick, brown plastic frames and a squared jaw that protruded when she spoke. She clipped her words, biting as if conversation were a meat snack. She sat still, her hands folded in front of her, showing off her manicured nails—her only apparent extravagance.

She wore no jewelry. (Garrett's father had disappeared when Garrett was twelve years old. Molly had wondered if Garrett's mother still wore a wedding band.)

Molly fiddled with her silk napkin, took sips from her water glass, patted her hair in place and checked her cell phone for messages. After a while, her smile began to hurt, so she let it fade a little at a time, until it disappeared entirely.

"My dear?" Paige Jenkins stared at her, one eyebrow raised.

"I'm sorry." Molly's cheeks burned with a sudden flush. "Did you ask something?"

"Ah," Paige said with a nod, her eyes narrowing. "Well, I wondered if Garrett had been candid with you about the financing for the house."

"As I said, she's completely aware—"

"Garrett's salary at the university did not allow for a great deal of savings. Luckily, I was able to help. I cosigned for the construction loan and provided the necessary security."

"Yes, that was very kind of you."

"Garrett is certain that I've made a good investment." Paige sat back. Her jaw tightened for a moment, making the muscles on her neck stand out.

"The wait staff certainly seems to take its time with food orders, don't they?"

Molly glanced at Garrett. He stared at her. Then, he looked away and turned to his mother.

"I discussed every detail of the house with Molly. She's an investment advisor for one of the better companies in Denver. It's her profession. And she knows all of the ins and outs. If any part of the deal had made her nervous, I don't think I'd have bought the house."

"Oh, my! We're lucky your girlfriend approved, aren't we?" Her voice was a paper cut. Molly flinched.

"Actually, I defer to Molly on financial matters. As I said, she's a professional. I trust her knowledge. In fact, you ought to let her look at your portfolio." He turned to Molly. His eyes shone with secret mischief. "You don't mind if I volunteer your time, do you Molly?"

She stifled a laugh. Garrett was defending her in a way she couldn't help but appreciate. He'd praised her work.

"Interesting," Paige said. An uncomfortable silence followed, interrupted by the arrival of the waitress with their food. Molly had ordered seafood pasta, tossed in garlic oil. Paige had ordered fried chicken and mashed potatoes. Garrett had ordered a steak, despite his mother's insistence that he *loved* the fried chicken the restaurant served.

After the waitress left, Paige put down her fork and dabbed at her mouth with her napkin.

"How is your food?" Molly asked.

"Fine," Paige said. "Tell me, since you are an advisor of sorts. What's your professional opinion of the stock market?"

Molly shrugged. "I don't tend to recommend the stock market to my clients."

Paige's mouth dropped open. "Why not, for Heaven's sake?" She shook her head, as if she couldn't believe what she'd heard.

Molly thought carefully before speaking. "Basically, the idea of a perfect market assumes that all buyers have equal access to information. Taxes are limited, which is important, because taxes alter the natural direction of the market—"

"Yes, yes, but you don't see any value in the stock market? The American stock market?"

Molly looked down at her pasta. There was supposed to be a mix of seafood, but there was more salmon than anything else. She didn't really like salmon. She felt a sudden rush of disappointment and anger. "I think," she said, "that the stock market is an interesting laboratory for the study of herd behavior."

"Molly is a contrarian at heart," Garrett explained with a smile, leaning forward, his elbows on the table. "But she understands the housing market. And I promise you, she believes in free markets. Which is a good thing, considering we're talking money and investments. I wouldn't trust a socialist finance advisor any more than I'd trust a skinny cook." He pointed at his mother's plate. "Speaking of food, your chicken is okay, isn't it? It sure looks good."

"I told you to order the chicken." Paige's voice was perhaps sharper than she intended. She sat back in her chair and looked away, folding her arms.

"I could be convinced to trade some of my steak for a piece of that chicken."

"You know I don't eat steak."

Garrett laughed. "I know. That's why I offered it. But I'm getting some of that chicken, one way or the other." He paused. "Come on, just a wing."

Paige tried to hide a smile, and then shook her head.

"Okay, a leg."

"You're exasperating!" She turned to Molly and explained, "He always does this. He makes me laugh. When he was young, I could never punish him. Not really. He'll say some foolish thing and I'd start to laugh and he'd be out of trouble, just like that." She finished with the snap of her fingers, nail polish flashing in the light of the ceiling lamp.

Molly smiled and took a bite of her pasta. If she had food in her mouth, she wouldn't be expected to speak. On the other hand, there was the taste of salmon. Garrett continued to talk about food and investments and old-world craftsmanship, skipping from subject to subject, peppering Paige with questions about her opinions, which for the most part seemed sullen and self-important.

At first, Molly had wanted to be part of the conversation. Now, she was content to watch Garrett steer his mother clear of anything important. More than anything, she wanted the meal to be finished. But a long hour passed before she gave Paige a tepid, obligatory hug and headed for his truck.

Once inside, he let out a sigh of relief. "What did you think?"

"Your mother is an interesting woman."

"Ha." Garrett slapped the steering wheel.

She sat silent for a few moments as he steered into traffic. When she glanced over, he was staring at her. "Watch the road," she ordered.

"I'm waiting. Real answer, please."

"She *is* interesting."

"Mother Theresa was interesting. So was Adolf Hitler."

"Now *you're* being interesting," Molly said.

He laughed again. "So, where on the continuum between Hitler and Mother T do you put Paige Jenkins?"

Molly frowned as Garrett turned right at the intersection. "Where are you going? I thought we were going to christen the house?"

"I changed my mind," Garrett said. "I want to finish the place first. So we're going to your apartment." He paused. "That's okay, isn't it? I guess I should ask."

"I left my clothes for tomorrow in your kitchen."

"I can bring them to you tomorrow. Or we could stop by now and grab them."

"No, that's okay." Molly frowned. It *wasn't* okay. She had a limited number of work outfits, and there would be a staff meeting in the morning.

Garrett took a sudden left, drove a block and took another left.

"We really don't have to go back tonight," Molly said.

"It's okay."

"Now you're making me feel guilty. Like I'm at the Hitler end of your bitch scale."

He laughed again, louder this time. "Well, say hello to my mother while you're there." He notched his voice up an octave in an attempt to imitate her voice. "*The stock market? The American stock market!*" More laughter.

"It's not that funny," Molly said.

He stole a quick glance and then turned back to the road. Though he seemed to tighten his grip on the wheel, his voice softened. "Don't let her ruin your evening, Molly."

"It's not her."

"Ahhh." He nodded. "Am I wearing a little thin on you tonight?"

"It's been a stressful evening."

Garrett's house loomed ahead, a silhouette, lit from behind by a quarter moon. Garrett slowed as he approached, easing to the curb. Molly frowned. Somehow, the Victorian architecture, quaint and comfortable in the daylight, seemed unnatural and misshapen when cast in black. Dormers and gables slumped against a sagging roof. The turret at the house's right front face seemed to lean inward, poised to topple into the entryway. The angles of the house were all wrong, as if the architect had cast Euclid aside and followed *Möbius* instead. A bay window tilted out from the second story, unsupported by columns, ready to spill into the neighbor's yard. *If we'd seen this place at night*, she thought, *I'm not sure he'd have made an offer.*

Garrett stared up through the windshield, a half smile on his face. "Beautiful, isn't it?"

No. It's disturbing.

"Do you want to come in?" he asked, opening his door.

"I'll wait here." The car was running, so she rolled down the window. What was it about the house that bothered her? The shape? A trick of the light? Or was it the house at all? She might be upset over something else entirely. She wondered if Garrett's jokes and his mother's snubs had transformed her view of the house. If the evening had gone differently, would she have found the odd shapes and unnatural angles charming?

For a moment, she wished that she'd excused herself for the remainder of the night. Her stomach turned. Was it the salmon pasta or was it the evening? She couldn't tell. Her ambivalence alone justified a premature end to the night. Of course, she'd miss the sex. Garrett was considerate and eager to please—a welcome change from her ex-boyfriend, who'd been a spectacularly selfish lover. (She doubted her ex knew anything at all about a woman's body, beyond what places he could stick his penis.)

Garrett was a saint by comparison.

But did she want him to spend the night?

As she weighed the pros and cons, Garrett returned, putting the car in drive and pulling away from the curb before she could decide. "Are you in a hurry?" she asked.

He winked.

She turned away, irritated again. As they drove past the house, she leaned out of the car window as if to glance up at the second story of the old Victorian house.

She closed her eyes instead.

What if a shadow or reflection in a window gave her a false glimpse of a shrouded figure? Just imagining such a thing gave her chills. If she saw something, would she believe her eyes, or would she go over and over what she'd seen in her mind, until the memory was hopelessly muddled. She shivered and shook her head. Perhaps it was a good thing that they were going to her apartment instead.

"Are you cold?"

"It's September in Colorado. I'm not cold." He didn't need to know how badly the house bothered her.

He nodded and drove on, faster than he should, his face blank, squealing tires on tight curves, swerving a little too close to the cars parked along the dark streets. *Damn. He really is in a hurry.*

But in the bedroom, he took his time. He didn't ask what was wrong. He didn't speak at all. Instead, he undressed her, touching her gently, urging her past her mood to a place where she could relax, nestled in the sheets, eyes half-closed, open to his fingers and his mouth. Lights out, the light of the moon was enough to see him, to drink him in. Garrett hovered over her, his muscles taut with tension that he would not release. She could see his half-smile, the one that made him seem younger. His gaze told her that he knew what he was doing to her. She began to shudder—too soon!—and felt a full-body surge that fired in every nerve ending, twisting her into the mattress, leaving her sweaty and spent.

After, she lay on her side. He'd wrapped around her, sending her into a quiet drift that felt perfect. She'd made the right decision. The events of the evening had faded and finally disappeared. She pushed back against him, forcing herself closer, until it felt as if they'd melded and became one person.

But when she woke up, he was gone.

* * * * *

Garrett pulled at the drywall bracketing the small room behind the kitchen, tearing away huge chunks with his crowbar. The small overhead fixture in the kitchen cast more shadows than light. Plaster dust swirled in the beams. Garrett covered his mouth and thought of the mask he'd almost purchased at the Home Depot. Did old homes have asbestos in the walls? It was a concern, but not enough of one to stop what he was doing. He would go to the store when the doors opened in the morning and buy some disposable masks.

Morning—just hours away. Garrett felt a rueful smile cross his lips. He knew better than to try to sleep now. He'd waited patiently while Molly dozed off, his arms and legs aching with the urge to action. When her breathing became slow and even, he slipped away. Back inside the house—his house— the need to make changes ignited him. His hands itched for the crowbar. Even the top of his scalp seemed to move. His heart ran ahead of his lungs, and he found himself gasping for breath as if he were out of shape. *My God*, he thought. *I'm happy. This is happiness. I'm doing what I want to do. What I was meant to do. This, finally, is right.*

He hooked the curved part of the crowbar behind the drywall at the base of a support beam and pulled, tearing loose another chunk. Because the light was dim, it took several minutes to notice the shoebox. Rather than touch it, he tapped with the crowbar. Stiff, but pliable. He reached out and felt the cardboard. When he tried to pull it free, he found that it had been wedged in tight between the beams. What kind of house was this? A treasure in every wall? He thought of the photos he'd found earlier.

He sat back and considered the possibilities. Someone walled up these little boxes. But who would take the trouble? In the case of the photos, why not simply destroy them? A fire would have made quick work of the old images. Instead, he'd found them 80 (perhaps 90) years after they were taken.

And now, he'd discovered a second box.

He reached forward, shifting on his knees, but a sharp pain stopped him. His knees had been a mess since a high school football injury. Sports had been a source of contention with his mother, and a subtle way for Garrett to rebel. A torn ACL ended the debate. Now, kneeling on the tile floor, he had to laugh. He'd forgotten the injury and the attending pain—another measure of how the house had captured him.

Careful not to irritate the knee, he slid closer and grabbed the box, which had been set in the wall on its side. His fingers slipped under the box lid for leverage. He pulled, but it would not budge. When he felt the cardboard tear, he stopped. He sat back on his haunches for a moment to think, and then tried again, trying to wedge his fingers under the box for leverage. He couldn't jam them in.

Then he thought of the crowbar. He grabbed it, and stuck the point between the cardboard and the baseboard. Because of the darkness, finding the right angle took a moment. He levered the box up. It moved.

"Ha." He grabbed the top of the box again and pulled, while levering the box from the bottom. The top tore, but the box moved again.

His heart beat against his chest. He dropped the crowbar for a moment and tried to calm his excitement. *I should have quit teaching long ago.*

Another try at the box popped it free without further damage. He opened the top. The dim light gave him just a glimpse of some sort of doll. He struggled to his feet, knees straining, and took his prize into the kitchen. Placing the cardboard box on top the stove—the lid carried the name "Denver Dry Goods"—he removed the lid and stared inside.

For a second time, he wished he had a face mask.

What the hell is this? He dared a single breath through his nose. The smell was musty, as if dust and mold had taken residence in the box. And there was another smell—a cross between sulfur and rot.

He stepped away and scratched his head. The figure inside wore hand-sewn silk stockings, garter and a bustier. The clothing style was old-fashioned, similar to the lingerie in the old photos he'd found. Garrett grabbed a screwdriver from his tool box. The silk garments were old and delicate, and the figure itself looked mummified. He poked with the head of the screwdriver, and the bustier split, revealing two round, fur-covered breasts beneath the cups. He tapped them again with the screwdriver, striking glass.

The dead squirrel in miniature lingerie seemed to grin at him from the recesses of the box.

He set the screwdriver down. The overhead fixture wasn't bright enough to show much. Garrett slid the box across the top of the stove, angling it under the light. Though he was loath to touch the dead animal, he reached in and gave the tiny breasts a squeeze, splitting the fur, revealing the two glass marbles that had been sewn into the flesh.

He pried the marbles loose, spilling them into the box—two opaque marbles with bright blue swirl lines. Garrett plucked them out and set them aside. The locksmith's brother had a pawn shop. Perhaps the man knew something about vintage children's toys. Could the marbles be valuable?

Garrett replaced the shoebox lid, careful not to breathe in the dead, musty air until the squirrel was covered up. He paused to stare at the box. *What kind of person sews marbles into a dead squirrel?* Not that it mattered—he wanted the damn thing out of his house. He slipped the box into a plastic trash bag, then slipped that bag inside another bag.

Later, as he stood watching the sun rise from the back porch, his gaze settled on an old cement incinerator block near the fence. Back in the day, people burned their trash in their own back yards. That practice had been outlawed to protect the air. Garrett stared at the incinerator, as if weighing the notion. Neighbors might complain. He didn't care. Some things needed to be burned.

* * * * *

When he woke, the sun was down. Early morning? Late evening? When had he gone to sleep? He tried to turn over, but he was caught up in his sleeping bag, and his arm had gone numb. He inched his way out of the bag, leaning on his other elbow for support, until he bumped his head on the wall. *What the hell? I need to get a bed in here.* He continued to struggle, finally kicking the bag free.

The room was black. He stood up, wavering at first, and then slid along the wall. He had an alarm clock plugged in somewhere. He hadn't set it, but he could discover the time. The red digital display glowed from across the room. Hadn't he gone to sleep next to the clock? He wasn't sure. He couldn't remember going to sleep.

The clock read 6:00. Was it morning or night?

He felt along the wall for the door. He found the window instead and pulled back the curtains. A dull band of gray lit the horizon beneath a blanket of black clouds.

A storm was coming.

Garrett stared at the empty pavement where he'd parked. The street lights were off. No lights in any of the houses—none of the neighbors seemed to have electrical power. But he did—the alarm clock was working. He turned, but couldn't find the red glow anywhere. *The power must have just gone out.* He grabbed the window by the handle at the bottom and tried to lift up. The old wooden frame stayed shut.

"Well, shit." His voice sounded strange, as if he were nursing a terrible cold. He cleared his throat and tried again. "Shit!" Better. He continued his journey along the wall, hand extended, looking for the door, but couldn't seem to find it. *Haven't I made the circuit yet?* Then his hands brushed the door frame. He grabbed the knob and pulled the door open.

The lights were on in the kitchen.

He turned back to the room. The alarm clock—working again—read 6:15.

Garrett felt dizzy for a moment. When had he last eaten? He couldn't recall. Nor could he recall crawling into his sleeping bag, though he clearly had. He worked his way into the kitchen and sat down on the folding chair by his tools. A small box sat on the stovetop, which gave him a start (*I burned you!*), but it was the antique box with the tiny lock, not the shoebox with the squirrel. He'd been looking at the old photos again. A few of the pictures lay face-up around the box.

For some reason, the woman in the photos had captured his imagination. What was the appeal? The woman was pretty enough, with real curves. But in the age of Internet porn, how could a few comparatively tame poses garner his attention? Part of the attraction had to be the way he'd found them, hidden in the wall. And the woman looked genuinely vulnerable. Her expression wasn't staged. Who was she? Was there a chance she was still alive? *If she is alive, she's over 100 years old.*

He wondered then what Molly would look like in a private photo. Just the thought of it fired him up. Would she ever let him photograph her? There was no harm in asking.

He had a digital camera.

He shook his head. Something was playing hell with his thinking. He felt dizzy and disoriented. He needed a shower and a hot meal and a full night's sleep. He tried to stand, but all of his remaining energy seemed to drain out through his legs, and after swaying a moment, he sat back down. The idea of showering left him cold, rooted to the chair. *I must be sick.* He seized on the notion, because it explained *everything.* He wasn't disoriented. He was running a fever.

He stumbled back to the bedroom, turning on the light as he went. His sleeping bag lay bunched in the far corner. He considered turning out the light so he could sleep, but the thought of groping for the bag in the dark changed his mind. He crossed the room and bent to fumble with the zipper. His field of vision seemed to slip sideways, and he fell, hitting the ground hard enough to lose his breath. When his head cleared, he found himself on his back with the sleeping bag still zipped. *Yup. A fever.*

He rolled onto his side and attacked the zipper again. Six inches down, it stuck. He could see where the teeth of the zipper had caught the liner, swallowing it like a snake on a rat. He shivered again—the floor was cold—and decided to slide into the bag the same way he'd climbed out. He shoved his feet into the open bag and inched his way down inside the bag's gullet. He heard himself grunting with the effort, and halfway in, he had to stop and rest. Laying still, he could feel himself drift.

When he woke again, he was still halfway out of the bag. His chest and arms were corpse cold—numb and lifeless. His head ached. His eyes had crusted over, gluing his lashes shut.

And the bedroom light was off.

* * * * *

Garrett tried using the cell phone to call his doctor, but the battery was depleted, despite being plugged into the charger for at least a day. *One more thing to fix.*

A hot shower made him feel marginally better. He might be able to get by with non-prescription drugs. He'd get the kind with alcohol and let it knock him out. Another night in the sleeping bag—this time, all the way inside the bag—would do him good. Then he could get back to work on the house.

So far, all he'd done was to tear out some walls. He'd need more drywall than he'd initially imagined, but that wasn't a problem. He had money in his checking account, courtesy of his mother. She'd been unsupportive when he'd first approached her about the house and the renovation loan. He ignored her reservations, and after she saw the plan, along with real estate sales figures, she seemed to change her mind. "When did you find the time to do all of this research?" she'd asked, giving him the opportunity to sell her on his knowledge and his enthusiasm. She stared as if seeing him for the first time. She maintained her silence for a long minute, and then said, "I'll see what I can do." Two weeks later, she arrived at his doorstep with a check—she had taken a loan on her own house in order to finance his plans.

But no gift from Mom comes without strings. If he'd had it to do over, he'd have saved his own money and bought the house without help. On the other hand, how long would it take a college prof to save a down payment for a house that size?

He rolled the truck window down as he drove, which did him some good. Clean, crisp air seemed to pass directly from his lungs to his veins. He drove with his left arm dangling outside. The sun and the rushing air felt good on his skin.

His first stop was the medicine aisle at the grocery store. He grabbed some off-the-rack nighttime syrup and headed for the deli without a pause. *I'm really hungry*, he thought. The deli sold rotisserie chicken. He bought an eight-piece. The smell made him salivate.

His second stop was the pawn shop.

The locksmith had a brother who might be interested in the old wooden box. Garrett took the box from the front seat, tucked it under his arm and went inside.

The store was dimly lit, but Garrett couldn't miss the mud and paper wrappers on the floor. Products sat on dusty shelves, seemingly undisturbed for weeks, perhaps months. He stared at what appeared to be a pump handle—rusted and broken. Who would buy such a thing?

To his left, a single glass case. Behind the case, the pawnbroker sat on a stool. A tiny cash register on the counter top looked as unused as the pump handle. "Hello," he said, nodding to the pawnbroker.

No answer. The pawnbroker had one cocked eye that stared off to Garrett's right. Was he staring at him, or past him? Garrett set the wooden lock box on the glass case. He smiled, searching the pawnbroker's face, trying to discover which eye he should look onto. "Your brother the locksmith thought you might be interested in the box."

The pawnbroker smiled. His smile drifted to the side, much like his gaze. His teeth were brown and crooked, but the smile seemed genuinely friendly, if a little odd. "Oh, you're the fellow working on the house."

"Yes, I am," Garrett said, a little mystified. He didn't recall telling the locksmith anything about the remodel.

"How do you like the old place? It was on the market for a long time."

"Fine. Say, how do you know where I live?"

The pawnbroker snorted. "Our cousin works at the construction supply store."

"Small neighborhood."

The pawnbroker nodded. "When someone spends money in this neighborhood, people talk. So tell me, what was in the box?" He pointed. "You found it in the walls, right?"

"A few old photos."

"Oh. Too bad." The pawnbroker grinned again, showing his teeth. "I thought maybe there'd be some vintage sex toys inside."

Garrett was silent. The pawnbroker kept grinning.

"Okay," Garrett said finally. "Well. Are you interested in the box?"

The pawnbroker shrugged. "Probably not. It's junk, really. Sorry."

Garrett glanced toward the back of the shop. His gaze came to rest on an old bed frame and a rusted set of springs. Behind the bed, a broken chest of drawers that someone had tried, and failed, to refinish in cream-and-gold. "Junk," he repeated.

Then, a thought occurred to him. He reached into his pants pocket and pulled out two small, round objects. "What can you tell me about these?" He set the marbles on the counter.

The pawnbroker sat forward. His smile disappeared. "Where did these come from?"

"I think they're fairly old."

"They are," the pawnbroker said. He fished a jeweler's glass from his pocket and fixed it against his right eye. Garrett watched the other eye drift off to the side as the pawnbroker studied the marbles.

"Clams," he said.

"Pardon?"

"They're called clams. They get the name from the white, pearl-like color. These are glass. The swirls come off the pontil—that's where the glassblower broke off the stem. They smooth the marble, of course, but you can find the point. Look! Look right here. See the little mark here?"

Garrett bent forward. The glass had a tiny blemish where the blue swirls began.

"These are very nice. How much do you want for them?"

Garrett had never liked to dicker. "How much are you offering?"

The pawnbroker shrugged. A tiny smile returned to his face. "Ten dollars?" Garrett didn't answer immediately, so the pawnbroker added, "Ten apiece, I mean."

"Done," Garrett said. The marbles were probably worth more, but he wasn't interested in doing the research necessary to get a better price. The pawnbroker snatched the marbles, pocketing them. Then he turned and pulled a small receipt pad from the top of the register. For the next five minutes, Garrett waited while the pawnbroker filled in the lines of the handwritten receipt.

"I don't really need a receipt. It's okay."

"I have to." The pawnbroker stopped writing and looked up. "It's the law."

When, finally, the transaction had been made, Garrett turned to go, box under his arm, but the pawnbroker wasn't done with him. "Wait! You don't want the box, do you?"

"Here, take it," Garrett laughed, setting the box on the counter top.

"Do you want a receipt?"

"Please, no." He started for the door.

"Sorry about the sex toy crack, but you know. Your house's history and all."

"What do you mean?"

"Didn't the realtor explain about the house before you bought it?"

Garrett's hand was on the doorknob. He'd almost been out of the shop. "Is this where you tell me about some murder that happened in the past?"

"Murder?" The pawnbroker snorted again. Garrett realized that snorts were laughter. "No murder. Your home was a bordello."

"What?"

"A bordello. A whorehouse—pretty famous for its time. During prohibition, some of the richest folks in five states came here to get a few drinks and some pussy. That's why I made the sex toy joke. You know?"

"Wow. I didn't know." Garrett pulled the door open.

"Well, thanks for the marbles." The pawnbroker ran his fingers through thinning hair, disturbing his comb-over. "By the way. Where did you find them? Were they in the wooden box?"

Garrett couldn't resist. "No. They were sewn up inside a dead squirrel."

* * * * *

His next stop was supposed to be the home supply store, but his cell phone rang just as he pulled into the parking lot. His mother needed to see him. He agreed to drive to her house, and then sat in the parking lot, his hands gripping the wheel, his eyes fixed on the supply store door. She'd sounded distraught. She often sounded that way. Crisis was a way of life for Paige Jenkins. A house payment could never be late—foreclosure was imminent. The tiniest weight gain was an eating disorder. Every headache was a potential tumor. But now she had a real crisis to stew in.

Paige's sister—Garrett's Aunt Rose—had been diagnosed with terminal cancer. When Garrett's father ran off, Rose had been very critical, blaming her sister for the marital breakup. Paige, never one to suffer criticism, went years without speaking to her sister.

After Garrett moved out on his own, Paige suffered from loneliness. Rose reached out to fill the void. The sisters settled their differences and began to build a tentative friendship. They traveled to garage sales together. They joined a baking class. Rose took Paige to roller derby night at the warehouse. Paige took Rose to her book club.

Then Rose's husband took a job back east. Rose moved away, leaving Paige lonelier than before.

Now, Rose was ill. What would Paige do? Garrett gripped the steering wheel tighter, squeezing the blood from his knuckles. He glanced down, surprised, and released his grip. But later, sitting on his mother's couch, he found his fists clenched again. He forced himself to relax and open up. He rested his right arm on the decorative pillow at the corner and extended his legs, careful not to disturb the throw rug.

"I sometimes regret not having given you a brother or a sister," Paige said. "Then you'd know. You'd understand just how painful it is to lose someone so close to you. It's not just that she's my sister. She's my past—the good part of my past. Carnivals and bike rides. Candy apples. Autumn days." She stopped to dab at her eyes with the corner of a handkerchief. The cloth was embroidered with the letter "P" done in fancy stitching. "There's no way to explain it and no way for you to understand."

"You're right, Mom." She was wrong, of course. He was perfectly capable of understanding loss. People died. Everyone with family and friends left sorrow in their wake when they passed. Paige was hurting, but she wasn't the first or last to mourn a passing. But he kept silent. His mother didn't need perspective. She needed a sympathetic ear.

Despite her anguish, Paige's voice was flat and steady. Only the open, downturned mouth and the touch of moisture at the corner of her eyes betrayed her emotional state.

Garrett's thoughts drifted. He wanted to be home, renovating his house. Rebuilding. Making something fresh out of something old. But he would do the right thing. Always, always, the right thing.

"Are you listening to me?" Paige asked.

He had no idea what she'd just said. He thought for a moment before speaking. "I'm listening, Mother. But I listen better when I don't interrupt. That's something I learned from you."

Paige sat back, one eyebrow raised. "Well." She dabbed at her eyes with the handkerchief again and took a deep breath. "You're a good son, Garrett. I don't say it often enough. You turned into a fine man. I'm glad I was able to help you buy that old house. I hope you make the most of it. I hope you've decided to settle down a little. It's not good to flit from one thing to another. From one person to another."

"I've always been here for you."

"I'm not talking about me," she insisted. "Not everything is about me."

* * * * *

The sun was down by the time he'd finished listening. He made his mother dinner, did the dishes (the only chore he could do for her—the house was immaculate) and left at the start of her favorite sitcom. Next, he drove to the supply store and purchased more sheetrock. Then he headed to Molly's apartment.

She might not be home. He hadn't called her in a day or so. She didn't even know he'd been sick. His visit would be a surprise to both of them. He hadn't planned it.

But that wasn't true—the digital camera on the front seat of the truck said so.

He rubbed his eyes. The fever seemed long gone. He was still a little weak, but his thoughts were clear and ordered. He slapped the steering wheel and headed for Molly's door.

Molly Harper's apartment was a modest single-bedroom place with a tiny kitchen and dining room, a bathroom and half the closet space any normal adult would require. A basket of dirty clothes sat by the front door, ready for a trip to the laundromat. A few dishes and plates filled up one side of the kitchen sink. The coffee table carried a stack of books next to an empty wine glass, stained red at the bottom.

Molly was beautiful and rumpled, dressed in a terrycloth bathrobe, her hair wet from the shower. The sight of her warmed him, but she seemed a little distant. "Big surprise," she said, an edge to her voice. "I didn't expect you. You didn't answer my text."

"My cell phone is acting up," he explained. (*But it worked when Mother called. Damn phone.*) "Are you angry with me?"

"No," she said, flopping back on the couch. She brushed her hair away from her eyes. "You're a flake. I've always known that."

"Really?" He sat down next to her on the couch. "You figure I'm a nut job?"

"Everyone's a nut job," she said, kissing him. "So tell me?"

"What?"

She pointed at the object in his hand. "What's up with the camera?"

II

Garrett forced himself to slow down. The pattern for the crenellated trim was a simple one, but he was not used to working with a chisel, and he'd already ruined one short but expensive piece of wood by rushing the work. Using the old methods of building was important to him. In his mind, the work didn't have to be perfect. A minor flaw was a welcome sign of handcrafted work. The second piece of trim looked better than the piece he'd ruined. The work was surer, smoother. He could finish the fluting with sandpaper before he fixed the piece to the top of the door.

Each of the upstairs rooms presented a challenge. The rooms were mismatched, and Garrett wanted an overall theme to tie them together. Visual cues like woodwork (and later, décor), would differentiate the upstairs from the downstairs, emphasizing the separation of the two residences.

The idea of thematic division had been Molly's. She thought selling might be easier if the two apartments were visually separate. Victorian both, but different.

Garrett sighed. Their argument over the camera had been upsetting. She hadn't taken his suggestion of private photos well. *Private photos are never private. Never! You're a nice man, Garrett, and you'd never think to hurt me, but it wouldn't matter. You'd show a friend, or someone would hack your files, or something else crazy would happen.*

He'd protested. She held firm, pressing her lips in a thin line, her eyes narrowed. *I know this from experience, Garrett.*

Her comment had surprised him. Had she posed for someone else?

She ignored his question. *Tell me something. You can have me, the real me, in the flesh, anytime you want. Why isn't that enough?*

A question he couldn't answer.

He found himself working around a small knot in the wood, slipping again with the chisel. "Damn!" He set his hammer down and examined the damage. The resulting blemish wasn't enough to ruin the piece. In a way, the tiny divot seemed to make the piece more charming than before in some way he couldn't define. Perfect wasn't really what he had in mind. Perfect meant machined.

Thoughts of Molly made him frown. He hated the bumps in their relationship. Why did he bring up the camera thing? Photos didn't even mean that much to him. He should have known that she'd react badly. She was full of spit and vinegar. He loved that about her, but calming her ruffles was a full time job. Why couldn't things be smooth between them?

He glanced up at the French glass doors. He could see his reflection, and it unsettled him. He was losing weight, and the lack of sleep darkened his eyes. He needed to put on a pound or two, and those puffy eyes had to go. He shook his head and turned back to the wood trim.

He considered his next cut. He bent in close. The wood had lovely grain marks, dark and irregular. He ran a hand across the surface. The crenellations were rough, but they'd be beautiful once he finished. He put the head of the chisel against the dim pencil mark he'd made, barely visible now. In fact, he was having trouble seeing anything.

Night. He stared out of the gabled window. The sun crouched behind the row of houses across the street. He looked at his watch. Six-thirty. The day had gotten away from him. He laughed. "I love this house," he whispered.

Thump.

The sound came from the next bedroom. Not the rustle of mice or even a footstep—the sound of someone slamming against the wall that separated the rooms.

Garrett went into the hall. The dark corridor left him momentarily blinded. He fumbled along, hand to the wall, until he found the door next to the one he'd been working in. He grabbed the doorknob and turned, pushing the door inward.

Blinded again. It took him several long moments to orient himself. The room was empty, except for a few pieces of old furniture that came with the house. A tiny end table sat next to a broken stuffed chair. A full-length mirror had been fixed to the far wall. The closet door was open. A wire hanger hung from the bar inside. Garrett turned to the right. A single nail marred the wall. A lightened rectangle revealed where a picture had hung, now long gone. A chill ran the length of his spine.

The light. It was daylight outside.

He lurched, staggered by the impossibility of what he was seeing. And from the corner of his eye, he saw movement, no more than a shadow's flicker, as if he'd stared at a bright light and the negative afterimage became suddenly animated. The figure came at him with frantic, jerking steps—the gait of a demented marionette.

He lurched away, bouncing off of the doorframe. Sudden, unreasoning fear turned his insides to liquid. Distilled fear flooded him, like the sudden terror of a nightmare. The room was not like the rest of the house. He was not welcome here.

If he stayed here, he would die.

Garrett stumbled into the hallway and shut the door. Darkness. Fumbling his way back, he peered into the room where he'd been working on the wood trim. The sun had set. Leaving a violet band behind the dark silhouettes of houses. Night.

He stood, hands on the frame of the doorway, shaking. *This is not possible.* His knees felt weak, and he needed to urinate. He wanted to leave. He wanted to climb in his car and drive away.

Instead, he forced himself to return to the adjacent room. This time, he found only darkness when he opened the door. He left again, returning with a flashlight. Every detail was as he'd remembered it—mirror, chair, end table and nail. But the sun had set, and the room had nestled into night, wrapping itself in tar.

He turned the flashlight on his wristwatch.

Just after midnight.

* * * * *

Sleep seemed impossible. He jolted awake at every sound, real or imagined.

Just after 3:00, he drifted off, only to awaken an hour later with a painful erection. He lay on his back, absently fondling himself. Eyes closed, half asleep, his thoughts drifted to the photos he'd found. The woman seemed so very unhappy—something he could relate to. He imagined her posing, embarrassed and aroused, taking direction from a stern husband. Garrett pictured the husband as a thin man with a pocked face and a goatee, never smiling. His eyes were smoke black, empty of pity.

She was silent, understanding that protest was useless. When he told her to touch herself, she did. When he told her what he would do with the pictures, she wept.

And suddenly, Garrett lurched in the sleeping bag, surprising himself with the ferocity of his orgasm. Then he lay still, panting, stunned and dismayed.

He started to ease out of the bag, careful not to make more of a mess than he'd already made, when a soft, shuffling sound, like bare feet on a wood floor, stopped him cold. He stared into the darkness, unable to see anything. He sat still for several long minutes, ears prickling. What had he heard?

Chilled by more than the night air, he felt his way to the wall and flipped the light switch.

The room was empty and silent.

* * * * *

The following morning, he returned to the university.

On the way, he phoned his mother—the fickle cell phone was working again—and wished her a safe trip. Paige had decided to travel east to take care of her sister Rose. "I may be gone for a few months," she'd said. "Rose is very, very ill." Garrett tried not to sound too happy about his mother's trip, but the thought of working on the house, uninterrupted, was exciting. Perhaps his mother would meet someone her own age and start a relationship. Perhaps she'd like Vermont and decide to move.

The visit to the campus cheered him even more. He'd taught classes for four years, but hadn't returned since his decision to remodel homes for a career. Whether the fall weather, crisp and breezy, or the sight of students rushing to class, he felt a sudden rush of nostalgia. He'd been happy here. He glanced at the college library as he passed. The thought of so many books made him smile. The third floor of the library held some particularly valuable books in a raised, gated section. Once a week, Garrett would request a key from the librarian, go to the third floor and browse. His field was graphic design, but his interests ran from mathematics to art history to spiritualism. Interest in the last resulted in a friendship and brief romance with one of the young assistant professors.

Pamela Miller taught in the physics department. She was an eye magnet everywhere she went, but within the physics department, she was a goddess. Auburn, shoulder-length hair framed huge green eyes. Short skirts and heels showed off her long legs. But it was her quirky love of the arcane that Garrett found most attractive.

Pamela's interest in the occult was an eccentricity that her peers tolerated. In reality, she was a skeptic, bringing a scientist's sensibilities to a field filled with debunkers and charlatans—and precious little serious research. "We're so far behind the old Eastern bloc," she'd told him. "They've been researching the unseen world since before the World War II. Our government is afraid to look silly. They won't fund a serious line of investigation. That abandons the field to amateurs and scam artists."

"So you believe in ghosts?" he'd asked.

Her eyes had narrowed, her tiny nose wrinkling. "No, of course not," she'd said, as if he'd asked her if she believed in the Easter Bunny. "But who can be sure? And it's fun to think about, don't you agree?"

Garrett shoved his hands deep into his pockets as he walked. *No, not so fun to think about.* But he'd thought about nothing else since the evening before, and he had to talk to someone. Pamela was the one person he could sort through the facts with. She wouldn't laugh at him. And she had a good mind.

He'd already decided what she'd say. She would tell him that he'd seen the adjacent room in the daylight. His mind had filed the image away, and in a moment of disorientation, he'd called up the image to fill the void. *The mind likes to fill in the gaps, so to speak.* He repeated the line to himself in her voice, imagining her smile and the tilt of her head. Seeing her again would be nice.

Crossing the student center plaza, he heard his name. A young man, short, with a yarn cap pulled over a spray of dreadlocks came rushing up, backpack in tow. His brown corduroy pants were too large, and in his effort to hurry, he'd adopted a hopping sort of run, tugging at his beltline as he went. Garrett recognized him. He'd been in a design course he'd taught the semester before he left the university.

"Mr. Jenkins! It's really cool to see you! Are you back?"

Robbie. The boy's name was Robbie.

Robbie came to a full stop just a foot away. If Garrett had opened his arms, the boy would have pitched himself into them. Instead, he tried to catch his breath and rearrange his clothing.

"How are you, Robbie?"

The boy beamed. "Great. So, are you teaching again?"

"No, I'm meeting a friend." Garrett pointed at the engineering building across the plaza.

"Oh, that's too bad. I thought maybe you changed your mind and came back." He frowned. "You were the best prof in the department. Hands down."

Garrett tried to remember, then took a guess. "You're a sophomore, right?"

"Nah. I'm a junior, this semester."

"Not long to go, then."

Robbie shook his head, tossing his dreads with the motion. "Long enough!"

Garrett reached out and touched the boy's shoulder. "It was good to see you, Robbie. I have to run. You keep after it, you hear? I think you're in the right field." He started away, then glanced back. "I hope you and Adobe are staying out of trouble." The boy laughed and waved.

The engineering building, home to the Physics department, was a series of five long wings, three stories tall, connected across the front by a ground-floor walkway. He entered the physics wing and headed for the third floor. Pamela was there, tucked in the corner of a shared office, staring at her computer screen. Her legs were every bit as long as he remembered. She turned her head as he approached, recognizing him. Her hands flew up to pat her hair in place, then brush the front of her blouse.

He smiled. "Hello stranger."

She blushed. "Garrett? What are you doing here?"

Garrett grabbed an empty desk chair and wheeled it over to her corner. "Do you have a moment for me? I need your expertise."

"Of course." She glanced at her watch. "I have a class in 15 minutes. I could be a few minutes late, I suppose."

Garrett sat in the chair, hands on his knees, staring at the floor. Then he raised his gaze, staring straight into her eyes. "Tell me again," he started, his voice lowered against the prying ears of the other teaching assistant—a short, thin man with dark, unkempt hair playing on a laptop. "Do you believe in ghosts?"

Pamela didn't answer immediately. Garrett watched as she stared, her expression shifting as if considering a series of possibilities. Perhaps she thought he was joking, or trying to reconnect. When she spoke, her voice was soft and low. "Tell me what you've seen."

Garrett explained what had happened the previous night. "It was nighttime in one room, and daytime in the other. That sounds crazy, but I'm pretty sure what I saw. I say 'pretty sure,' because the experience left me a little disoriented. And when I went back, the room was dark. I couldn't see anything, let alone a light spot on the wall where a picture used to hang." He smiled, self-conscious. "I sound like a lunatic, don't I?"

"I don't think you're crazy," Pamela said. She seemed to be measuring both him and his words. "Though I have to say, you look tired. Are you pushing yourself too hard?"

Garrett shook his head, chuckling. "No, no, quite the opposite. I don't have any real deadlines. I work when I want. I'm working a lot of hours, but that's because I'm enjoying what I'm doing."

Her smile seemed forced. "I'm glad the new direction is working out for you."

"It's not that I don't miss the campus. I do." He shifted in the chair, glancing over at the dark-haired man, who had been staring at them. The man returned his gaze to his computer.

"How is everything else going?" Pamela's voice seemed to have acquired a forced brightness.

"Good. Great. Except the house has me wondering." He leaned closer, dropping his voice to a whisper. "I'm there alone most of the time. But I never *feel* like I'm alone. I don't mind, not usually. There's an odd sort of comfort for me there. It's like I'm home. Like I'm welcome. Until last night." He sat back, weighing his thoughts before speaking again. Pamela waited, silent.

"What I haven't said is that I think I saw something. Maybe *someone*. Scared the crap out of me." He shivered with the memory. "It was like a shadow, only not a full shadow. Pieces were missing."

"Like arms and legs?"

"No. It was like a partial image. A silhouette." He paused. "No, that's not right. A silhouette is solid black. This was an outline, and not even a full outline."

"Was it a man or a woman?"

"I couldn't tell," Garrett admitted.

Pamela nodded. She stared at him for a while. Then she sat back, her gaze narrowed. "You're not sleeping well." It was a statement, not a question.

"I sleep okay. I'm really not in a sleeping mood."

"Doesn't that girl of yours let you sleep?" Her laugh was shrill.

He didn't answer.

"I'm sorry," she said, looking down. "That was rude. But I can't help but notice that you look tired. Exhausted, really. And you've lost weight."

"I forget to eat sometimes. But what about the—"

"Ghost?" She met his gaze again, her eyes harder and brighter than before. He sat back, a frown on his face. "There are no ghosts, Garrett." Her voice had softened, but only a little.

"But I saw—"

"Ghosts don't exist. Suppose for a moment that one really existed—an existence on another plane or in another dimension. And suppose that ghost could somehow physically appear. That would take energy. We live in the physical universe. The laws of physics apply. I hate to reference movies, but you often see lights flicker and die before a ghost appears. That's meant to signify some sort of power tap. That didn't happen to you, did it?"

Garrett shook his head.

"Changing state takes energy. Think of water and steam. Or ice and water."

"What about poltergeists?"

She laughed. "Most poltergeist activity takes place in the presence of young girls reaching puberty. Talk about a power source!"

Garrett felt suddenly foolish.

"But you believe you saw something. That much is clear." She cleared her throat. "I won't sugar this, Garrett. You're a friend. And you're a big boy. You're not taking care of yourself. You look like you haven't slept in days. When someone is tired, their mind can play tricks."

"That's too easy." Garrett felt her words sting.

"Sometimes the easy answer—the simple answer—is the truth."

He nodded.

"I am intrigued by what you've told me, though. And you are an honest man. Some people who claim to have ghostly encounters are selling something. I hear from bed and breakfast owners and fortune tellers and authors. Sometimes, people who say they've experienced the supernatural are just lonely. Sometimes, they need attention. You're none of the above. So, like I said, your story interests me. If you'd like, I can investigate the house. I could roll out the equipment this weekend—"

"I don't think so." He stood up, hands in his pockets, smiling. "I figured I had an actual haunted house on my hands. Or that I was crazy. Seems like the betting odds are on crazy."

"I didn't say that." She brushed a strand of hair from her forehead. "You're leaving?"

"You have a class to teach, remember?" His smile widened.

She nodded. "Did I piss you off?"

"No, you were honest. I do look like shit." He fought to keep his voice smooth and friendly. He suddenly wanted out of the office. He wanted to go home. To his house.

"You don't look like shit." A sadness seemed to have crept into her green eyes—downturned at the corners, softened by the threat of tears. "You always look good, Garrett. But you look tired to the bone."

"It was good to see you again, Pamela." He gave her a slight bow, and turned to go.

"Garrett?" Her raised voice caught the attention of the other teaching assistant. The man lifted his glance, his nose extended, sniffing the air.

Garrett turned back.

"The thing about a ghost is, if you see one, it's probably not real. Physical manifestations require power."

He frowned.

"Watch out for the ghosts you *can't* see."

"Why is that?" he asked.

She tapped her temple with an index finger. "Because they're in your head, Garrett. And that's where the *real* danger is."

* * * * *

As the sun set, he returned to the second-floor room that had frightened him the night before. Garrett didn't think of himself as a coward, but the thought of encountering the shadow—or whatever the apparition had been—left him dry-mouthed and weak. So he forced himself up the stairs, flashlight in one hand and a package of light bulbs in the other. He would focus his evening's work on that room, fear be damned.

He paused outside the door, listening. The house was silent, which set his nerves on edge. With a deep breath, he turned the doorknob and reached inside, fumbling for the light switch. Where was it? He slapped at the wall, his breath catching in his throat. No switch. He pushed the door open and looked inside. The switch was placed higher than he'd remembered. He reached up and flicked the light on, and then looked around the room. Nothing out of place.

"Idiot," he whispered.

The night's first order of business was to remove the wainscoting. The three-foot high decorative trim that circled the room was a cheap pressboard, coated in white paint. The paint, thick and bright, struck him as a recent addition. *Somebody ruined this room.* He would remove the wood, clean the walls, and paint over everything in tan or brown. Something earthy. He could add a touch of wood by placing crown molding around the tops of the walls.

He fetched his tools from the room next door. In the end, a crowbar would do most of the work, but he brought the rest of the toolbox as well. Screwdrivers made nice chisels.

He found a spot where the wainscoting had pulled free from the wall. He tried to wedge the crowbar into the gap, but the point wouldn't quite fit. The claw end of his hammer did, however. He was able to pry the gap open enough to let the crowbar do its work. The wood tore loose with a splintering sound. Peering behind the gap, he could see that the trim had been attached with nails. The wall was solid, and took the separation with only minor scuffing. He would make quick work of the job.

Garrett tore the wainscoting free, panel by panel. On the far side of the room, he found some of the wood fixed with screws, which slowed his progress a little. He smiled to think he was actually using a screwdriver to turn a screw.

When he came to the far wall, he moved the mirror—a floor-length, freestanding model. He lifted it from the side and carried it to the center of the room without looking into the mirror's face. He was a rational man, but there was no sense in testing his convictions. He'd begun to believe that the house was haunted.

The next wood panel came loose in one piece. When he saw the paint beneath, he frowned. Letters ran into the adjacent panel. Someone had painted a message, beginning with the letters "t" and "h." He hurried to remove another segment, tearing at the wood. In his haste, he put a divot in the wall, which bothered him. He'd been so careful!

The wood came loose—nails for this panel—and he grabbed the top, pulling with both hands. Grunting with the effort, he tore the wainscoting free, revealing the message underneath:
They leave.

Two words, painted in thick brush strokes, two-feet high, with an angry splotch for a period. Garrett stared at the message, mesmerized. What could it mean?

The message came from the naked woman in the photo.

He was sure of it.

He stood still, wood panel in his hands. How could he know that? He couldn't possibly know. But he was sure.

He turned to go. He had to get to a coffee shop or restaurant—any place with a WiFi connection. He needed to find out something about the house and its owners. He needed to find out about the woman. The Internet wouldn't work in the house. He needed to get out.

* * * * *

"Molly?" He'd called her on his cell phone, excited to share what he'd discovered. But as the ring tone sounded and she answered, he realized that he hadn't spoken to her in a while. How long? He didn't know.

"Garrett? Is that you?"

She sounded worried. That was a good thing. Worry was better than anger.

"I had to call you," he said, speaking in a rush, hoping to distract her from any hard feelings. *He'd been inconsiderate. How could he have neglected her? It wasn't like him.* "I found out some amazing things about the house. You won't believe it. Are you doing anything right now?

"Well, I was sleeping. It's after midnight."

He glanced at his laptop. It was nearly one in the morning. What was he thinking? "God, Molly! I'm so sorry! I guess I got caught up in my research and lost track. Can you forgive me?"

"What's going on, Garrett?"

The worry in her voice was gone. She was irritated. Distant.

"I'll talk to you tomorrow," he said.

"No. I'm up now. What do you want?"

He should have hung up. Instead, he hung on, silent.

"Garrett?"

"It's not that big of a deal," he said. He struggled to slow his voice. "It's just that I found out who the girl is."

"Who what girl is?"

"The girl in the photo."

"I'm sorry," she said. "I'm half asleep, Garrett. What girl are you talking about?"

Garrett realized that he'd never mentioned the photos he'd found. He paused for long moments, wondering how to explain what he'd found and what it meant to him. The whole thing was so confusing. "I found some old photos in the wall," he said at last. "A lot of the photos were of a young woman. It turns out that she was the wife of the guy who built the house back in the early 1920s."

"And that's important why?" Molly's words slurred. She sounded very tired.

"The house was a bordello. You know what that is?"

"I know what a bordello is," Molly said. Now, she sounded angry.

"She was the madam of the house."

Pause. "So?"

"She was this guy's wife. She married him when she was really young. His name was—let me look at my notes—Robert. Robert Laughlin. He made his fortune in finance. When the stock market crashed, he took off and left his wife with the mortgage. Her name was Winnie."

"Okay."

"There's more. A lot more. Winnie had no means to pay the mortgage. So she opened a bordello. A little liquor, a little prostitution. The stuff I read said that she got the liquor by providing sexual favors to the bootleggers."

He heard Molly yawn. "Sounds like there's lots of history there, Garrett."

"It's just that I found her picture here, hidden. And I could find out who she was—"

"On the Internet," she finished.

"Of course." He sat still for a moment. He could tell her that the pictures he'd found were nudes, but becoming obsessive over some old nude photos would make him seem creepy. And she would wonder about the photos *he'd* wanted to take.

"I haven't called in a while," he said.

"I know."

"I'm sorry."

"Don't be." She yawned again. "So are you taking a break from the remodel to play on the Internet?"

"No, not at all. I was remodeling." He remembered the message on the wall. "In fact, I found a message on the wall when I pulled off the wainscoting. I think the message was from Winnie."

"What did it say?"

"They leave."

"Pardon?"

"They leave," he repeated.

"What does that mean?"

"Damned if I know," Garrett said. "Say, we really have to get together soon. I have some things to tell you."

"Sure," she said. "That would be nice."

He frowned. "You don't sound too excited about it."

"Garrett. You get into an argument with me over taking nude photos, and then you don't call me for days. Now you want me to jump around because you call? Seriously? Listen, it's late, and I have to work tomorrow. I'll talk to you later." The phone clicked before he could respond.

* * * * *

He noticed the discrepancy while vacuuming the hallway to the right of the kitchen. But before that, he's seen signs, so the discovery wasn't much of a surprise. The first of those signs was the kitchen floor. He'd torn up the cheap vinyl, hoping that he could restore the wood floor beneath it. The wood was in good shape, with a dark, beautiful grain. But a gap ran down the middle of the kitchen, bisecting the floor. It was clear that a wall had originally stood there. The distance from where the old wall stood to the right-side wall in the kitchen was too little, even for a cramped, narrow, Victorian-style kitchen.

And the right-side wall was wallpapered, unlike the rest of the kitchen. Had one of the house's owners moved walls to accommodate appliances?

Then, while vacuuming his plaster mess from the carpeted hallway, he discovered that his cord, plugged into a kitchen socket, wouldn't reach far enough to finish the job. The vacuum went as far as the window that looked out over the back-yard. The window had been placed at the junction where the outside walls of the hallway and kitchen met at right angles. Staring out, Garrett wondered why someone would place a window in a corner, where the dominant view was a perpendicular wall extending into the yard. Turning back to his left, he realized that the cord extended down 12 feet of hallway to the corner of the kitchen.

If the outside wall starts here, then why is the interior wall 12 feet down the hall?

The wallpapered wall in the kitchen had to be a false wall.

He paced his way along the vacuum cleaner cord and peered into the kitchen. If the gap behind the wall went all the way back to the end of the kitchen, the enclosure would be fairly large. Smaller than a room, perhaps, but larger than a walk-in closet. A pantry? That made no sense. Why wall up a pantry when remodeling a kitchen? He stared at the stove against the right-side kitchen wall. Who would put wallpaper behind a stove?

Bootleggers?

He examined the gas line behind the stove. An old, dirty flex line ran into the wall at the base of the floor. Was the gap between the inner and outer wall for gas lines, wires and vents? That would make sense for a two-foot, or even a three-foot space. Not for a small room.

Garrett walked back down the hall and stared out of the window. There were no windows on the wall that extended out, but there was a small, rectangular vent a few feet above eye level. He backtracked to the kitchen. No vent on the inside. Whatever the vent's purpose, it had been walled up along with the room.

Picking up a hammer, he tapped his way along the right-side wall, listening for hollow spots. The walls in these old houses were sturdy—built to last. He couldn't hear a difference. For a moment, he held the hammer out, ready to strike. He could solve the mystery with a single blow.

The sound of the cell phone stopped him. The ring tone—an old Tom Jones song—identified the caller. He considered not answering, but only for a moment. His mother would continue to call until he answered. In many ways, she behaved as a child. For his part, he tolerated her tantrums and lent a patient ear to her complaints, understanding the gaping wound at the center of all of her insecurities. When Garrett's father left, Paige was forever transformed. What had been strident became shrill. What was strong became hard and brittle.

"Hello!" he said, forced cheer in his voice.

"Hello. Am I calling at a bad time?"

"No, Mom. What's up?"

"I made it safely. I just thought I'd call and let you know. In case you were worried."

"Thanks, I appreciate that." Silence. "So how's Aunt Rose?"

"She's not well, Garrett. It's worse than I'd expected." She launched into a lengthy explanation of his aunt's illness and symptoms.

"Sounds terrible," Garrett said at last. He'd wandered back into the kitchen, set the hammer down and picked up the box of photos. "Your sister is lucky to have you there, I think."

"Family is supposed to take care of family." Paige sighed. "I miss my apartment."

"Of course you do. You don't travel much, Mom. That apartment is your world."

"Remember that you promised to water my plants. You have a key. Every other day. The ferns take a lot of water. You won't forget, will you?"

"I won't forget."

"I'd hate to come home to an apartment full of dead plants."

Garrett smiled in spite of himself. A sudden image of his mother's deathbed came. Shriveled, she would whisper, "If only your father hadn't left. If only you hadn't killed my plants." He shook his head. "Your plants will be fine." *If the damn things die, I'll buy new ones.*

"How is Molly?" His mother's voice changed with the topic, becoming crisp and businesslike, as if checking off a list.

"She's fine."

"And the remodel is going well?"

He looked around the kitchen at the scraps of vinyl flooring and plaster dust. "Smashingly," he said.

* * * * *

The cursed cell phone did not work so well later that evening. Garrett tried to call Molly. Either his cell or hers was malfunctioning. He couldn't seem to make a connection.

At first, the prospect of another evening alone buoyed him. He wanted to finish his assessment of the kitchen. And he did his best work at night.

But.

He hadn't done a good job of keeping in touch with her. In fact, he'd been very selfish with his time. His focus on the house hadn't been malicious. This was the life he'd chosen, and he wanted to immerse himself in the remodel right from the start. And time seemed to slip away—proof that he was truly enjoying what he was doing, maybe for the first time in years.

On the other hand, he missed her. And she might misunderstand his silence better if he explained. He ought to call her. But how? Payphones were a thing of the past. He could just hop in the car, of course. The cell phone seemed to work better outside of the house. And if he couldn't get the phone to work, he'd stop at the convenience store and ask to use their phone.

He *was* a little surprised that she hadn't contacted him.

He wondered what she was doing with her time.

He grabbed his jacket and headed for the door, taking his phone. On the way, he thought of a dozen things that might have held him back, kept him inside the house, from the dimmer switch he'd bought for the upstairs bedroom to the brushed nickel fixtures he'd bought for the downstairs bathroom. But he ignored the house's call and jumped in the car.

Two blocks down the road, he tried the phone. After four rings, the call went to voicemail. Surprised, Garrett hung up and glanced at his watch. Eight o'clock. Surely she'd had time to get home from work. Where was she?

He turned the car around. He'd go back home. On the way, he left a message. "Molly? Hey, Sweetie, it's me. I tried to call you, but no answer.

And I didn't want to come by uninvited. Give me a call when you get this." He thought for a moment, and then added, "If I don't answer, keep trying. My cell phone is giving me fits these days. Time for an Android." He chuckled, then hung up. But by the time he reached the house, all traces of his smile were gone.

* * * * *

He forced himself to work on the upstairs apartment again. Since his encounter with the ghost, if that's what it was, he'd not heard or seen anything out of the ordinary. In fact, the house was fairly silent for an old building. And the lights didn't flicker, though the wiring was ancient. Solid home, quiet ghost.

He'd decided to paint the room where he'd found the message. *They leave.* He'd thought a lot about the message, and decided that it was Winnie's accusation against her husband, and perhaps against men in general. Her husband left her at a time when women had fewer economic opportunities. Had he been the photographer that took the pictures Garrett found? Probably. The young girl in the photos was clearly uncomfortable with the idea of nude photography. Then, when the financial going got tough, the bastard bailed on her, leaving her with one time-tested way to pay the bills and save her life.

Garrett tried to find a picture of Winnie Laughlin on the Internet—perhaps from her days as a Madame—but had no luck. Sometime during the week, he would take a day off and go to the library. Surely he'd find something there. Then his suspicions would be confirmed. Molly might like to tag along. She was a reader. She loved libraries and bookstores.

Molly. Where was she? He'd been checking his cell phone every 10 minutes, not wanting to miss a call that hadn't yet come.

Stop it. Get to work.

He opened a can of paint with a screwdriver. Earlier, he'd set a paint tray, brushes and roller on a plastic tarp. He needed to tape the tarp down and cover the wood floor. Though the hardware store had given the can a good mechanical shaking, Garrett needed to give the paint a stir before pouring it out. He sat on the floor with a stir stick in one hand and a roll of masking tape in the other, unable to move.

Was Molly seeing someone?

What if she was? He didn't own her. People ought not to own each other. If she wanted to see someone else, she should. He licked his lips. His mouth was suddenly dry. He dropped the stick and turned to stare at the tape. Molly was a woman, not a child. She would do whatever she wanted to do.

And if she went her own way, it would be for the best. Already in his thirties, Garrett hadn't had a dating relationship that lasted more than a year. Odds were, the thing with Molly would have been over in a few months anyway. She was a nice girl. But nice people make demands, too. Nice people try to figure you out, analyze you and change you. And nice people cheat.

He pulled a strip of masking tape from the roll. He would get up in a minute, and he'd start taping the tarp to the floor at the base of the wall. He would paint the room and make it new. A fresh start for a sturdy old room. *Old can be good. They don't build houses like this anymore. They make them out of plastic rods and bubble wrap. You can hear every bump, every footstep. Not here. Still as death in this house.* He sighed, and the sound perished as it passed from his lips.

He sat back, dropping the roll of masking tape. He'd spent his life trying to connect with people while maintaining a piece of himself. When his father left his mother, he'd understood for the first time that relationships didn't last. Nor should they. His father had always been an intrusion—at least, that is how Garrett remembered it. The man came home late, worked in the kitchen at the dinner table until late, his eyes on his paperwork instead of his family. On the weekends, his father drove them to museums and tourist attractions. A petting zoo with wolves and a Capuchin monkey. The world's only llama mummy, "discovered in a local Native American burial site." *Are you having a good time?* His father scowled from the rearview mirror, his hands gripping the steering wheel. If Garrett was tired or hungry, he'd ruin everything. He learned to be wide awake and full.

When his father left, Garrett's mother had a brief period of euphoria. Ice cream every night. VHS rentals and pizza delivery. Then the bills came due, and the loneliness set in, and Garrett learned what his new role would be. When she despaired, a shutoff notice for the power company crumpled in her lap, he cheered her with jokes. When she was angry, a broken plate or glass bearing witness to some outrage, he calmed her with soothing words and a dust pan. When she needed to be alone, he found his own way, immersing himself in books, even writing his own stories. And when she needed company, he was hers.

And what did I want? Garrett lay back on the floor, feeling the hard wood beneath him. He wanted this house. But that was selfish, wasn't it? People in a relationship didn't have personal goals. They had couples' goals. Hopes and dreams were subordinated, postponed or discarded.

In his junior year of high school, before the injury that tore his ACL, Garrett played wide receiver for the football team. During the homecoming game, a close, hard-fought battle between rival schools, Garrett fought off the defender and caught a touchdown on a fade route. He'd been airborne—stretched out, the ball at his fingertips. He'd managed to drag his toes inside the lines and keep a tight grip on the ball when he slammed to the ground. When he realized that he'd scored, he jumped up and did a brief dance of victory, a silly outburst of adolescent exuberance. The coach would have none of it. He grabbed Garrett by the faceguard and screamed at him, spitting his words. "You don't celebrate! You're not the only person on this team! Your quarterback threw that ball. He didn't do a dance! Your other receivers blocked the players that would have had your head. They didn't dance! Get your mind right, Jenkins!"

Garrett sat up. He grabbed the roll of masking tape and pitched it across the room. Incomplete. *There are teams, and there are individuals.*

But he really liked Molly.

"This is silly," he told the walls, and he felt doubly foolish. He was overreacting to Molly's failure to call. And he was talking to an empty room. He stood up and replaced the lid on the paint can. There would be no painting tonight.

He tapped the cell phone in his pocket. What should he do instead? He didn't own a television.

Somehow, reading didn't seem distracting enough. If only there were something he could be excited about.

The gap behind the kitchen wall?

He'd forgotten about the mystery space. He smiled. Could there be any better therapy than knocking a hole in the wall with a sledge hammer?

He decided to attack the space from the hallway, rather than the kitchen wall. Knocking holes behind the stove might result in a disaster. He really didn't know where the gas line or electrical conduits were. There weren't any wall sockets in the hall space. Putting a hole there would be worth the risk.

Before swinging the sledgehammer, he tapped the wall, looking for hollow spots, but as before, the walls were too solid to yield any clues. He chose a spot, chest-high and halfway to the kitchen from the window. By his best guess, the spot was dead center. The hammer head punched a hole with the first easy swing. There had to be framing boards, but his spot was clearly between them. A second, harder swing punched another hole. Pulling down, he tore a small flap of wall loose. Setting the hammer aside, he took a look through both holes. Too dark to see anything. The ceiling light at the far end of the hall was no help. He needed a flashlight.

He ran upstairs, taking the steps two at a time. His heart pounded. When he did not immediately find the flashlight—he thought he'd left it in the room with the painted message—he began to curse. The frustrations of the evening found him thrashing through his renovation supplies. At length, he found the flashlight in the adjacent room, though he couldn't remember moving it.

Back to the wall, he aimed the flashlight beam through one hole, and stared through the other.

Years earlier, he'd watched, with some amusement, as a popular television journalist opened a sealed basement wall in a building once owned by Al Capone. Live television at its silliest—the journalist uncovered an empty soft drink bottle in an otherwise empty room. Garrett thought of that moment as he pointed the flashlight into a room that had been walled up for more than half a century. The beam played across a four-post bed that took up most of the enclosed space.

A bed. *Please, no bodies. That would be too much.*

He grabbed the sledge hammer and took another swing, this time with zeal. In moments, he tore through the wall, leaving a pile of plaster rubble at his feet. Grabbing the flashlight, he stepped inside. If there were a corpse, he'd find it and be done with it.

But there was no corpse. The bed was sized something between a queen and a twin, with four thick oak corner posts. The top posts were affixed with handcuffs. The outside wall, to Garrett's right, featured a wooden shelf, complete with candles, a riding crop, paddle, and several other metal accessories. The floor of the room was sprinkled with rodent waste. On the far side of the bed, beneath the vent in the wall, he found a large envelope. He pinched the packet. More photos?

He glanced behind him. The dim amber light should have put him at ease—a lit exit from the darkened room. But he was not comforted.

He hadn't checked under the bed.

He knelt, flashlight in hand, and grabbed the edge of the bedspread. Taking a deep breath, he lifted the fabric and thrust the beam underneath.

More rodent poop.

He took a deep breath, and stood up. Above him, a metal ring hung from the rafters. Garrett supposed that ropes or cords might have been tied there. The room was a sex dungeon—tiny, and perhaps a little tame by modern standards, but a dungeon just the same.

He sat on the corner of the bed, still holding the envelope. He tore the flap carefully, certain of the photographs he would find. He could feel the stack. When the flap was open, he slid the contents into his lap, and turned the flashlight on the first photo.

Winnie. She lay naked on the very bed he on which he sat now, arms manacled, legs spread—her expression passive, resigned, as if she'd given in to whatever compelled her to pose that way. He could feel his heart race, both with anger at the indignities to which she'd been subjected, and with excitement at the prospect of further revelations. The realization that he was victimizing her, as surely as the photographer had, gave him pause. He closed his eyes. He could take the stack of photos into the kitchen. He could stuff them in a trash bag. He could take them to the dump. No one else need ever see them. Surely that would be what she'd have wanted.

Unless. Finding the photos seemed serendipitous. What if he was meant to see them? What if the photos were part of a story she was trying to tell?

He shook his head. What was he thinking? Winnie was long dead and past caring about old photos. Ghosts weren't real, and they didn't send messages. In fact, though he thought of the woman in the photo as Winnie, he couldn't prove who she was one way or the other. All of which added up to a single thought—flip to the next photo. He watched his hand shuffle the top photo to the bottom of the stack, then move the flashlight beam across the next print.

A second shot of the bedroom. A man sat on the edge of the bed, dressed. In the foreground, blocking much of the photo, a woman's face, too close for focus. The man looked like Garrett. The thought gave him a sudden start, and he looked up suddenly, half-expecting to see a woman behind him, blocking the hole in the wall, her back to him, echoing the photo. On closer inspection, Garrett realized he'd been mistaken. The man wore vintage clothing and had a thin mustache. Garrett had never grown a mustache. The man in the photo sat staring into his lap as Garrett had done, but the man's wrists were manacled. A leather crop sat on the bedspread to his left. Garrett gave an involuntary glance to the side. Was the crop on the shelf the same as the one in the photo? He couldn't tell.

The photo showed only part of the woman's face, but the shape of her mouth seemed familiar. Garrett checked the previous photo to be sure. The woman in the foreground was Winnie. Older, but most definitely her.

Good for you. You turned the tables, didn't you? Smiling, he flipped to the third photo.

He stared down at the picture, unable to understand what he was seeing. A chill shot down his back, and he dropped the flashlight. For a moment, the room was dark. He kept his eyes on the amber light from the hallway, blindly slapping the bed beside him, searching for the light. His fingers grabbed the barrel, but the light was out. Garrett shook the flashlight, and a feeble beam crept across the room. He turned the light on the photo. *No! This can't be!* His mouth went dry. He could feel his tongue swell in his mouth, and he nearly gagged. *What is this doing here?*

He stood up, photos in hand, and lurched toward the hole in the wall. He stumbled down the hall and into the kitchen. He flipped the light switch on, and positioned the stack of photos on the work table directly underneath the ceiling light. Taking a deep breath, he forced himself to look at the photo. And the next. And then, shaking, he set the stack aside and went to the sink, where he vomited.

* * * * *

Molly met him at the coffee shop, as he'd demanded. She came wrapped in a sweater and jacket—the evenings were getting cooler. She seemed to know that something was seriously wrong by the expression on his face. Garrett didn't know how he looked—but he knew how he felt. Hidden under the table, his hands shook. He couldn't draw a calm breath. He refused meet her gaze. Instead, he stared at the logo on his paper coffee cup.

"Garrett, what's wrong?" She slid into the booth, facing him.

"Would you like some coffee?" he asked. His voice was gravel in a tin can.

"What is it?"

He tried to speak. The words wouldn't come. He finally shook his head and grabbed a photo from the pile on his lap. He put it on the table.

Molly turned the photo around and stared at it. She frowned at first. Then, when she realized what she was seeing, her expression turned to disbelief, and then to horror. Her mouth hung open and slack, her gaze darting from the exit to the empty wall, but always back to the photo—the damn photo.

"It's you, then." He sank into the booth, as if he could disappear.

The photo was a close-up of a woman performing fellatio. Garrett had been reasonably certain that the woman was Molly, but he'd held out some hope that she'd convince him otherwise. A good lie would have been balm on his wounds.

"Where did you get this?" she whispered.

"I found it in the house."

She didn't seem to comprehend what he'd said. "I mean, where did you find this? On the Internet?"

"No, it was hidden in the walls of the house. I found a secret room behind the kitchen." He explained his discovery of the room, the bed, the sex toys, and finally, the photos.

"There are other pictures?" she asked. Her voice had drained to a tiny squeak.

He nodded, and set a few of the pictures on the table. The one on top showed two women together, one pinning the other with a strap-on device. Molly's hand flew up to her mouth, her eyes wide open. She started to speak, then stopped. Her expression went blank. She flipped through the pictures, her eyes narrowing at each new revelation.

"I recall you saying that if you let someone take pictures, they'll show up eventually." Garrett reached for his coffee, but couldn't muster the strength to pick it up. His mouth was dry, but caffeine wasn't what he needed. *This is a coffee shop. I should have asked her to meet me at a bar.*

"And you found these in the house?" Molly's whisper had a harsher edge.

"Yes."

"I don't understand, Garrett. What's the game?"

He stared at her. She seemed angry now.

"I mean, you almost had me with this one," she said, tapping the first photo of the girl performing oral sex. "My ex was a real asshole. I found out about the camera after the fact. He swore to me that the digital files were all erased, but he was a liar, and I always expected this sort of thing to happen." She slid the photo aside and tapped the one with two women. "But this? This never happened."

"What do you mean?" he asked He could feel anger rising inside of him, beginning to overwhelm his sadness, even his nausea. "The picture's right there."

"And how did you get the picture?" she asked.

"I found it in the room."

"You found it in a walled up room? What, then? A ghost put it there?"

He didn't answer.

"What I don't understand is what you hoped to get out of this. Was this supposed to convince me to pose for you? Are you an idiot?" She hissed the last question, trying to keep her voice down.

Doubt crept in for a moment. Garrett looked away. The barista stared at him, as did a young girl with a computer at a nearby table.

"You did this. And it's sick, Garrett." She sat back, sagging in her seat, as if someone had suddenly tapped off her anger like steam from a kettle. "I thought you were a nice guy. I thought we were a cute couple. I thought we were normal."

"There is no normal," Garrett mumbled.

She shoved the pictures back at him. "You made these."

"What do you mean?"

"Oh please, Garrett!" She stood up. Something in her manner, the weariness in her eyes, the resignation in her voice, seemed final. "Don't lie."

"I'm not lying. I found these. In a small, hidden room."

She leaned on the tabletop, putting her face just inches away. "You were a graphic arts teacher, Garrett. Photoshopping is right up your alley. You made these." She shook her head and stood back. "Jesus! What do you take me for?" She turned and left him sitting alone with his coffee.

III

Showering. The hot stream from the showerhead steadied him. He put a hand on the tiled wall and closed his eyes, feeling the water sting his scalp and the back of his neck. Vapor filled the bathroom, fogging the glass doors that enclosed the bathtub. He could smell mold—the tiles were old, crusted, sealed with black and gray caulk. He could feel grit under his feet. The tub was filthy.

And someone was in the room with him.

The realization startled him. There had been no sound, no flicker of the lights. But he was no longer alone. He stood straight, head and shoulders back, water hitting his chest now, rolling down his torso and legs. He listened. The only sounds he could hear were the showerhead and the gurgle of the drain. The smell of mold had turned; now more like wet clay. His eyes burned. He hadn't been sleeping well. He reached for the shower door, then hesitated.

"Hello?" He'd tried to sound fearless, but his voice wavered.

No answer.

He pulled the shower door open. The room was empty.

He'd been feeling the presence of the house for some time, but he hadn't caught a glimpse of anyone. Once, after a day of putting up plywood, he'd stepped into the hallway near the secret room and seen a cloud of black speckles, like the shadow he'd seen in the upstairs room. But there was no shape he could discern, and the speckles disappeared when his head cleared. He realized then that he hadn't eaten in some time. He forced down some saltines and peanut butter, and the speckles did not reappear.

But the feeling of being watched never left him. He felt it most keenly when he changed clothes or showered.

* * * * *

He put the cell phone on the charger and stared at it, as if he could will the damn thing to work. He couldn't make a call unless he went outside. He might well have missed incoming calls. He'd never know. Charging the useless piece of crap was an exercise in futility, but he did it anyway. The phone might suddenly ring.

Night time. Time to renovate. Garrett couldn't decide if he should focus on an upstairs bedroom, or continue installing the new appliances in the kitchen, so he opted for both. Upstairs, he carted chunks of wall to the window at the far end of the hall, dropping them down to the pile that had begun to cover the back porch. When he grew tired of hauling debris, he headed back downstairs to the expanded kitchen. He'd torn out the walls of the hidden room, moved the gas and electric lines against the new back wall, and sealed his work with drywall and plaster. He was not certified to do the work, but he wasn't worried. According to the blueprints, the gas and electric lines were situated behind the west wall, and indeed they were once again, though the wall had moved more than eight feet. If the city inspectors gave him trouble, he'd bribe them. *Show green and the cattle will graze.*

He tried for the sixth time to move the new gas stove—a Wolf four-burner—but the damn thing weighed a ton. The delivery men had wrestled with the stove for half an hour. Garrett could tell they were struggling, because the excuses started almost immediately. "I'm having trouble wheeling past the construction work up front," the fat one had said, mopping his face with a scarf. Garrett finally had to assure the men that there'd be no trouble if they dug a few grooves in the floor. The wood wasn't important. His latest idea was to lay a new, grooved-wood floor on top of the old floor anyway. He'd first hoped that he might sand down the original wood and refinish it, but the flooring was too old and too dry, and each thing he tried, from sanding to staining, left the wood looking worse. He gave thought to having an expert look at the floor. After all, it was nearly 100 years old. But the house was in transition, and he couldn't have people wandering through, staring at everything. He'd had to ask the delivery men to leave before they finished placing the oven for just that reason, and now he was stuck trying to slide the appliance into place without the benefit of a second set of hands. He might as well push a car without wheels.

Discouraged, he headed back up the stairs. Two of the bedrooms were painted, but weren't finished. The one with the painted message looked plain, empty without the wainscoting. He had no intention of returning the original wood pieces to the walls—they'd been cheap and ugly. Still, he'd been surprised by the expense of putting nice wood in place. Part of the problem was the lack of selection—wainscot was not in high demand—and part of the problem was the fellow at the building supply company. The man contradicted himself constantly.

Quote one price, deliver another. Promise one delivery date, then change it. Garrett had called him on his bullshit several times. The man seemed genuinely upset that Garrett wasn't satisfied, which only meant that the bastard had a long, practiced history of bilking the public. Garrett would have ordered his materials elsewhere, but even the inflated price of the local shop was lower than the other prices he'd been quoted over his damn, worthless cell phone. So he put up with the contradictory price quotes and contradictory delivery dates. *Even the man's body is a contradiction.* Long thin arms, a round, florid face, spindly legs and a pot belly that came from sitting in front of a computer, cheating people. "Potbellied people cheat," he whispered. The thought amused him, so he burst out with a laugh that echoed down the hall.

"I could buy a two-wheeler," he said, suddenly thinking of the stove again. But the stove had cost him a small fortune, and he'd be damned if he'd spend another penny on it. Workers built the pyramids for a loaf of bread and a jug of beer a day, and they did it without two-wheelers. If he could rock the thing back and slide some 2 x 4s underneath, he could lever the oven into place. It was worth a try. He raced back down the stairs. He'd need wood, of course. There was some on the lawn. He'd asked that the last few deliveries be placed there. Too much trouble to clear a path, and the renovation was at a critical stage.

On the way, he stopped at the stove and tried to tilt it back. The thing wouldn't budge. He doubted he'd be able to wedge the blade of a two-wheeler underneath, let alone 2 x 4s. He'd need to ask for help.

"Like anyone's going to help me," he muttered. "Maybe when Mother gets back, I can put her to work." The absurd thought cheered him for the briefest moment. *When is she coming back, anyway?* She hadn't called, and he hadn't called, at least the cellphone hadn't rung or been dialed. If he hadn't started to worry about finishing the house, he'd have taken a day off and headed to the phone store, found a smiling 20-something with a sweater vest, name tag, and clipboard and shoved the phone up his ass. This thought made him laugh again. "This is a house full of laughter," he said. "That makes it a home." He glanced at a pile of debris in the great room. "Home, sweet home." He turned to the hall that led to the front stairway. "Do you agree?" he shouted. He liked to imagine that he could include Winnie in his discussions. She hadn't answered back, yet.

Her presence, though, was undeniable, if only for the number of photos he'd found. He'd lined the walls of upstairs hallway with her pictures, out of the view of nosy delivery men. He'd found more than 70 photos in walls and ceiling ducts. He'd even found one behind the wooden mantelpiece over the fireplace in the great room. That small print of an older Winnie in leather, sporting a lash, had been taken in front of the very fireplace that became the photo's hiding place. Garrett wandered back up the stairs to stare at the gallery again. He paused at the first photo he'd found—a younger, vulnerable Winnie. Further down the hall, he paused again to stare at what seemed to be the oldest shot of Winnie. She wore a man's suit, cut to her figure—a daring choice for the era—complete with a Fedora. At her feet, a young blonde girl in lingerie and a choker, staring up with apparent adoration. Garrett nodded in salute. Winnie may have started out as a victim, but she'd turned the tables quickly enough. Hadn't she been a notorious Madame? Someone had said so, once. He tried to remember. Perhaps he'd read it on the Internet. The laptop worked on occasion.

At the end of the hall, near the bathroom, a whiskey bottle sat on a decorative table next to a small foil tray. On the wall above was the most recent photo, found in one of the upstairs bedroom walls. Winnie, sitting in a garden, perhaps in the backyard (though any traces of a garden had long since dried up, shriveling to nothing). A squirrel sat at her feet, nibbling a treat. That struck him as funny, though he couldn't say why.

Garrett glanced down at the table and the whiskey bottle. "Someday, I'll put a plant there, or maybe a candle." He crossed over and grabbed the half-empty bottle by the neck. He wasn't much of a drinker, but whiskey had sounded good on one of his infrequent trips to the store, and a sip now and then seemed to hit the spot. A whiskey high was different than beer. Warmer, mellower, without the bloat. He took a sip. "Burns so good," he shouted. He'd been saying the same thing for days, as if following a ritual.

And why not? He'd disconnected from society, society's expectations, and society's rituals. He could replace them with his own. He was his own boss now.

"And so saying, it's time to get back to work." He set the bottle back on the end table and headed for the upstairs bathroom. He hated grout jobs. They were messy and easy to botch. And he'd abandoned this one in mid-job, afraid that he'd ruined the floor tile. He opened the door and flicked on the light, gaze cast down, avoiding the mirror. He'd learned not to look into mirrors without steeling himself. Too many glimpses of things from the corner of his eyes. If he faced the mirror and stared directly into it, prepared for what he saw, there was less chance that he'd be startled. Better still, if he could avoid looking into the mirror at all.

The floor was as he'd remembered it. "I thought one of you would get to work on this in my absence," Garrett called out. Perhaps there was more than one spirit at work in the house. Winnie would be one—the friendly one, the melancholy one. Then there was the spotted thing he'd seen in the upstairs bedroom. That one was malignant. Were there others? When he had time, he'd research the people who died on the premises. Perhaps he'd learn something about the people that haunted his house.

He knelt to grab the bag of grout. He'd have to mix a new batch. The old batch had hardened in the plastic tray. Did he have another tray? He'd probably need to buy one. He sighed. This job would have to wait.

That bothered him. He wanted to finish something—to check it off the list. And the job he finished should be one that nagged at him. If he could just move that new stove!

He sat back against the door jam and closed his eyes. When he reopened them, it was dark.

He'd turned the bathroom light on, hadn't he? He pulled himself up, grabbing the wall for support, and flipped the switch back and forth. The bulb had burned out. He peered down the hall. He could see the gray flicker of light at the other end, coming from downstairs.

Then something black passed between him and the light.

He froze in place. The black shape had been fragmented—shards he couldn't put together. He tried to piece the memory of his glimpse into a discernable shape. He couldn't. He crept down the hall, his right hand balled into a fist, raised, brushing the wall as he went to keep his bearings in the dark. Whatever was waiting for him would get the first blow in, he decided. But that would be all.

He paused where he thought he'd seen the shape move, left to right, across the hallway. Solid wall. The door to the bedroom on the right was another 15 feet ahead.

A step sounded behind him.

He felt the blow on the back of his neck, so keen was the imagined attack. But after stumbling, he realized he'd not been struck at all. He stared back down the hall into the brown darkness and glared. Jokes. "Fuck you, fun and games." He shook himself, and then headed back to the stairway. He ignored the creak behind him. "Tricks. Smoke and mirrors."

Down he went. With each step, he forced himself to refocus on the stove. Surely he could slide the thing. The idiot delivery men had left it just a few feet away from the wall. Perhaps if he braced himself properly, and pushed the bottom of the stove instead of the top, he could get it to slide.

Delivery men.

No wonder he'd had his supplies placed on the front lawn.

Groceries.

He'd called the supermarket the day before. How had he forgotten that? He'd paid in advance, over the phone, using his bank card. He'd told them to put the grocery bags on the porch. He hadn't wanted to be bothered. Now he thought of groceries, and the frozen pizzas that were surely thawed. Wasted money! The thought grated on him like the bathroom tile and the immovable stove. He had to see if any of the neglected food could be salvaged.

He doubled back to the front door. Night had fallen. Would he need a flashlight? Probably. Any reputable delivery service could place grocery bags near a door, but he hadn't thought to include a tip, so there was no telling where the cretins would hide his food. He took a deep breath and opened the door.

And froze.

Snow.

He stepped into the storm in stocking feet. His groceries sat on the front porch, covered in three inches of powder. The street lights were soft orbs, nearly swallowed by flurries. He cupped his hand over his eyes, shielding them from the blowing ice. The cold cut through his tee-shirt and sweat pants, sending shivers down his back, but he still couldn't believe his eyes, his skin, his bones.

What day was it?

He shuddered.

What month?

He stood swaying in the storm, trying to remember. He rubbed at his forehead, eyes closed, He tried desperately to trace the last few weeks. He saw himself tearing down walls, putting up beams, painting and repainting dry wall.

Then he pictured the whiskey bottle, sitting on the table next to foil. An aluminum foil tray. A frozen turkey dinner.

Christmas.

Not possible. He stepped back toward the house. He felt dizzy and drained. He missed the doorknob on the first try. He steadied himself with one hand on the door frame and reached again with the other, eyes focused on his fingers, grasping the cold brass. He turned the knob and stepped inside. His stocking feet were wet, stiff with the cold. He glanced at the floor. He'd left damp footprints on the wood.

Christmas. How long ago?

A wave of panic hit him like a punch to the solar plexus. He flinched, doubled over, hands on his hips. He had to be mistaken! Snow in September in Colorado? Not unheard of. Surely it was still September.

He needed to check the date. He broke for the kitchen. His cell phone was there. He could check the date.

The cell phone was plugged into the charger. He tore it loose, turned the phone on and waited for service. The logo appeared. Garrett set the phone on the table—unable to stand the suspense. He glanced at the stove again—more technology that didn't do what it was supposed to.

Unable to wait any longer, he snatched up the phone and stared at the display.

Service unavailable.

He started to throw the phone, but stopped himself. If he left the house, the damn thing would work. He was sure of it. He pocketed the phone and went looking for his shoes. He needed shoes to leave the house. Where were they? When was the last time he'd gone outside?

He searched for his shoes, upstairs and down. Then he searched again. Where could he have left them? He tried to remember his last trip downtown. He'd been calling for supplies, calling for groceries. When his cell phone gave him trouble, he took it to the back yard and called. He could do that now, couldn't he?

He'd need his shoes to go outside.

Stymied, he began searching places he would *never* have left them. Kitchen cupboards. The bathtub. The basement crawlspace. At length, he found them perched halfway up the attic stairway. He could not recall leaving them there, but his faltering memory was no longer a surprise.

He pulled on the shoes and raced for the door.

Car keys.

He nearly shrieked with frustration. *Forget the car. Go down the street and make a call. If the cell phone won't work, smash it and run down the block to the convenience store. Use their phone.*

Call Molly.

Five steps outside of the house, he slipped on ice, his legs kicking up into the air as he fell. His head hit the sidewalk and bounced. He lay still, eyes closed, and took a silent inventory. *Please, nothing broken.* He shifted on the wet concrete. His tailbone ached, and the back of his head had begun to scream. He opened his eyes. Snowflakes, glistening in the light from an upstairs window, drifted down, settling on his face.

It was cold.

He had no coat.

* * * * *

"Molly?"

She recognized Garrett's voice, but she didn't speak. She didn't hang up either—he sounded distraught. Enough so that she closed her eyes, ground her teeth and listened.

'Molly?" Softer now.

"I'm here," she said. "What can I do for you, Garrett?" She tried to sound businesslike. Distant.

"I need help."

Silence. She nearly hung up the phone. But something in his voice was so fragile, so frightened. In the months after they stopped seeing each other, she'd wondered how things might have been different. He'd been an attentive man. Unselfish. Willing to give everything except—

"Something's wrong," he continued.

There was always something held back. Something hidden by the smile and the manners and the good heart. Something darker. And the barrier between them had doomed their relationship, even before Garrett had disappeared into his damn house.

"I . . . didn't know who to call." His voice broke.

"What about your mother?" Even as the words left her mouth, she regretted them. Her voice sounded thin and cruel. *This is not who I am.*

More silence.

"I'm sorry," she said. "It's just been a long time since I heard from you." She sighed and then said something else she'd probably regret. "How can I help, Garrett?"

He wanted to come over to her apartment. She refused, suggesting instead that they meet at *Gabrielle's*, an all-night coffee shop a few blocks away. Even that was too close for her comfort, but it was late, and the coffee shop was open. And public.

"Thank you," he gushed, which made her feel worse. Garrett didn't sound like himself. Was he drunk? If he was drunk, she'd leave him in the coffee shop and shut off her phone. She paused, hands on her hips. *And if he follows me to the apartment, I'll call the police.*

"I should never have agreed to meet him," she whispered after hanging up. Then she thought about his voice, all tremors and pain. She'd always known there was something bruised under the man's veneer. Even the best actor gave himself away over time. Garrett couldn't fake perfection forever. Nor could he hide the sort of pain he was surely carrying. While they'd dated, he'd let bits of his life slip, like pieces of a puzzle, and she'd built an ugly picture of his childhood. Supposition, of course. And much too late to rescue their relationship.

At the coffee shop, she ordered a hot chocolate and found a corner booth away from the late night crowd—drunks and poets, the homeless and the college students. She undid her coat—the shop kept warm air blasting from overhead vents—and resisted the temptation to check her makeup in the restroom. From her seat, she could see anyone entering the shop. When the thin man with the stringy beard slid into the booth across from her, she was startled, and then horrified. "My God, Garrett! Is that you?"

He winced. "I know, I know. I got a look at myself in the front window." He rubbed one eye with a fist, then leaned forward, as if to speak in confidence.

Molly pulled back, pressing against the back of the booth seat, her expression turning from shock to repulsion. "Garrett, when was the last time you bathed?"

He blinked. "I don't know." He looked away. His shoulders began to shake. Was he cold?

No. He was crying.

He rubbed at his eyes with the back of his sleeve, his face still turned away. He mumbled something and started from the booth.

"Garrett! Sit down!" The sharpness of her voice surprised her. He nodded, his face still turned, his chin tucked into his left shoulder like an embarrassed child.

Molly slid out of the booth, taking her purse. "Stay here. I'll be right back. Don't go anywhere." When he nodded, she went to the front counter to buy him a hot chocolate. "Give me one of those muffins, too," she said. Garrett looked as if he hadn't eaten since she'd last seen him. He'd lost 20 pounds at least.

She set the muffin and hot chocolate in front of him. He stared at the food, his mouth open and slack, as if he'd never seen food before. "Eat, Garrett," she said, her voice softer than before. He reached for the hot chocolate, pulling back when his fingertips touched the hot cup. Then he broke off a piece of the muffin and stuffed it into his mouth. He chewed slowly and swallowed with some effort.

Molly slid back into her seat. She'd had a moment to gather herself. She patted the back of his hand and, steeling herself for the smell. "I think you've had some kind of breakdown."

Garrett shook his head, mumbling through a bite of muffin. "No, it's Winnie."

"Who is Winnie?"

"The girl in the picture. In the walls."

"I'm sorry, Garrett. I don't understand."

His expression shifted from frustration to anger and then despair in the space of a few moments. His blue eyes seemed darker than before, nearly black, an illusion enhanced by the dark circles under his eyes and the dim lighting in the coffee shop. Then, worse still, Garrett tried to smile. His lips trembled with the effort. Unable to hold the shape of the smile, his mouth collapsed into a loose, open look of anguish. "The house has me."

She listened, nodding encouragement. A wisp of hair slipped across her forehead. She let it dangle and focused on Garrett.

"I went outside to look for supplies, and it was January. Snow."

"Yes, it snowed last night."

"No. Last night it was still September."

She frowned, trying to understand. Had he begun taking drugs? Such a thing seemed impossible, but it would explain much about his appearance, his behavior, his conversation.

Garrett rubbed his nose with the back of his hand and tried again. "How long has it been since I spoke to you?"

She frowned.

"How long?"

"Months." Her lips barely moved with her terse answer.

"No," he said, a look of anguish distorting his face. "Days. Days! My cell phone wouldn't work—she didn't want it to work—and I meant to go to the convenience store, but I forgot, and then—" He stopped suddenly and sat up straight. His eyes narrowed. She turned around to see what he was looking at so intently. Behind the booth was a plain wall. "I don't think she wants me to call you," he said, his voice soft and curiously flat. "The house." He stared directly into her eyes. "The house has me by the throat."

His words chilled her. "You need to move out."

"I can't," he said. His lip trembled again. "I have too much money in the place. *My mother's money.*" He looked away. "I believe I've botched the remodel."

"You might need some professional help, Garrett—"

"I can't afford professionals. I had to do the work on the house myself."

She closed her eyes. "Not that kind of professional."

He stopped speaking, though his lips continued to form words. He broke his gaze and looked away. She had to take his hand again to get his attention.

"Garrett. What did you mean when you said you'd spoken to me days ago?"

He stared at the hot chocolate, scowling now as if the beverage were his nemesis. He pushed at it with a fingernail, and then barked a laugh, startling her.

"Oh, Garrett," she whispered.

"It's like this," he said, his voice suddenly even. "I wanted a few days to myself, to enjoy working on the house. I thought of calling you, but the cell didn't work, and that was enough of an excuse, I suppose. I was being selfish. And I thought of you. Every day. And it seemed like a week, I think. No more than 10 days, or two weeks. It's hard to say. But then I found snow outside, and thought, I've got to call Molly. And the cell phone worked—outside—and I then saw the date. The middle of January. *January!* It didn't seem possible."

He laid his head flush on the tabletop, wrapping his arms around himself like a canopy. His shoulders shook once. She let him alone.

Eventually, he sat up. His effort to regain some dignity—brushing lightly at his eyes, patting his hair in place, smiling again—was a complete failure. She tried not to stare.

"So, you've moved on, haven't you?"

She nodded. "But I'm here with you now. As a friend. And as a friend, I'm advising you to get yourself to a doctor. You've had a breakdown, Garrett. You might even have had a stroke. I don't know. I'm not a doctor. But I know this much—that house is no good for you. You have to get out of there."

He nodded, but the way his gaze darted and the grim-lipped nod gave her to believe that he was not sincere in his agreement.

She grabbed his hands. "Garrett!"

His slack, open-mouthed look returned.

"You have to get out of that house! You can stay at a motel—" He frowned. "No. You can stay at my apartment. On the couch. You're coming home with me. And tomorrow, I'm taking you to a doctor."

"No, I need—"

"Should I drive you to the emergency room?"

"—things from the house. Just a few things. My wallet." He swallowed. "And you're right. I have to get out of there. Thank you."

"You should come straight home with me."

He shook his head. "I need those things. I won't be more than a minute."

But when she drove him to the house, he went in alone, insisting that she wait outside. "I know you don't believe in ghosts, Molly," he said. His voice seemed weary, but clear. "But they believe in you, and they don't like you. *Winnie doesn't want you here.* It sounds crazy, but you'll be safer out here." He stepped from the car, and then bent down to peer back at her. "I really liked you, Molly." And then he was gone.

So she waited. And waited. She stared at the snow-covered piles of building supplies. She stared at the bags of refuse on the front porch.

After a half hour, she told herself that it was time to go. She'd checked her watch, minute after passing minute. She'd tried honking the horn. Once, she thought she saw him peering out from a window, though she couldn't be sure. And her uncertainty gave her a chill. She hated the house. She would never have been able to live in it.

After an hour, she left, angry and hurt. As far as she was concerned, the story had ended, and there would be no epilogue. When she reached her apartment, she blocked his cell phone number and went to bed.

* * * * *

When the call came, she was racing down the highway, 15 miles an hour faster than the law permitted, trying to pass an 18-wheeler that had been lagging on every hill between Denver and Colorado Springs. She'd offered to drive a prospectus to an important investor. She was certain the call was a cancellation—the investor had cancelled two previous meetings. Her boss imagined that the investor might keep the meeting if Molly, the pretty assistant, delivered the papers in person. One hand on the wheel and one on the phone, eyes on the 18-wheeler, she gave the caller her customary, "Speak."

Silence.

"Hello?"

"Molly?" A woman's voice, shaking.

"This is Molly," she snapped. She pulled around in front of the big rig, nearly dropping the phone. "How can I help you?"

"This is Paige Jenkins. I wonder if—"

"Paige?"

"—maybe meet for coffee?"

"I'm sorry. I can barely hear you." Why was Garrett's mother calling? Had something happened to Garrett? Had he hurt himself?

"I need to see you!" Paige's voice blared through the cell phone, much louder than before.

"What's wrong? Did something happen?"

"I need to see you. Can we meet somewhere this afternoon?"

"I'm working," Molly said. "I'm out of town, actually."

"When will you be back?" A hint of the Paige she knew had returned, her voice becoming stern.

"What's this about?" Molly asked, ignoring Paige's question.

Silence.

"I'm pretty busy right now, Paige—"

"Have you noticed anything wrong with Garrett? Anything odd?"

"I haven't seen Garrett in some time, Paige," she answered. She did not mention her last meeting with him—it was none of Paige's business.

"Oh no." Paige's voice cracked.

Molly gripped the wheel, trying to focus on the road.

"Please, I need to see you. Something's wrong with Garrett, and you're his only—" Paige paused, and Molly thought she heard a stifled sob. "You're his only friend."

Molly glanced at the rearview mirror. The truck had dropped back, struggling with another hill. There only the backseat, the receding scenery, and her reflection, head shaking side to side; no, no. "I'm sorry Paige—"

"He won't answer the phone. I went over to the house. I saw him in an upstairs window, looking down at me, his face as plain as day, but he wouldn't answer the door. He just stood there, staring at me." She paused again. "I'm afraid."

Molly scowled at the mirror. "All right, Paige. I'll be back in town tonight. Should I meet you at the house?"

"No, no, that wouldn't be right. Meet me at the coffee shop you two used to go to." She named the street.

"You know about the coffee shop?" Molly asked, surprised.

"Garrett used to tell me everything. I know all about you." One last pause. "But there are things you don't know about him."

* * * * *

"Garrett's father left when he was 12 years old." Paige had wrapped her fingers around the coffee cup, but had yet to take a sip. Her nails were chipped ragged.

"He told me. It was a hard time for him."

"For both of us," Paige corrected. "I'm sure he told you that I had to support him alone, without financial help. Every day was a challenge. I had no time for a life of my own. Garrett was everything to me." She glanced down at her coffee cup, but didn't drink. A strand of hair tumbled across her forehead. She pushed at it once, twice, and then gave up.

Molly sipped her hot chocolate, resisting an urge to glance at her watch.

"Not having a father damaged him. He never stuck to a single thing in his life," she continued. "Other than his degree, of course, and he'd have quit college if I hadn't insisted that he finish. Then he took the job teaching, and I thought he would finally come into his own, but I was wrong. And the women! He went from one to another—" She glanced up, her face suddenly pale. "But you don't want to hear about other women," she said, reaching out to pat Molly's hand.

Paige's touch was cold and dry. Molly suppressed a shudder and settled back in the booth. Paige stared for a moment, her face running through a series of emotions—the knotted brow of surprise, the narrow gaze of anger and finally, the slack, empty look of helplessness. "It's my fault, too, you know," she whispered.

Molly didn't answer.

Paige sniffled. "I think I asked too much of him. He should have had more time with friends. Boys need that. But when I came home from work? That was our time. I worked so many hours! Sometimes two jobs. And then there was laundry and cleaning to do. We couldn't live like pigs, after all. And when the day ended, I wanted my son to be there. Everything I did, I did for Garrett. Was that so much to ask?"

She seemed to want an answer, so Molly shrugged.

"But he might have been more focused as an adult if he'd had time to himself." Paige shook her head, her lower jaw jutting a little. "Damn his father, that's what I think. What did I know about raising a boy? If Garrett had been a girl, I'd have had some idea what to do. I am a woman, after all." She pushed the coffee cup away, not having taken a sip. "I don't much care for this coffee."

"I'm sorry," Molly said. "The hot chocolate—"

"And he tried *so* hard to be the man of the house. That's what I called him—*my little man*." She looked directly into Molly's eyes. "He loved that."

Molly felt her face flush hot. She put down her drink.

"He was the most loving boy in the world. There wasn't anything he wouldn't do for me."

A sudden, horrible thought took Molly by surprise. She blushed, certain that the notion showed in her expression.

Paige's mouth flew open. She sat silent, her lower teeth exposed, her eyes lit with the fire of sudden understanding. She leaned forward. "I know what you're thinking."

Molly reached for her purse.

"How could you think such a thing?" Paige demanded.

"I didn't say anything, Paige. You've done all the talking."

"Don't you dare go there," she said, flecks of spit hitting the table.

Molly pulled her coat on.

Paige spoke quickly. "You misunderstand me. When I say he would do anything for me, I mean that he spent all of his free time with me. We were best friends. We watched television together. We made cookies." Molly started from the booth. "*Don't go!*"

"This was a mistake," Molly said.

"No, no it wasn't. I have to tell you!" her voice desperate, as if she were compelled to confess, not confide. "I know what he's doing. This house. This lack of focus. I read about it. I know what this is."

Almost against her will, Molly waited.

"His childhood," Paige said. "He missed a real childhood. And he'll never get it back. He'll never have an adult relationship, because he's a child forever. His father crippled him. *I crippled him.*"

Molly took a deep breath and sat back down.

Paige's shoulder's sagged, and she reached out for Molly's hands, as if ready to accept absolution.

"You were the most important person in his life," Molly said. "But I think maybe you took advantage. Keeping Mom happy isn't the child's job. Did you know he's never had a relationship last beyond a year? He told me once that women want too much—that they're never satisfied. Where do you suppose he learned that?"

Paige hung her head and wept. "You make it sound like he's twisted—"

"We're all twisted," Molly said.

"No. Garrett's a good man. He's charming—"

"Yes, but he has no friends. You said so."

"He's smart—"

"He knows graphic design. I'm not so sure about house renovating."

"He cares about people—"

"From a distance."

"He deserves to be happy!"

"So do we all." Molly sat back down. She was tired. Her eyes burned. *I need to get out of here. I have to work in the morning. This isn't my concern.*

Paige grabbed her by the sleeve. "*I am begging you!*" she whispered. "Come with me to the house. I need to see that he's all right." Her broken nails cut into Molly's skin, and when she tried to pull free, Paige's grip tightened. "He stopped answering my calls while I was away. And now this? If I go to the police, they'll put him away. I can't lock my own son up. Can you understand that? I can't do it."

"This isn't my concern," Molly said. "Garrett stopped calling me months ago."

"I know he treated you poorly," Paige said. "But he respected you. I could hear it in his voice. He thought the world of you. If you'll just tell him he needs help—"

I already did. And then I left him in that house.

A wave of guilt coursed through her, and she grimaced. Garrett frightened her. She'd washed her hands of him, wanting a finish to their story. But he didn't deserve to be abandoned. He was sick.

"I'll go," she whispered.

* * * * *

The skies were clear and bitter with February cold. Garrett stood by an upstairs window, staring at the street below. Molly's car was gone. She'd left him.

He lifted a hand to pull the curtain aside. His hand held his wallet. He stared at it, stupefied. How long had he been carrying the thing? Wasn't that what he'd come back to the house for? He dropped the wallet and tried to wiggle his fingers. They were stiff and numb.

He licked his lips once—so dry and sore! He reached up with his free hand and touched his mouth. When he pulled his hand away, his fingertips were stained with blood. His stomach gave a lurch, and he tried to vomit. Nothing came up. The pain doubled him over, and he cried out, his lips cracking with the effort.

How long had she waited for him? Ten minutes? No, it was longer. Had she tried the door? Had she seen what he'd done to the house? The house! That was why she'd left him. He was certain of it.

He shifted from one foot to the other, and his legs nearly buckled. How long had he been standing in this room? Was it even the same night? He searched his memory, desperate for even one detail—something to anchor him. He couldn't think.

He backed away from the window, taking small steps toward the hallway. *I need help. There's something seriously wrong. I might have had a stroke.* The thought cheered him. He stepped into the hall.

"Oh my God," he whispered. He stared at the hallway in horror. He shook his head side-to-side, unable to grasp what he was seeing. He wandered the back of the hall, touching the wood and plaster, as if feeling were believing. At the far end, he sat down and put his head in his hands.

"Look what you've done," he whispered. "Look what you've done."

Though he hadn't believed it, he'd agreed with Molly when she'd told him that he needed a professional. He hadn't wanted her to be angry with him. He'd have agreed to anything. But now? He stared down the length of the hallway and began to cry. He was damned. And he'd taken his poor mother with him.

Despite his inability to remember the past days and weeks, memories of his earlier life, from childhood to the job at the university, seemed clear. He traced his pattern of mutable goals and altered passions like the irregular path of a tear coursing down a cheek—left, then right, but always, always down. And now, he would abandon still another path, leaving the wretched walls of this house as a monument to his mother's stupidity for believing in him.

He wondered if she would be surprised when she found out how badly he'd failed. Would she forgive him? Yes—her love was unconditional. His head was muddled, but he was certain of that much. The thought gave him no comfort. He stared at the pocked walls and open beams. He'd failed the house as well. He truly loved living here. There was the final irony.

He took a deep breath and stood. The black, speckled shape that had sporadically haunted him reappeared, this time in the guise of a swarm of flies, nearly blotting out the light. Frozen in place, he waved his hands in front of his face until his vision cleared. The specks thinned and then disappeared. The only buzzing he heard was the low hum of a crushing headache.

What the hell was that? God, I need help. He thought of Molly, but that ship had sailed. He'd asked her to wait outside for him, and she'd gone away.

He began walking down the hall, toward the stairs that led to the front door. He'd leave the house, and when he was far enough away, three or four blocks, he would call for an ambulance.

He stared at the battered walls, tripping on debris as he walked. There was no way to fix the mess, not this time. Whether he wanted to stay on or not, he had to leave. This was not the time or place to make a stand. His mother would forgive him this last abandonment. When he was well, he would think about finding a way to pay her back. He would make things right.

The thought of quitting the rubble he'd created gave him an enormous sense of relief as he moved to the top of the stairs. He was ill. This disaster wasn't his fault. He would get help and then rebuild his life. Later, he would find the thing that he was meant to do, and the person he was meant to do it with. He would start over.

He paused at the top of the stairway. The lights in the entryway were off. The darkness didn't bother him. He was comfortable here. *I really do love this house.* Was there had been any way to undo the damage he'd caused? Maybe he could call in a contractor to help. He could look for extra financing to pay for the repairs. Perhaps his mother had a card or two up her sleeve. An IRA? He glanced back down the hall.

No. Too much damage.

A crippling sense of shame washed over him. He had to leave the house. There was no other way.

He gripped the bannister carefully—now was not the time to trip and fall. He counted steps to the bottom, and then shifted left to the front door. Fumbling, he found the light switch and turned it on.

They leave. They leave. They leave.

He spun in place, staring at each wall in turn. Scores of two-word accusations slashed the entryway walls and ceiling. The brush strokes were angry, bold and somehow familiar. Despair gripped his heart like a fist. He'd failed Winnie as well. One more man had chosen to leave her, leave her house.

"What can I do?" he called out. "I've ruined everything!"

Silence.

"I have no choices!" He whirled in place, his hands outstretched. "Tell me what to do!"

He stopped, his head cocked to the side, as if listening.

Garrett stood still, hands in front, one folded over the other, shoulders slumped, his head hung low. The house sighed, settling with a creak and a pop.

* * * * *

Molly stopped her car at the curb, directly in front of the walkway that led to the front porch of Garrett's house. Paige had followed in her own car, pulling up directly behind Molly. The lawn was a landscape of snow-covered shapes, rounded and gray in the moon's dim light. Molly turned off the engine and headlights, and then opened the glove compartment. She wasn't going inside without a flashlight. She checked the batteries, then stepped from the car door. Jamming her hands into her pockets, she sank down into her coat, shivering. Paige's car sat running, lights on. Molly waited a moment before walking to the driver's side. Paige sat, hands on the steering wheel, staring at the lawn.

"Paige?" Molly tapped at the window.

Paige turned, her mouth twisted in fear. She glanced back to the lawn again before finally turning off her car's engine.

Molly waited long moments while Paige sat still. She tapped at the window again. "I'm cold. Are we going in?"

The car door opened. "What is all of this? What have they done to his lawn?"

Molly didn't answer. She waited until Paige stepped from the car and then, together, they walked to the front door. One stack of drywall, crumbled and ice-covered, looked like cake frosting, glistening in the soft glow of the street light. A wet bag of groceries had split and spilled under the weight of snow. A notice, bearing the city's official logo, had been pinned to the front door. Molly pointed her flashlight at the notice and shook her head. "Shall we go in?"

Paige stood, her back to the door, staring at the piles on the lawn. "You should knock," she whispered.

Molly knocked on the door. The cold night air swallowed the sound. After a few moments, she tried again, louder this time.

"He might not be home," Paige said.

"He's home. He's not answering." On impulse, Molly grabbed the doorknob and turned.

The door opened a crack.

Molly stared. She hadn't expected the door to be unlocked. Now they had a choice. They could stand on the porch, shivering, or they could go inside. Neither woman moved.

"Should you call out to him?" Paige asked.

Molly glared at the woman. "I'm here because you asked me to be here. What do you want me to do?"

"I don't want to barge in on him—"

"What do you want?"

Paige seemed to shrivel with her words. "Don't be angry," she said. "I'm frightened of what we're going to find."

A cold wind gusted through the porch, stinging them both with ice. Molly covered her eyes for a moment. When the wind paused, she grabbed Paige by the elbow and pulled her into the house. The threshold was dark. Molly fumbled for the light switch.

"Oh, Molly." Paige's voice was a low moan, drawn out over long, slow moments.

Then grandeur of the entryway was gone. The room had been split in two. A passageway formed from plywood sheets and bracing, tunneled to the rear of the house. To the right, Sheetrock closed off all but a small doorway, blocking the stairway that rose back and away from the barricade. Every inch of wall space had been covered with a repeated cryptic message:

They leave. They leave. They leave.

Molly stared. She seemed to recall Garrett telling her what the words meant, but she couldn't remember the explanation. She'd been too angry with him to listen.

From the ruts gouged in the old wood flooring to the holes and dangling wires above them, the room had been dismantled. Destroyed. A bag of rotted groceries sat in the corner, bracketed by tiny piles of rodent waste. The smell of putrefied meat and vegetables would have been worse, but the room was ice cold. Molly could see her breath.

"Garrett?" Molly's voice sounded thin and frightened. No one answered.

Paige stood behind her, shaking. "He's here, isn't he?"

"How could I know that, Paige?" Molly peered down the plywood tunnel. The lights were off in the rear of the house. The passageway reminded her of an open mouth. She couldn't see the tunnel's end. Gripping the flashlight, she turned back to Paige. The woman seemed to have aged five years in five minutes. Her hair was disheveled. Her mouth had gone slack.

"I can't go in there."

"We may have to."

"No." Paige shook, more like a convulsion than shivers.

Molly stood up. She hadn't intended to go through the tunnel, but watching Paige break apart made her angry in some way she couldn't define. *Doesn't she understand that Garrett is in trouble? That he needs help? She's his mother, for God's sake!* Molly lifted the flashlight. "We have to find Garrett. And I'm not doing this alone. You're coming with me."

Paige seemed to shrivel under the weight of the words. She sank back against the front door, one hand behind her, the other hand up near her throat as if to ward off an attack. "I'm afraid."

"So am I." Molly waved the flashlight. "Come on."

Paige nodded, her mouth trembling and wet.

I should call an ambulance and let the paramedics handle this. Instead, Molly turned toward the tunnel. She hunched over and took a step inside. The flashlight beam played out into an empty room ahead. She couldn't see a thing. "Are you coming?" she demanded, inching forward.

"Yes." The reply was a timorous whisper.

Molly scowled and plunged ahead into the tunnel. As she neared the end, a sound stopped her. She stood still, bent forward, listening. What if someone were waiting for her, hidden? She imagined a face, peering around the end of the construction, ghastly white, smiling. The thought gave her chills. She nearly turned back.

No! Paige was behind her, and the thought of the two of them inching backwards because Molly was afraid was unacceptable. Molly took as deep a breath as her cramped posture would allow, and forced herself to move ahead. She crept into the cold, dark room and panned with the flashlight. The beam fell on a kitchen range. The appliance was new, much nicer than the old gas stove that came with the house. But the top of the range had been dismantled, and huge dents disfigured the sides. A sledgehammer lay on the floor next to the battered appliance.

"What the hell?" she muttered, as much to herself as to Paige.

Paige?

Molly peered back into the tunnel. Garrett's mother was nowhere in sight.

"Paige!" she shouted, anger in her voice. No answer.

A noise came from behind her—the same noise she'd heard earlier. She whirled, pointing the flashlight like a handgun. Nothing. She stood dead still, listening. The only sound she could hear was her own shuddering breath. She turned the beam to the right. Was this the kitchen? The walls had been torn out. She looked for a light switch, but the flashlight was too dim. She tried to move, but her feet were rooted to the ruined floor. Across the room, the flashlight beam danced in the open walls—her hands were shaking.

She forced herself to take one step, and then another. The flashlight beam leveled out, fixing on the room beyond the kitchen wall. Photos were thumbtacked to the walls inside. She crept closer, listening for any sudden movements. "Garrett?" Her voice was a rattled whisper.

Closer. She could make out the photos in the recesses—black and white pictures of a brunette in leather. The wall behind the kitchen appliances had been torn away, leaving 2 x 4 framing and dangling wires. Behind the open wall, a bedroom decorated with the image of Winnie. The photos had to be Winnie—the woman Garrett was obsessed with.

That's what this whole disaster was about. Obsession.

She slipped around the sink and between the joists, entering the tiny room with the bed and the photos. Inside, she realized the room was little more than a closet. The bed was a shabby antique with dusty sheets. The shelves were makeshift carpentry, exhibiting all the hallmarks of an amateur—tilted and square-cut.

She felt, rather than heard, movement behind her.

Shuddering with electric shock, she whirled, flashlight extended like a weapon, panning the darkness in a frantic attempt to see whoever was stalking her. The hall was empty. Fired with adrenaline, she stepped from the room, flashlight in front, turning into the hallway. Empty. She turned back, shining the light toward the living room tunnel.

Behind her.

She whirled again, pointing the flashlight back into the room. No one. But she'd heard a sound!

"Fuck!" Molly backed into the living room, turning with the light beam as she moved, panning back and forth until she reached the entrance to the plywood tunnel. Near tears, she peered around, then ducked into the tunnel. She tried to move quickly, but hunched over, chin in her chest, she could only go so fast. She heard a sound at the mouth of the tunnel behind her. She didn't dare look back. She plunged forward, a moan turning into a shriek as she banged her head on the boards above her head. She burst into the entryway and dropped to her knees, turning to look down the tunnel.

No one there.

She flopped down to the floor, cold and frightened.

After long moments (time seemed to freeze for her), she pulled herself up. She still had to find Garrett. And now Paige was missing. She stared at the cut-out door to the stairway. Garrett had loved the stairway, with its fine polish and dark wood. Why would he wall it up? She took a deep breath and held it, trying to calm herself.

Up the stairs.

She paused with each step, glancing behind her often. The light from the entryway lit the stairs nearly to the top, where the brown shadows swallowed the light. She kept one hand on the bannister while pointing the flashlight into the void. Paige had been frightened. Why would she rush off into the dark?

Then she reached the top step.

The hallway stretched before her. She'd stood here once with Garrett, months earlier, dreaming of a future that would never be. A sliver of melancholy slipped in with her fear, leaving her shaken and drained. *Paige would never have come up here alone. She's on the lawn waiting for me. What am I doing?* She sighed, and the sound pierced the cold silence of the hall. She raised her hand and pointed the flashlight.

The walls had been torn away, from the front end of the hallway to the back, the exposed bracing festooned with photo prints. Garrett had eviscerated the ceiling, laying open vent ducts, conduits and insulation. Carpeting had been slit open and tugged free in huge, coiled strips. Plaster dust whirled in the beam of her light, drifting specs that danced like confetti. "Oh, Garrett!" Molly whispered.

She crept down the hallway. Her light reached the rear of the hall, to an open window, where frigid air had frosted the wooden frame. Her flashlight beam made the ice sparkle.

Then she heard another sound. This time, the scuffling was clear enough to locate. The bedroom door ahead on the left. She froze. Soft footsteps? A rat? She couldn't tell, not for sure. She pointed the flashlight at the wall framing, and found a spot where the holes went clear through, but the thin beam was swallowed by shadows.

This is crazy. I can't do this. Then she heard the sound again, followed by a moan.

Paige?

Molly took a deep breath. She could go downstairs and check to see if Paige had returned to her car. But if she hadn't, Molly would have to force herself back up the stairs, and she didn't think she could do that. She had to check the room now, before her nerve failed her. She walked forward. Two steps, then four. The door was open, though Molly could have squeezed between the open wall framing if she'd dared. She rubbed her watering eyes with the back of her free hand, and forced herself inside.

The sound came again, to her right. A chill shot across the back of her neck as she pointed the flashlight. Something thrashed in the mouth of the closet. Molly moaned, nearly dropping the flashlight. Not a rat—

She caught a glimpse of a pale visage, open-mouthed, doll's teeth flashing in the dark. Eyes wide, with black, pin-head pupils. The specter thrashed in a pile of paper and building refuse, sending plaster dust into the air.

Molly stared. She knew the woman in the closet.

"Oh my God, Paige! What happened? Are you all right?"

Paige Jenkins lay on the closet floor, trying to cover herself with chunks of drywall. She thrashed again, legs askew, whimpering. Molly moved the beam down, out of the woman's eyes, and tiptoed forward. "It's all right, Paige. It's me. Molly. What happened?"

Paige stopped moving.

"Are you hurt?" Molly came closer still. She kept the flashlight beam on Paige's legs. "Can you tell me what's wrong?"

Paige took a ragged gasp of air. Her eyes bulged, and she would not meet Molly's gaze. Spittle dripped from her open mouth.

Molly knelt a few paces away, holding her free hand out. "I'm here for you, Paige. It's me, Molly."

Paige did a double-take, as if coming awake at the end of a horrible nightmare. "Molly?"

"Yes, it's me. Molly. You're going to be okay. I'm going to help you." Molly inched forward, now just a yard from Paige and the mouth of the closet. She glanced into the closet and tried not to shiver, resisting the temptation to point the beam into the empty shadows. What would she see?

Paige leaned forward, her mouth dropping open even further, her tongue brown and shriveled, her gaze meeting Molly's gaze, then raising up over Molly's shoulder. Paige's eyes went impossibly wide as she spoke, her voice raw like sandpaper.

"Don't look behind you," she said.

* * * * *

Later, when the team of paramedics arrived, gurney and emergency equipment bustling down the hall in a burst of noise and light, Molly directed them to Paige's closet and then backed away. Let the professionals do their work. With so much activity, she felt safe, or perhaps just disconnected from the black magnetism of the ruined house. She wandered to the end of the hallway and peered out of the open window. Below, wood, snow and drywall made a huge icy pile that would take a bulldozer to clear. Shivering, she shut the window.

To her right, she could see the outline of a bathroom—gutted. Molly still had her flashlight. She pointed the beam inside. The toilet had been lifted from the floor and pitched into the bathtub, cracking the basin in two. On the wall, a decorative rack held a plush red towel. A flower vase with a single dead rose sat above the sink.

She started down the hall. Her senses seemed jumbled, as if her head had been clogged with a cold—clouding her vision and blocking her ears. She felt dizzy and sound seemed to come from a distance.

So when she heard the creak, it surprised her.

The sound was distinctive, and she thought she'd heard it before. A twisting, stretching sound that made her think of sitting on a stuffed chair in a short skirt, skin chaffing against vinyl. She stopped.

To her left, a closed bedroom door. No holes in the wretched walls for her to peer through. She stared at the door for long seconds, and then heard the sound again. A rubbing sound, but not vinyl. What was it?

She stared at the doorknob, then stared at a photo tacked to the wall joist. A woman in her late thirties, perhaps early forties, wearing a leather bustier and dark nylons, wielded some sort of flogging device. The ends of the whip were tied in tight, tiny knots. In the foreground of the photo, a young man, naked and bound, grimaced in pain. Molly stared. The man didn't interest her. He was pretty, but he looked foolish. The woman's expression, though, fascinated her—part enjoyment, part anguish.

Another creak.

Down the hall, one of the paramedics came up from the street, carting an oxygen tank. Molly hoped that Paige would be all right.

Her hand gripped the doorknob.

Garrett.

She turned the knob. As she did, she had a sense that this would be a moment she would remember forever. Like grabbing her college diploma from the dean after walking across the stage. Like fetching coffee for her boss on the first day of her job at the investment firm. Like turning down her first proposal, and watching the man she liked (but did not love) mouth the word associated with female dogs.

This will change me. She pushed open the door.

Creak.

The sound of rope on a rafter.

The window in the room was open, and a February wind pushed the body in a gentle arc, twisting to face her. His mouth was a grotesque, frozen parody of who he'd been—tongue spilling from blue lips, frosted eyes protruding from their sockets. Despite the cold, the smell in the room was horrible. Garrett had filled his pants at the moment of death, and his skin had begun to decay.

In her mind's eye, she could see him jerking at the end of the rope—the frantic, spastic dance of a marionette.

As if from a distance, she heard the sound of a train. Trains take you away—take you to somewhere new. A comforting sound, that groaning whistle. But it was not a train. Molly dropped to the floor, moaning. And eventually, one of the paramedics found her.

After

July 25, 1933
The Weekly Chronicle
Local Legend Sentenced

Heads are spinning this week over the conviction and sentencing of local legend, Winnie Laughlin, the first woman in the state to be convicted of "contributing to the delinquency of a minor." Judge William Boroughs Kent of the Municipal Court ruled that Laughlin "tended to cause delinquency," resulting in truancy. The trial put a fitting end to a series of unsuccessful charges against Laughlin, ranging from the sale of alcohol to tax evasion.

Hailed by supporters as a woman "ahead of her time," Winnie Laughlin was abandoned by her investment banker husband at the cusp of the Great Depression. Without friends or family to sustain her, Laughlin turned to scandalous behavior, including the sale of alcoholic beverages and the life of a "sporting girl." In subsequent years, her home was a notorious independent house of prostitution.

At her trial, Laughlin made no effort to conceal her vocation, choosing instead to boast, "My girls and I have avoided the foul *life of a slave. Because I am a professional, and because our girls are above the cut, we are able to charge $3 instead of the usual $2. The house keeps the standard fee, so my girls are able to save and plan for their futures."*

Under further examination by the judge, the former Mrs. Laughlin denied reports of white slavery. "Anything my girls do is done with full understanding and consent. Unlike the sour old maids who populate your courtroom, my girls neither dry up, nor resort to the conceit, deception, and hypocrisy of marriage."

The jury took less than 10 minutes to deliberate, finding Laughlin guilty.

The specific charges leading to Laughlin's conviction involved the abuse and debasement of a young boy of 16 years. Though large for his age, and acknowledged to have misrepresented his circumstances, the young man was discovered in what the police described as "shameful circumstances." This reporter learned that the boy was rescued from the Laughlin house wearing suggestive leather implements, much like the harness used to restrain a plow horse. The boy (name withheld out of respect for his family) has been remaindered to his loving parents in hopes that he might return to a productive and rewarding life as an honest Christian.

Laughlin's previous legal misadventures had ended in acquittals, a great frustration to the current city administration, who saw Laughlin's house as a community blight. An unnamed source from the prosecutor's team allowed that help in obtaining a conviction came from an unlikely source. A "ringer" house supplied certain tips, so that police could raid Laughlin's operation at a precipitous time. Ringer (or ring) houses have a central office with several locations, much like a chain of supply stores. In this case, the ringer house may have been one of Laughlin's direct competitors.

Though Colorado was the first state to pass a law against contributing to the decency of a minor, this case marked the first time since the law was enacted in 1903 that the defendant was a woman.

Judge Kent levied the maximum sentence against Laughlin, whose disgraceful and unrestrained response earned her an additional jail sentence for direct contempt of court proceedings.

June 7, 1958
The Weekly Chronicle
Obituary: Winifred Laughlin

Winifred "Winnie" Laughlin, 58 years, of Denver, Colorado, passed away on Wednesday, June 4th. She was born March 2,

1900 to Duncan and Leda Hornsby of Greeley.

Winifred married Robert Laughlin, an investment broker, in 1923. When the stock market crashed, Robert left for parts unknown, leaving his wife nearly penniless. Winifred became something of a local legend through her association with bootleggers, gangsters, and prostitutes. Her home was rumored to be a "house of ill repute." In 1933, she was convicted for "contributing to the delinquency of a minor," the first woman to be jailed for that offense. In 1935, and again in 1938, she was convicted of solicitation. Throughout her legal difficulties, she kept possession of her Denver home, owing to sizeable personal investments.

In later years, Winifred became something of a women's rights advocate. Officials noted that only women visited her during her stints in prison, and she was said to have been very popular among fellow inmates. In 1940, she founded the "Laughlin School for Women," a finishing school that enjoyed some popularity until the early 1950s.

In the final years of her life, Winifred battled illness and personal financial setbacks. In February, several women's clubs pooled resources to settle a longstanding dispute with the Internal Revenue Service, allowing Winifred to continue the remainder of her life in her beloved home.

Winifred, mourned by friends, was not survived by family. Funeral services will be held at the Aspen Bough Women's Club on 17th St. in Denver on Monday, June 9th.

Scandals of Old Denver
Tom Bryant, Author
(Pernicious Press, 1966)

"...she was one completely crazy bitch. She hated men. I mean, she loathed them. Strange for someone in the pleasure business, but then, you see people in customer service all the time who'd just as soon their customers die, foaming at the mouth. And this gal really had a hot poker up her twat for anyone with a Willie, you know what I mean? She destroyed a lot of men's lives. Regular customers found themselves divorced and ruined. Who tipped off their wives? And poor schmucks who ended up addicted to that riding crop of hers! I'll tell you this: she'd have been kinder to slide a blade across their throats. But kindness wasn't her thing."

* * * * *

When Paige passed away, Molly attended the funeral, even though she'd only visited Paige once in the hospital.

During the visit, the doctors told Molly that Paige had suffered a stroke.

Her private room seemed comfortable, decorated in earth tones. Monitoring equipment had been built into the wall, silent and hidden. Someone had turned on a television, leaving the volume muted, like the wall color. Paige lay on her back, her head turned toward the window blinds. Every five minutes or so, she would turn and look at Molly, as if to assure herself that she was not alone, and then turn back.

"Do you want me to stay?"

No answer.

"Do you want me to leave?" Getting out of the room was something that Molly wanted very much to do, but she had a question that she needed answered. If Paige wanted her to stay, she would stay.

When the nurse came to check on Paige, Molly pulled her aside. "Can she talk?"

"Oh, yes. She can talk. She's having trouble with certain words, but she was speaking earlier. Why? Is she having trouble now?"

Later, when the nurse had finished with blankets, television volume, a glass of water with a sipping straw and a promise of JELL-O, and they were once again alone, Paige turned her gaze on Molly. "I'm very tired, and seeing you reminds me that my son is dead."

The sun was setting, leaving the room dusky. The last blush of the day painted the blinds, but night would fall soon, and Molly did not intend to share the darkness with the old woman. "I'm leaving then. But first, I have a question. When I found you in the upstairs closet, you told me not to turn around. Do you remember that? I've been wondering. What exactly was behind me?"

Paige regarded her silently. The machine in the wall gave a single tick. Another minute passed.

"I don't recall saying that." Paige's voice was thick and gauzy, as if she'd tried to speak through bandages. But her eyes were sharp, like a kitchen drawer full of knives. Molly stood to leave. "Perhaps I tried to warn you about my son."

Molly forced herself to approach the bed, to touch Paige's hand and smile gravely. "I'm so sorry for your loss."

Molly recounted the visit during Paige's funeral. A second stroke had taken the woman in her sleep, or so the hospital said. Stroke or not, a broken heart was a powerful adversary. And there was nothing Molly could do to make things better.

The funeral was well attended. Paige had work acquaintances and neighbors who made the trip. She hadn't belonged to a church, so the service was held by the funeral home at the gravesite.

Early spring in Colorado could be brutal, and the icy winds put an edge to the service. Molly had forgone a warm, cream-colored outfit to wear black. The thin material of her pants suit was raw meat for the wind. The dark wood coffin, resting on supports over the open grave, was topped by a bouquet of roses. The wind blew the flowers across the polished surface, spilling them to the ground. The speaker—a pastor, or perhaps a funeral home employee—continued with his ruminations on the meaning of life and death. A man in a gray overcoat and fedora stepped from the crowd and put the roses back on the coffin. When a second gust of wind spilled the flowers again, the man returned them to the coffin a second time, holding them in place, one hand on the coffin and the other on his fedora. When the final prayer ended, the man stepped back, and the wind sent the roses flying.

The sight of the man struggling with the wind and flowers touched Molly in a way she couldn't explain. She'd felt so distanced from tragic events that it was a relief to have some moment of grace bring tears to her eyes. She was glad she'd gone to the funeral. Paige was not a bad woman, and her sins had been repaid tenfold.

After the funeral, she discovered that Paige had made provisions for Molly in her will. The bulk of her estate was passed on to a series of local causes, but a sizeable endowment went to Molly, with the following note:

You were the best thing in my son's short life. Thank you. P.

Molly had been surprised that there was any estate to be divided, given the damage to the house, but the lawyer, a gabby sort who seemed to like Molly, explained that the house had been sold as-is to a group of buyers that included several paranormal investigators. That news gave her pause because it introduced the question she'd refused to ask herself.

Armed with her inheritance and her personal investments, Molly found herself without money concerns, an interesting state of affairs that she'd never anticipated. She used all of her available vacation time to take a break from work and headed for the mountains west of Denver. Time away would let her think through her changing circumstances. And a road trip sounded delicious.

She packed her car and took to the road, her iPod loaded with traveling music—mostly classic rock. She loved Skynyrd and Zep and Lou Reed—musicians long gone, still firing tracers through the air waves. And each song stripped away the investment banker, vest and coat, until all that remained was Molly, hair flying, a car going 20 miles an hour over the speed limit on a quarter tank of gas, and the tunes.

She found herself in an old mining town, took a room, and slept. She got up once to go to the bathroom and grab a drink of water. In the morning, she explored the town, which consisted of a bar with the worst nachos in history, a convenience store, and a gift shop.

She had no one to buy gifts for.

On the third day, she headed home.

Back in town, she stopped by Garrett's old house. The lawn had been cleared, and some landscape work was evident. Bushes nestled in the flowerbeds that flanked the front steps. A new tree blocked the view of the living room window. The dead grass was gone, replaced by turf.

She regarded the house from her car for a long time. She stared at each window (though she might not have, had the sun set). She gave thought to knocking at the door. Would they let her in to see the changes to the house? She decided against trying. There was no point. Her reason for going inside was to find an answer to one remaining question, and a daylight visit would not give her an answer.

* * * * *

Molly tried dating soon after the funeral, but she found herself skeptical of men and their intentions. Her cynicism seemed to spill over to her own gender as well. What did people want from a relationship? Was anyone ever honest with others? With themselves? She came to the conclusion that honesty was secondary in a world where people were simply too damaged to relate.

A year after Garrett's death, Molly bought a house. She had a brief relationship with a man from her department at the investment firm. The affair ended badly. Molly blamed herself, though placement of fault no longer seemed important.

As the years passed, she had many quiet nights to remember, to analyze Garrett's death. Had he been haunted by the vindictive ghost of a Madame in an old house of prostitution? Or, faced with a lifetime of commitment issues and the stark realization of repeated failures, had he broken down?

The photos he'd shown her had to be his own work. He knew how to Photoshop an image. He'd taken headshots from Molly's pictures and transposed them onto pornographic images.

But she'd felt something in the house. Something malevolent. Something dangerous.

Was she fooling herself?

Paige could have answered her questions. She'd said she hadn't remembered saying not to look behind her, but she was lying, lying. Molly saw it in her eyes.

In the end, Molly put her questions to rest one night in her new condo. Sitting in front of a fire, a blizzard outside and a glass of wine in hand, Molly came to a realization in mid-sip. She could only go by what she knew first-hand. And she knew this much:

When Paige had said not to turn around, she'd obeyed.

She knew what she'd see.

THE HONEY GATHERER

This last tale does not involve the supernatural, though the story is as dark as anything I've ever written. I wrote the novella as an exercise, at a time when I was uncertain if I understood story dynamics. The question, "What is a story?" is something every serious author asks at one time or another. I found myself struggling to come up with a meaningful answer.

Beginning authors often write autobiographical tales, but I never did. To lift events from one's life seemed like cheating, and besides, people are seldom honest with themselves, and the result looks flat and false on the page. But in my quest for something I knew was a story—the kind that grabs you and won't let go—I fell back on a series of events that took place in three different cities over a space of two decades. In the process, the characters came to life, asserting themselves, and any resemblance to real events began to dissipate.

I still don't know enough about story to explain why this narrative takes you by the throat. The setting is real enough—I worked in restaurants for a long time. (No, don't worry—no one consumes human flesh in this one.) Perhaps the characters, each doomed in their own way, are tragic enough to warrant undivided attention. But I think what lingers is the fulcrum the plot rests on—too bizarre to be fiction.

As for Laura (not her real name), I still think of her. And I wish I'd kept the photo.

There is some soul of goodness in things evil
Would men observingly distil it out;
For our bad neighbour makes us early stirrers,
Which is both healthful, and good husbandry:

Besides, they are our outward consciences,
And preachers to us all; admonishing
That we should dress us fairly for our end.
Thus may we gather honey from the weed,
And make a moral of the devil himself.

William Shakespeare
The Life of King Henry the Fifth
Act IV. Scene I.

I

The night I met Laura, the girl who broke my heart, was also the night Leon told me he had cancer. Everything that happened later tumbled out of that night. God was setting up his Rube Goldberg machine— stacking rows of dominos, setting levers and switches, everything arranged in anticipation of a sudden whirl of motion. My memories carry the added weight of dramatic irony. I know who won, I know who lost, and I know who ended up face-down on the carpet.

I worked as a cook then. Laura had been waiting tables at lunch for a few weeks, learning the restaurant's table system. When they introduced her to the night crew, I thought she was cute. She had brown hair and a pretty face. Her body was rock hard; I remember that. When they got to me, she held out her hand, but I had steak blood all over me, so I just waved hello. She dropped her hand and started to giggle, and when I saw that smile, I got hungry.

I have a few pictures of her, but none of them caught that smile. (The photo the crazy photographer took did, but Leon ended up with it.) A camera freezes things. Laura Beck was alive. She resisted being frozen.

Her trainer whisked her away to wait tables, and I went back to the line to cook. It was a weekday, so it wasn't very busy. The heat was bad, rising off the grill, out of the fryer vats, from under the heat lamps and the salamander. I was sweating like a fat woman at the beach. My shirt had a salt ring and my thighs rubbed when I moved. Manager Tom had been promising to fix the air conditioning for weeks, but he didn't have to sweat with us because he never worked the line. Repairing the AC ranked somewhere below replacing the broom on his list of priorities. Besides, Nixon had frozen wages and prices, and if we didn't fix the air conditioner last year, we couldn't fix it this year.

Things were going well despite the heat. I had Davy Milford working with me, and he was busting his tail trying to please me. A few days before, he'd been flirting with the girls and talking instead of cleaning, and I called him on it. "Listen," I told him. "Everybody makes the same money here, and there's nothing anyone can do about it, so we all need to do the same work. If I have to carry you on my back because you're not paying attention, then you owe me part of your check." After that, he kept his mind on work.

Manager Tom sat grousing in the corner, hoping to catch me doing something wrong. Normally, he'd have been on the new girl like blood on an apron, but the cash shortages had him all worked up, and he wanted someone to abuse.

"What's your time on the lead ticket?" he demanded, suddenly at the food window, trying to look up under the wheel and read the tickets himself, something he couldn't do because he was too short, and he didn't have x-ray vision.

"We're at five minutes on the lead ticket, Manager Tom," I answered.

He closed his eyes and whistled a sigh. "Don't call me that. I've told you not to—"

"Your name is Tom and you're the manager," I explained. I had my poker face on. No expression, no clues. I kept my hands moving, setting plates, wiping the counter. All the while, I was swallowing a laugh.

Manager Tom ran a hand across his forehead, probably a holdover from when he had hair to run his fingers through. "Don't screw with me tonight, Wilson. I don't have any patience for you."

"I wouldn't dare," I smiled. I set two rare steaks in the window, a tiny opening in the wall that separated the cooks from the waiters. I pinned the ticket under the first plate and called for Leon. Davy was watching, so I had to push a little more. "You can call me *Cook James* if you like, Manager Tom."

The little man pursed his lips and nodded to himself, as if he'd made a decision. His eyes narrowed, a difficult trick, since his eyes were tiny little brown pellets to begin with. I was supposed to be afraid of losing my job now, but instead, I was laughing, because it occurred to me that those little brown pellets looked just like rabbit poop.

"Can I call you Cook James?" Davy asked after Manager Tom left the line.

I took the spatula off the grill and brushed the tip against Davy's bare arm. "Is this hot?" I asked as he yelped.

The rare steaks were still sitting in the window, so I called for Leon again. Davy put a chicken salad on the staging counter. "Those shortages are making Tom crabby," he said with his little gee-whiz voice. "I wish they'd figure out who's stealing, so things could go back to normal."

"Manager Tom is a jerk whether there are shortages or not," I said. "And the stealing isn't going to stop, because he's a stupid jerk. He leaves the office door open half the night, with the cash box just sitting there on the desk. He ought to put up a sign— *Please steal my money*. Someday, somebody's going to walk out with the whole deposit, and Manager Tom won't have a clue."

"What, are you going to put it under your shirt?" Davy asked.

"Hah, why bother? You could roll by the office with a mop bucket, throw the box into the dirty water, and mop your way out the back door in front of everybody. Wet money dries out."

I flipped a halibut filet on the grill, and the thing fell apart. "Damned halibut," I wailed. I'd have to piece it together on the plate when it was done cooking. Halibut's a delicate fish, and it looks like crap when you grill it—you can never get good marks on it—but Manager Tom liked grilled fish because it wasn't as fattening. He was trying to keep his thirty-year-old belly from turning into a little round flesh pillow, so I had to grill the halibut rather than bake it, which is what I ought to have been doing.

Then I remembered Leon's steaks. I turned around and started to holler for him, but there he was, standing in the window, a blank look on his face.

"Are you going to run those steaks?"

Leon looked down and stared at the plates like he'd never seen beef before. "These are mine?" He shook his head. "Where is my head at tonight?"

I started sliding the next order into the window, pushing Leon's plates off the edge. He grabbed them, still shaking his head. "Sorry guys. Sorry." He paused, and looked right at me. "We need to talk later, okay?"

"Sure," I said. "What's up?"

"Later," he promised.

That ticked me off. I hate it when somebody stops you to tell you that later, they're going to stop you to tell you something. I don't like to wait for the punch line. I don't like to wait.

Every so often, Laura would come by with her trainer, running orders, or delivering other people's food. "Are you going out after work?" I asked. No use waiting, I figured. If I didn't ask her, one of the other guys would beat me to it.

She shrugged. "I might. Who's going?"

I thumbed at Davy. "We are. And probably Leon. He's the old guy, the waiter." Leon was twenty-eight, older than the rest of us by half a decade. His age made him a bit of an authority figure to the cooks. But only a bit, since he was goofy as hell. Mostly, we made fun of his age.

"You can come out with us," Marjorie said. She was Laura's trainer, a tall blonde with great legs and no chest. With the exception of Leon, the cooks and the wait staff didn't mix much. I figured that Laura would get the hint, but she gave me that smile again and said, "Let me know where you're going. I'd like to go along."

We'd already made plans to do midnight bowling after work, but that didn't sound so great now. I told her I'd get back to her. Meanwhile, I was doing some furious thinking in hopes of coming up with another plan. Maybe Leon would think of something.

Leon. Sharing Laura with Davy was like bringing along your little brother, but Leon was another matter. That old man loved young girls, and I didn't want to go head-to-head with him. I looked pretty good back then, too thin maybe, but women are supposed to like thin guys. I didn't have a lot of luck with dating, though. I figured I was too nice for my own good. Everyone knows, nice guys finish last.

I got a jump on the closing work so I could get out about the same time as Laura. I was bent over, scrubbing the cooler doors, when Leon tapped me on the shoulder. "You busy?" he asked.

"Yes."

"The thing is," Leon whispered, his fish-mouth close enough to spray saliva on my cheek, "I've been having these headaches. They had me worried, so I went in to see a specialist." He looked serious now, pasty and twitching, so I stood up and let him talk.

"And they found something."

I waited. He frowned, like I'd forgotten my line. "What did they find?" I finally asked.

"Cancer." He spit the word like a mouthful of sour milk. "I have a tumor."

"You're kidding." But Leon didn't have a great sense of humor. I guessed he was probably not joking. I looked down at the floor and shuffled around a little. "What are you going to do?"

"I've got to have an operation," he said. "They want me to go under the knife right away. The thing is. . ." He paused. "I know it's the busy season here, and I don't want to lose my job."

"They wouldn't fire you for that."

"Tom already told me I couldn't take a vacation this month. I had an idea that I might need this operation, and I didn't want anyone to know I was ill. They treat you different when you're ill. So I asked about a vacation, and Tom got angry with me."

I started to laugh. "You're screwed up, man. You have cancer, and you don't want Manager Tom to be mad at you?" I went back to wiping down the cooler. "Tell him what's going on. He's a jerk, but he's not a heartless jerk."

Leon put a cold hand on my arm and thanked me for the advice. "I want you to do me one more favor," he said, almost whispering. His voice was thick and low. "I don't want anyone to know about this. I don't want to be treated differently." He paused. "If you see me feeling sorry for myself, even for a second, I want you to get after me. Joke all you want. Cut me down. You do anyway. Just don't let me get maudlin."

I assured him that I would do my best. "You still want to go out tonight?" I asked. I thought of Laura. "If you want to skip it. . ."

"No," he assured me. "I need to be with friends. Laura's going too, isn't she? She's nice. I've been working lunches with her for a while now. Anyway, I leave the day after tomorrow. There's a clinic in Michigan that's going to do the operation. I don't want to be alone tonight." He hung his head, and I thought I saw a tear threatening, so I turned away.

* * * * *

We went bowling. It sounds boring, but if you wanted a few beers at the end of a shift in a little town like Fort Collins, Colorado, you didn't have a lot of choices. You could go to one of the college bars and not hear a thing over the music, or you could go to your apartment. I had one room, two chairs and a bed. We went bowling.

Being restaurant employees, we spent the first fifteen minutes arguing over the stakes of the bet. There had to be a bet in bowling. I was worried that Laura might not get into the whole thing, but she was as loud as any of us, so I guess she had restaurant experience. At first we were going to play teams, but everyone wanted to pair up with Laura. We finally settled on breakfast at the pancake house for high score—the three losers would pay for the winner's meal.

That was fine with me. I'm no pro, but I can bowl as well as any schmuck. I have long arms, and when I pay attention, I can wind up and throw a wicked hook. Pins will fall. Usually, bowling was more about beer than anything else, but having Laura there, watching, gave me a little extra motivation. That, and the chance to show Leon up again.

Leon wanted to be best at everything, and he often was, but he was funny about the way he did it. He would become intense and focused, almost desperate, like someone on the bomb-squad, hunched over high explosives, his forehead wrinkled and his eyes pinched shut. I was just the opposite. I fooled around, took things casual, and if I won at whatever game we were playing, it ticked Leon off all the more.

Laura was a pretty fair bowler. She knew what she was doing, so Leon's "let me show you how to hold the ball" routine didn't fly. I bought a pitcher of Coors and a coke for Davy, who managed to sneak a few sips of beer from my glass as the evening went on.

Davy wasn't a good bowler, and he was pitching gutter balls like a child. Laura picked up a few spares, but Leon and I were knocking down strikes, so it was pretty much a two-man race. While we bowled, we talked about the night's work. Davy bragged about how I harassed Manager Tom, which made me look good. Leon complained about his tips, which he did every night. I could never tell if his service was so bad that people didn't tip him, or if he just liked to complain. That night, a table had stiffed him, and left a cartoon pamphlet about Jesus instead.

After showing off the written material, though, Leon sat thinking, looking like a robot that someone had switched to "standby." Weird, but I didn't care. It gave me a chance to talk to Laura.

"I had an odd thing happen tonight," she said. "One of my customers asked if I was a model, and he offered to take pictures of me. Marjorie said he's a regular, and he tries the same thing with every new girl—"

"The Photographer!" Davy and I started laughing. "That guy is a trip. I suppose he tipped you really well." Even Leon smirked for a moment before going back to his catatonic fugue.

Laura shrugged. "He tipped okay. What's the deal? Is he a creep?"

"I don't know," I told her. "I don't even know if there's film in his camera."

"Oh, he showed me some pictures he'd taken. I don't know that much about it, but they looked pretty good to me."

I didn't know how to tell her. "I think he wants gals to pose nude for him," I said, finally. Laura looked stricken for a moment. "Why?" I asked. "Did you agree to pose for him?"

"Just some outdoor shots," she assured me, though she looked a little uncertain.

"Well, you should watch out for him."

"Why, would he attack me?"

"No, I don't think so," I mumbled. "He just wants pictures."

Laura gave me a small, sharp smile. Her eyes locked on mine, and I knew then that she knew plenty about men and the tricks they played. "A man who wants me to take off my clothes? Are you serious?"

I tried to say something funny, but the subject started me thinking about what she looked like naked, and my mouth got gummy. I left the corner pins with my next ball.

Leon was still hitting, so he went up in the score. He was feeling pretty good about winning. "I've got this locked up," he boasted. He stood in the lane, hunched over, his bony butt pointed back at us like a weapon, and after a long pause, he went into his stride, and the pins all fell. He snapped his fingers and grinned. "Hell, if I lose this, I'll buy everyone's breakfast."

He should never have said it. Guys like Leon freeze up when the game is on the line. He left the ten pin on the last frame; and I ran the frame, three straight strikes, beating him by two pins. They were pulling pitchers off the tables—last call had come fifteen minutes earlier—so we paid the tab and headed off to the pancake house to cash in on Leon's mouth.

The waitress was a sour old woman in her thirties. She had glasses with thick plastic rims, just like Leon's. Davy wondered out loud if maybe the waitress was Leon's sister, and we all had a pretty good laugh at that. Then we ordered breakfast. I got strawberry-stuffed crepes. They were good, but there wasn't a lot of food there for a guy with an appetite. "I'm still hungry," I said.

"So am I," Davy agreed. He'd ordered a tall stack of pancakes, but as near as I could tell, Davy could eat anything. He was a thin little guy, too, one of those people that are immune to calories.

"You're all welcome to order more," Leon said. He was being grand, not gracious, and I felt obliged to make him sorry that he'd offered. I asked the waitress for another round of menus, which pissed her off, but what was she going to do, refuse the business? We were having a good time, and she wasn't. Work stinks. Too bad.

Laura ordered a second plate of French toast, which I thought was pretty cool. I've been out with girls that take a bite and a half of whatever dinner I buy them, and then complain about how full they are. Full of crap, maybe. Then they hit the refrigerator five seconds after they get home. Not Laura, though. "If you guys are going to pork out," she said, "then I'm going to join you at the trough."

By then, I guess I was in love with her.

Leon ordered a second breakfast too, but he didn't eat it. He cut the pancakes into bite-sized pieces and pushed them around the plate a little, but he was busy thinking. Laura noticed, and offered to pay for the second breakfast.

"No, no," Leon said. "That's not it. I don't mind. Money doesn't mean that much right now." He faced the window, looking melancholy, but I could see his eyes reflected in the glass. He was watching us watch him. Then he dropped the bomb.

"You guys are my friends," he started. "I don't want to lie to you. The fact is, I got some bad news from the doctor today. It seems I have a tumor. A brain-tumor. I'm going the day after tomorrow to have it operated on."

"Leon," Laura whispered.

"Oh my God," Davy said.

I sat and wondered what happened to not wanting any special attention, which he was getting plenty of with his announcement. "I have to be honest," he repeated.

We were silent for a moment. I don't think anyone knew how to comfort him. I didn't. Then I remembered that he'd wanted me to joke him out of any maudlin moments, so I did. "Well," I said, "when they cut your head open, make sure they take the biggest mass. The smaller one is the brain."

Davy snorted his soda through his nose, and that got a laugh, but nobody thought I was as clever as I did. Laura shifted around in her seat, trying to smile. I was sure I'd ruined something. Leon didn't seem willing to get me off the hook, so I launched into an explanation. "I knew about the tumor. I was the first one Leon told. He made me promise to pick on him if he started to feel sorry for himself."

By then, it was nearly three in the morning. We were starting to wind down, so the conversation became philosophical. To people in their twenties, the only three subjects worth discussing are death, sex, and philosophy. Leon's cancer made death a touchy subject, and though Laura was sitting pretty close in the booth (I could feel her right leg against my left), we left sex alone. We would have to make do with a discussion of good, evil, and the nature of humankind.

The waitress made a snide comment about a third round of entrees, and Davy stated his opinion that her poor service, her lack of a smile, and her general bad attitude were indicative of an evil nature. "She's vile," he said.

"She's tired, and we're having more fun than she is," Laura offered.

"That's right, that's right." Leon seemed eager to agree. I nodded too.

"I wonder if she knows how bad she sucks as a waitress," Davy said.

"How good of a cook do you think *you* are?" I asked. That got a laugh. "Really, I don't think most people recognize their own shortcomings."

"I'm honest about mine," Leon said.

Davy and I both laughed, so Leon had to protest. "I am, I am honest," he insisted. "I get spacy sometimes. I'm not the fastest waiter in the world—"

"That's because you're old." Davy was quick.

". . .and I trust people a little too much." Leon ignored us. "And I'm a giving kind of person, giving to a fault, so I sometimes end up being used."

"Wait a minute," I said. "Are these your shortcomings or your virtues?"

We started to laugh again, Laura as loud as Davy this time, and Leon slumped back in his seat to pout. I decided to rescue him. "Leon's right, though. He's pretty honest with himself." I didn't know that to be true, but it seemed like a nice, generic thing to throw out, so I did. "But in general, I think most people don't recognize the things they do wrong. They tell themselves that they're good guys."

"There are evil people out there," Laura said.

"The ones that don't tip," Leon added. I think he was serious.

"I don't think they know they're evil," I said. "Hell, if Adolf Hitler was here now, right in this booth, he'd tell you what a swell guy he was."

"No way."

"Sure. He was a patriot. He was righting the wrongs of the Versailles Treaty. It cost a bushel of Deutsche Marks to buy a turnip after World War One. He fixed the economy. And besides, he liked dogs and small children."

"He had one testicle," Davy added.

"What? What?" Leon was one step behind the discussion, as usual.

"But surely he understood that he was a butcher, don't you think?" Laura asked.

"I don't think so. Read *Mein Kampf.* Hitler was the hero of all of his stories."

"Hitler killed five million Jews," Leon assured us.

"If he was here now, he'd defend it," I said. "And you know what else? If Hitler was sitting here now, you'd be the fourth best-looking guy at the table, Leon."

It took him a second to do the math.

"It makes you wonder," Laura said when the laughing died down again. "Can you really do all those things, and lie to yourself? Tell yourself that deep inside, you're good?"

"Hitler used his political beliefs to defend himself with."

Laura nodded thoughtfully. "Does anyone *ever* think they're evil? What about Charles Manson?" Five years had passed since the Beverly Hills murders that left a pregnant actress and others dead. Even then, he was a symbol of insanity and evil.

"Manson thinks he's a messiah," Davy said. "I read an article about it. He thinks he's Jesus Christ."

"Everyone sins," Leon said. We all stopped. It seemed an odd comment to add. At the time, I thought he'd run out of things to say, and had decided to pitch in a little Sunday school gem. I would have argued with him. The lack of perfection in the human animal is no cause to lump the rest of us together with the likes of Manson and Hitler. But, there was no point. Leon couldn't keep up with ethical relativism, or theology, or even late-night beer talk. After all, he was just a waiter.

* * * * *

One more thing happened that night. We ended up back at the restaurant parking lot, picking up cars (Leon had driven everyone to the bowling alley), and Laura's car wouldn't start. It cranked, but it wouldn't fire. Leon and I had a tug-of-war over who would get to drive her home, but she was in a logical mood, and opted to go with the guy who lived closest to her apartment. Leon looked like he might be a sore loser about it, but then suddenly changed his mind. "Well, this might be goodbye for now," he said, removing his glasses and tucking them into his shirt pocket. "I'm leaving the day after tomorrow for that operation I mentioned."

Laura threw her arms around him. "I'll miss you," she said. "Get well and hurry back."

He latched onto her. "Just a hug? Are you afraid to kiss a dying man?" It was so contrived, so goofy, so Leon. She fell for it anyway and kissed him.

Davy drifted off during the goodbyes without saying much. I told Leon to keep in touch, and let me know how the operation went. "If I can, I will," he promised ominously.

Then I drove Laura home. She told me I didn't have to walk her to the door, but I did. I was a gentleman. A cool breeze had her shivering, and I put an arm around her. She didn't complain.

Then I put my foot in it. I asked her if you had to "die to get a kiss" from her. I could see the anger and disappointment in her eyes, and I figured that I'd blown it again. My mouth was my worst enemy. "You're a jerk, aren't you?" she asked.

Then she slid up against me, and kissed me anyway, her tongue slipping into my mouth. I was so surprised that I just stood there, probably grinning like an idiot. I think of that kiss sometimes, especially when a cool summer wind happens by, and the air smells like wild flowers (with a hint of manure, blowing in from the cattle feedlots in Greeley). There won't be another kiss like that. I'll never believe the way I did that night. I believed in truth, and goodness, and I believed in love.

So I said goodnight, and I left. I didn't invite myself in. I was a real gentleman.

II

There are no heroes in my story. (Maybe Laura. But she was the kind of person who was heroic because she made it out alive, with a piece of herself still clean.) In my own way, I made a hero's journey that summer. I had something to learn, but the truths I had to discover were ugly little worm-riddled secrets, and there was no glory in the knowledge. No enlightenment at the end of the tunnel.

I didn't think like that back then, of course. We were young Americans, and the world was ours. It was 1971, and if we'd opened our eyes, we might've had a sense of our limitations. Nixon had implemented a wage and price freeze, trying to shore up a crumbling economy by decree, as if any President could repair a complex world with a series of executive orders. But we were young, and young people imagine themselves both immortal and pure.

After that goodnight kiss, I was anxious to see Laura again, but I had to give up my night off to cover a shift for the restaurant. The other lead cook, Brian, an old guy in his thirties who'd worked for the restaurant since dirt was formed, ended up in jail for auto theft. He'd been drinking at Pandora's Box, a bar in Old Town, and took someone's black Toyota pickup. He claimed he'd mistaken the truck for his own, and thought he'd lost the keys, which explained why he put a rock through the driver's-side window and hot-wired the ignition. The problem was, Brian didn't own a vehicle. He'd owned a pickup years ago, but he sold it when his license got suspended for the first of his four DUI arrests.

I believed his story. I think he saw the pickup and thought, hey, it's my pickup! Where are my keys? Drunks do crazy things. The cops didn't believe him, though, and the restaurant needed to cover his shift. He wasn't going to be back any time soon.

The crew held a goodbye party while I worked. Davy told me that Leon had tearful hugs for everyone, and everyone had to "kiss the dying man." Near the end of the night, Leon hit on Laura, but by then he was plenty drunk. I chalked it up to the beer.

I meant to make it to Leon's party myself, but when my shift was over, I was too beat to move. I worked long hours at that restaurant. A dinner shift started at three in the afternoon, but the day guys were lazy, worthless bastards who never cleaned up after themselves, never stocked up for the next shift, or even changed out the trash cans. At any given time, two-thirds of them were on work release, mostly for drug or alcohol-related crimes. I couldn't just waltz in at three and start cooking dinner. I had to arrive an hour or two early every day and clean, stock my cooler, and check the reservation books to see what surprises Manager Tom had booked for the day. With Old Brian gone, I started at noon, doing prep alongside the chain gang. Then I'd cook dinner, sweating like a pork roast. By the end of the day, I was tapped out, which explains why I waited to do anything about Laura.

And it wasn't as if I never saw her. We worked together.

We did go to the park for a picnic the day after Leon left. Davy tagged along. We played on the swings, ate bologna, and rolled around in the dandelions. Davy brought his camera. I used up a roll of film on her. She was self-conscious, and I think I made her mad, snapping away like an idiot. I didn't care.

"Are you tired of that yet?" she asked me, pointing at the camera.

"No. Pretend I'm your photographer friend."

"But I'm not sitting on your lap," she joked.

"Very funny." I felt a stab of jealousy. Not a good sign. "Where are you from?" I asked. No one in Colorado was from Colorado. If she said California or New Jersey, I would leave her to walk home.

"Wisconsin."

"You're lucky," I laughed, without explaining. "What brought you here?"

"School," she said. "I had a friend at Colorado State University, and he said it was a good school. I want to get a degree in—"

"Where's this friend?" I interrupted.

"He's not a friend anymore," she said. She looked off to the mountains, lost for a moment, which made a nice photo. "What got you into cooking?" she asked.

"It was the farthest thing possible from English Literature."

"I love literature. What's your favorite book?"

"Anything by Jane Austin."

"You're kidding," she said. "I love Jane Austin! Guys don't usually like her, though. They think her characters are too whiney and selfish."

"Her characters are realistic," I said. "They're young people. They think about love, money and themselves."

That got a laugh. We sat in the grass and talked about books. I trashed Dickens; she defended him. She trashed Melville, and I made fun of her. All the while, I kept my eyes on hers. They were like a book, really. I got lost in the dream of them, imagining what she was like and calling it true. When I glanced at my watch, I found myself late for work. It must have been a good conversation.

Laura was at the restaurant nearly every day, covering shifts for waitresses with the usual emergencies— breakups with boyfriends, apartment evictions, and monthly biological trauma. And Leon was gone. Someone had to cover his shifts as well.

So we were both busy, but it wasn't like I ignored her. We did the flirting thing. One time, I saw just a glimpse of her hair at the left side of the order window. I stood waiting for her to do something. All of a sudden, her face comes out in front of the window, her chin bobbing across the shelf, no expression on her face, just a head, moving left-to-right. Then she was gone. I thought, what the hell? Then her head goes bobbing back the other way, only she was starting to laugh, and I laughed too.

"What are you doing?"

"I'm trying to get your attention," she explained.

"You look like a retarded puppet," I told her. It was sort of romantic.

There was also the burglary thing to worry about. Someone had hit the restaurant and made off with an undisclosed amount of money. The details were kept secret. I think Manager Tom was hoping someone would know too much and give their self away. All we knew for sure was that the theft was an "inside job" and that unless the money was returned, the police would step in, and Manager Tom "wouldn't be able to protect us." Whatever that meant.

I wouldn't have given it a second thought, except that the money walked out the night we went bowling, and the first person the police talked to when Manager Tom was done protecting us was me. On his way out that night, Tom saw my car still parked on the lot. We'd gone to the bowling alley in Leon's car. That made me a suspect.

I made the trip downtown to talk to a detective. They put me in a little room with a table, some pencils, and a legal pad, in case I wanted to unburden myself. The room smelled of other people's guilt, clinging to the walls like cigarette smoke. I thought I was a good guy, and yet here I was, answering questions. Go figure.

The detective had the idea that I was a hard-case, something he must have picked up from Manager Tom. "Are you happy at your job?" he asked.

"I love my job. How about you?"

"We're talking about some missing money here," he reminded me.

"Really? I thought we were chatting about our careers."

"Taking money is wrong," the detective explained patiently. "It makes you feel bad, even if you're a thief. People who steal from their employers work out elaborate rationalizations to help them feel better about what they've done. The people they work for are jerks, jerks who deserve to have something stolen from them."

"Nice guys work for jerks too."

The detective shrugged, and patted his shirt back into place. "I understand you have some college under your belt. What was your major?"

"English Lit."

"Why did you leave?"

I knew where the conversation was going. I cut to the bone to save time. "I had a run-in with a professor. He was a jerk."

"And I see from your file here that you had an arrest for assault last year. A bar-fight?"

"The guy was a jerk."

"You think everyone is a jerk, don't you?"

"You're not proving me wrong," I noted. He was too easy. I stood up. "I've got a bad attitude. If that's against the law, book me. But I don't steal. Either you're fishing, or you're stupid, because this is wasted time."

"Sit down," he barked.

"Screw you," I said. I headed for the door. For a few seconds, I thought the guy was going to blow a gasket and jump me. He was a cop— he could have gotten away with it. Instead, he sat sputtering in the chair while I headed down the hall.

That night, Laura asked if I wanted to go somewhere after work, but I was worried about the detective, and pissed at Manager Tom, so I wasn't in the mood.

"Too bad," she said. "I had something I wanted to show you." She wouldn't tell me what it was. She was angry that I wouldn't take her anywhere.

Work went badly. One table ordered medium-rare steaks, and returned them because they looked "pink inside." I guess they wanted the burned, dry sort of medium rare. Manager Tom was pretty sore, having to kiss up to a bunch of diners, or maybe he'd heard from the detective that I was uncooperative. Either way, his body language was classic Manager Tom, complete with folded arms, drumming fingers, rolling eyes, and overly polite manners. Cold, distant, passive-aggressive, self-important little prick. By the end of the night, I was furious.

Laura was done an hour before I was. She asked me to walk her out to her car, and I did, but I think I spent too much time venting about the boss. She slapped a manila envelope in my hand, and said, "This is for you."

"What is it?"

"I told you. I posed for that photographer guy, and he gave me a print. I thought you might like it."

She started to get in the car, but I stopped her. "Well wait a minute here," I said.

"I've got to go," she said. We kissed again, but it was hurried and clumsy. Then she was gone. I stood waving.

I opened the envelope. The flood lamp at the back of the restaurant lit the parking lot enough to get a good look at the picture. Laura was standing against a wall, smiling at the camera (or perhaps the Photographer). There was a framed picture on the wall behind her. She was wearing a short skirt, and a white tee-shirt. Her head was back against the wall. She looked out of breath. The shirt was wet, and you could clearly see her nipples through the material.

I stood staring at the picture for a long time. She wouldn't have given it to me, I reasoned, if she didn't want me. It was a sign, the kind of sign a guy prays for after years of dealing with mixed signals and misread clues. She wanted me. And I wanted her. The photographer had caught that smile of hers. How had he talked her into posing that way? No matter. The picture was suddenly my most prized possession. I put it back in the envelope and took it to my car.

I slept in late the next day, and worked the next evening. The days clicked by, just like that, one after the other, until Leon was back.

III

A lot of soldiers were coming back from Nam with limbs missing, so it shouldn't have been such a shock to see Leon with a shaved head, covered with a cheap wig. But seeing him shocked me anyway. He didn't look ill. In fact, he looked healthy. But that wig was a sign-post, reminding me that people get sick and die, and I couldn't take my eyes off of it.

Everyone in the restaurant gathered around to congratulate Leon on his return. He was gracious, seemingly overwhelmed by the attention. He shuffled and nodded, blushing like a glass of white zinfandel. Laura gave him a big hug.

I went off to set up for my shift. While I was working, the owner poked his head onto the cook's line. Ross was a thin, razor-nosed man in his early sixties. He was pleasant enough to your face. He took pains to remember our names and shook everyone's hand at the annual Christmas party. I'd been cooking at the restaurant for two years, which is a long time to stay in one place in this business, so it didn't surprise me when he wanted to chat.

"Too bad about this missing cash business," he offered.

"Too bad for you," I said. "I'd be pissed off."

He closed his eyes and nodded solemnly. "I understand they had you down at the police station. I hope it wasn't too unpleasant."

"No, it was instructive." He frowned. "I've never been there before," I explained.

He smiled. "You're a good boy, James. Tell me, how are things going around here?"

An order came up on the printer. Salmon, which was ironic, because Ross was fishing. "Things are going great."

"Tom treating you right? Is he doing a good job here? I value your opinion."

I tried to keep from laughing. In this business, if there's a theft problem, it's usually the manager that's doing the dipping. Ross was having second or third thoughts about Manager Tom. "Tom treats me okay," I said, trying to be casual. "He does a good job here. This is a complex operation, and he keeps a lot of balls in the air. He's a hell of a juggler." Tom was a jerk, but he was our jerk. Ross would have to go elsewhere for dirt.

But the visit got me wondering. Was Tom playing fast and loose with the cash? It wouldn't surprise me.

Davy was my only help on the line again, and we got rocked. They were on a wait at the front of the house, and people were willing to sit for more than an hour just to get a table for dinner. I had dozens of steaks on the grill at once. Most of them were rib-eyes. Rib-eyes are fatty steaks, which is why they taste so good, but the fat drips onto the burners and starts fires, so I had to keep moving the steaks around to open spots to avoid scorching them. Davy was snowed on his side of the line, and by seven o'clock, we were buried. When Laura popped her head in the window to ask what we were doing after work, I was a little short with her. All I really wanted was a hot shower and eight straight hours of sleep.

The wait staff finished before Davy and I did. Laura asked me to join Leon and her at the bowling alley, and I promised to meet them, but I wasn't in the mood for the noise. I just went home.

* * * * *

The moment I figured out that Laura and Leon were a couple came the following night. I'd tried to call her all day, and I was a little peeved that she wasn't there, patiently waiting to hear from me. When I got to work they were together, grinning like loons. "We have something for you," Leon said. He emphasized the word "we," like it was a big deal, and I started to get a little uneasy. Laura held out a small wrapped package, tied with thin red ribbon. I didn't take it.

"What's this?"

"A present," Leon explained. "You're our best friend, you know."

Laura was still holding the package out. Leon grabbed it from her and shoved it into my hands. I pulled on the ribbon, and the paper came loose. A trophy. The plaque on the front said, "World's Greatest Bowler." I stared at it as if it were a bowl of cereal.

"Do you remember?" he asked me. "You kicked my butt in bowling, just before my operation. We thought you'd like it."

I was being ungracious. "This is very nice," I said, smiling.

"After work, we're going downtown to TJ's," Leon said. TJ's was a pub in the old part of town—a small place, but they usually had a live band, and the beer was cheap. "You should join us."

"Sure," I said. From the corner of my eye, I could see her watching me, wondering if I was angry. I just smiled and smiled.

* * * * *

Three nights later she was pounding on my apartment door. "I need to get that picture back," she said. It had rained earlier. The night air was cold. She stood shivering, her arms crossed in front of her chest.

"Why?"

"I told Leon about it, and he asked me to get it."

A gust brought the first drops of another rainstorm. "You're freezing," I said. "Come on in."

She rushed inside, grateful for the warmth. "It's cold out there!" She paused. "Do you have the picture?"

I glared. I'd already lost her. The whole restaurant was cooing about what a "wonderful couple" Laura and Leon were. Still, I had no intentions of returning the picture. She'd given it to me, and that meant something. Or it meant nothing, in which case she was an arbitrary bitch, and she wasn't getting the picture back.

"It was a gift."

"I told Leon about it, and he thinks it would be wise if you returned it," she said.

That put me on a low flame, simmering. "And what do you think?" I asked.

"I think I don't want to argue with him," she said.

I nodded. "I can understand that. But if Leon wants the picture, Leon's going to have to ask for it in person. You gave it to me."

She wouldn't meet my eyes. I felt sorry for her for just a moment, and then the whole thing just struck me as funny, and I started to laugh, which was the wrong thing to do. She was caught in the middle, shivering like a child, and I was laughing.

"I think I'll leave now," she stammered.

When she left, I slammed the door. No use letting her think I was sorry.

* * * * *

I expected her to come back, of course.

I waited, and a day later, I was still waiting.

One of the mysteries of life is why the nicest, prettiest girls end up with the misfits. Leon had always seemed like a nerd to me. With his new hair, he was some sort of super-nerd, a complete pud. I couldn't figure out what she saw in him. Was there a vulnerability that she mistook as sensitivity?

Perhaps she needed a "project." Guys love to buy junk cars and restore them. Girls date "junk guys" and rehabilitate them. When guys are done with a car, they sell it, and get a new Junker. God help Leon when Laura finished "fixing" him.

I finally had a day off, and spent the morning hanging around the house. I wasn't too surprised when Leon came knocking. He had a car salesman's smile. The hairpiece sat on his head like a butterball on a baked potato. "Hey, how are you James?" he asked.

"Fine." I kept the door half-open.

"Well, are you going to let me in?"

I turned away, back into the apartment, leaving the door as it was. Leon followed me in with that energetic, old-man bounce of his, like somebody hopping with a stick up his butt. "How are you?" he repeated.

"What do you want, Leon? I'm kind of busy here."

"Really?"

There was a paperback on the kitchen sink. "I'm reading."

"Oh, that's great! What book?" He grabbed the book and stared at the cover. *Modern Critical Theory*. He frowned. "What is this?"

"It's a text, Leon. What do you want?"

Leon put the book down, relieved to change the subject. "Hey, Laura told me to come by and pick up that picture. Do you have it handy?"

Now, I knew Laura didn't tell him that. And I knew that Leon knew I knew. We were dancing, doing the steps civilized people do when they're pretending to be noble and courteous and considerate. But I was feeling surly and rude and honest, so I stopped dancing.

"I don't want to talk to you right now, Leon. And you're not getting the picture. Laura gave it to me."

Leon blinked, and stood there with his mouth open. Long, silent seconds ticked by. I had to rescue him—robbed of convention, he was helpless. "Now is when you go home," I told him.

He started for the door, and then stopped. "She loves me, you know." I smiled. The man could be honest after all.

"But she gave me the picture."

Leon turned and squared up. He was big, and I had to consider how a battle was going to come out. I was angry enough not to care, but after a few seconds, Leon started to waver. "She wants me to have the picture now. And I'm wondering what it means that you want to keep it."

"It means I like looking at her tits." Leon winced, but not as bad as I was wincing inside. I was doing what I did best, shooting off my mouth to throw smoke and cover my tracks.

"If you're in love with her, I guess I understand you wanting to keep it." He surprised me. It was a clever thing to say. I had the photo out of the desk drawer and into his hands before he could blink.

He gripped the photo like a table full of women holding onto a tip. "Thanks," he said. "This is—"

"That's all right, Leon," I said. "You should go now. I have reading to do. Don't worry, we're still friends." I stood by the door after he left, and then I spotted the book. I threw it across the room and spent the rest of the evening trying to wash away the taste of my last words with a six-pack.

* * * * *

"Do you think they'll figure out who took the money?" Davy asked.

We were knee-deep in orders, and one cook short on a Friday night. Davy had gotten clumsy with a pan of gravy, and we were slipping across the kitchen tile like cattle on skates. I didn't want to talk. They'd fired Manager Tom. No one mentioned the money, but we knew what it was all about. Ross brought a manager in from another one of his restaurants.

Big Chuck was no surprise. He was a fat guy in his late thirties, with a mustache that made him look like a sea lion. He had a jolly laugh, a quick temper, and he liked to flirt with the waitresses and talk about sports. I missed Manager Tom.

"I don't think they'll figure out who did it," I said, slapping steaks on the plates like a dealer throwing down cards.

"Do you think it was Manager Tom?"

"Maybe." But another idea had occurred to me. Why not Leon? He'd been there, watching Laura and I drive off that night. He'd been the last one to leave he parking lot. He had an expensive operation to pay for. Why not Leon?

Of course, I wanted it to be Leon. Laura had chosen him over me, and I wanted her choice to be a disaster. I wasn't comfortable with the vision of paradise they were showing the crew. As I cooked, sweating and slipping on gravy, Laura and Leon were telling Marjorie and the others about their dinner date the previous night. "The booths were tall, made out of dark wood, and they served water in pewter goblets. It was like the Middle Ages," Laura said.

"That's so romantic!" Marjorie gushed. Leon nodded, as if to admit a difficult truth.

"We just talked and talked."

I stared through the window. "Did you get any?" I asked in a serious voice.

It was the wrong thing to say. Marjorie laughed, but she was the only one. Even Davy shook his head.

Later, when business was done, and I was penned into the back half of the line by garbage and bits of meat, Laura poked her head into the window. Davy was off on his fiftieth bathroom break, so we were alone. "We're going out tonight. Would you join us?"

"I don't think so," I said. I pushed my way over the trash and faced her. "I'm going to be cleaning in here for the next two hours."

"I'm sorry you're hurt," she said.

"This isn't hurt. Sticking your hand in the fryer? That's hurt."

"I'm sorry."

"Your sorry isn't worth crap to me, Laura."

She knew I was mad, but she faced me straight up. Suddenly, the anger dribbled out of me, and I felt stupid. I was a young man in my early twenties, standing in garbage, earning a few cents above minimum wage, no prospects, with the full attention of my heart focused on a girl who belonged to someone else. And whose fault was it? I knew the answer.

"Catch me tomorrow," I said. "Things went like crap tonight, and I'll feel better tomorrow. Tell Leon we'll go bowling again. I feel like winning another breakfast."

She gave me a thin smile and left. Marjorie had been hovering behind her, listening, I guess. She stuck her head through the window, whispering, "For what it's worth, James, I think she chose the wrong guy. She's a sweet girl, but I can't believe she chose that liar."

"What do you mean?"

She gave me a sardonic frown. "Come on, James. Cancer? Who has brain surgery and goes back to work in two weeks?"

* * * * *

The rumors had already run through the restaurant. Most people were willing to give Leon the benefit of the doubt, despite the whispers. We were, after all, the children of Camelot. We believed what we were told. Watergate would change that, and leave a nation slightly less naive and full of bitterness.

As for me, I hadn't thought to question Leon's story. If asked, I'd have said he was a friend. Friends don't lie to each other.

I thought Davy, my fresh-faced little partner, was unaware of the gossip, but I was mistaken. At the end of the shift, we walked out to the parking lot, tired and dirty, without so much as a thank-you from Big Chuck. I asked Davy if he'd heard the rumors. "Oh yes," he said. "I even did a little digging at the school library. I don't think he had any kind of tumor."

"How did I miss this? Does everyone know?" I asked.

Davy snorted. "Everyone except you and Laura."

IV

All the dominos were in place, waiting for the first one to fall. Everything else would follow in quick order, the Rube Goldberg mechanism sending rows of sprawling dominos across our lives.

The first domino was a ketchup bottle.

Davy had the night off, and there were no other cooks to call for help. Big Chuck made a show of working with me at the two-spot, but he was gone most of the night. I worked alone.

Leon was in a foul mood. We were busy and short-handed, the two-pronged fork that has skewered restaurant employees since the business opened. No one was in a good mood, but Leon was angriest of all. One customer returned a medium steak. He slid it into the window and off the ledge. I caught the plate just before it hit the grill. Apparently unaware that he'd almost sprayed bits of porcelain over the food I was cooking, he stuck his face through the window. "She wants it medium! Do it right the first time!"

I checked the steak, opening the filet where the customer had cut into it." I held it up, showing Leon the steak. "It's a perfect medium," I said.

"No pink!" he shouted. "Do it right, and stop arguing with me!"

"I know you've only been waiting tables for a decade," I said. "So let me help you out. Medium is pink."

"Screw you!" Leon shouted. His lower lip jutted into full pout. He put both of his hands on the ledge, as if he meant to climb through the window. Thinking better of it, he pushed away, slamming into Marjorie, who was returning a bottle of ketchup from one of her tables.

The ketchup flew, striking the counter behind them, shattering into a million pieces, spraying ketchup against the walls, over the counter, and onto the bus boy, who was leaning back in Manager Tom's old corner. A dime-sized spot splashed back on Marjorie's white blouse. She stared at the stain like it was a bullet-hole. "Oh my God!" she said. "What's wrong with you, Leon?" The bus boy stood with his arms outstretched, covered in ketchup, looking like De Niro at the end of *The Taxi Driver*.

Leon had an apology handy, but Marjorie wasn't listening. "Why did you come back here? You should have stayed in Michigan with your fake doctor."

The other waiters froze. Leon pretended he didn't know what she meant. "What do you mean by that?" he asked. Mistake.

"I mean, you're a phony. You never had surgery. What kind of person would pretend to have a disease?"

"I had cancer," Leon insisted.

"Great. Show me the scar."

"What?"

"Show me the surgery scar, Leon."

Leon shook for a moment, and then headed out the door. "I don't need this," he hissed. Marjorie turned, and looked directly at me through the window.

Leon's losing it, I thought. But I didn't know how bad things were until the following morning.

None of the day cooks showed for work. Apparently they didn't like Big Chuck any more than the rest of us. Chuck called me in at nine in the morning. The sun was shining and everything.

I was setting up the line for lunch when Leon showed up. He was off, so he came dressed in street clothes. He called the waiters around, and when they were quiet, he began a little speech.

"There's been a lot of talk lately. Every place you go, you hear gossip, but there are rumors, and then there are rumors. Sometimes it's time to cut to the chase, and call a spade a spade. Lies have been told, and backstabbing—"

. . .has been stabbed, I thought.

"I think you know what I mean," Leon added, but I don't think anyone knew what he meant.

"Anyway, I'm only going to do this once." He grabbed his hairpiece, and lifted it, holding it up for a second or two. Then he put it back on his head, and left.

No one moved for a while. I stepped back, out of sight. It's one thing to sit in a pancake house and discuss the mind of a Hitler or a Manson, but it was another thing to come face-to-face with such a thing. I could imagine Leon approaching the bathroom mirror, leaning closer, his dull eyes glaring at the top of his head, his mind a black, empty, howling void.

When Leon lifted his hairpiece that morning, I saw the brownish-red square, complete with cross-stitching, cut into his skin. The wounds were less than a day old. Leon had taken a straight-razor to his head to keep the lie going.

* * * * *

Big Chuck let me go home for an hour that afternoon to shower before the night shift. Leon was waiting at the apartment. He sat in front of the door, his hairpiece pulled low over his eyes like the brim of a ball cap. He had no expression on his face until he saw me. Then he looked miserable.

"I need to talk to you," he said. "I need some advice."

I let him inside. "Listen to me," I started. "Let's say, hypothetically, that a guy wants a vacation but the job won't let him go." Leon started to protest, but I waved him off. "Let's say he tells one lie, a silly one at that, not meaning any harm, but it gets him what he wants, and more. He gets a little attention, which always feels nice."

He was all ears, so I kept going. "No harm done so far, but when he gets back from vacation, the poor guy has to answer a lot of questions, and each lie compounds the first one. Soon, he's chest-high in lies. What can he do?" Leon shrugged helplessly, his eyes anywhere but on mine.

"Here's the thing," I finished. "The shit-storm will die down, but the guy's got to get right with his friends. He's got to let them know that everything got out of control. No malice intended."

"Laura," he nodded. I'd meant myself, but I guess Laura needed to hear the truth, too. Leon grabbed my hand and shook it. "Thanks for the advice," he said in that goofy way of his, which made me feel like the old Leon was back. "It was kind of you to talk to me."

That night, no else came in to work. I ran the kitchen alone. I was pretty much fed up, and would have quit, but I thought it was wrong to leave a place in the middle of a shift. I kept my head down, which is why I didn't know that Leon had quit, no notice, or that Laura had broken up with him; something I'd have guessed in an instant if I'd looked into her eyes.

* * * * *

He was in his car, hunched behind the wheel, staring at the back door of the restaurant when I came to work the next day. When I went inside, I found Laura up against the wall, her lips clamped and her mascara running. She looked really cute. "He's out there, isn't he?" she asked.

"Leon? Yeah, he's in his car."

"We broke up last night, and he's been following me." She turned, a pleading look in her eyes. "Dating someone is all about trust, and he lied to me. He lied to everyone. How could I trust him?"

I shrugged. I was standing over her, one hand on the wall, feeling protective and smelling an opportunity, but the look in her eyes—a flutter, a hint of panic—made me step back.

"He wrote me a note."

"Were there threats?" I asked. "Because if there were, you can take the note to the police."

"No, no," she moaned. "The note was fine. But he left it *inside my apartment*. I lock my doors, James. He came inside, and left it on my table."

The sick feeling returned, like a sour ball of spit at the back of my throat. I thought of the razor cuts on his head, and I was suddenly afraid for her. I stepped out the back door, thinking that I would confront him then, but Leon's car was gone.

After my shift that night, I went back to my apartment. I'd been home long enough to open a beer and head for the shower, hoping to rinse off hours of grease and smoke, when the phone rang.

"James." The voice was just a whisper, and I almost hung up the phone. Then I heard something like a sob, and I realized who it was.

"Laura?"

Silence. Then, "Never mind. I'm sorry." She hung up.

I was out of the door in a moment.

When I got to her apartment, she wouldn't answer. I banged on the door, calling out to her. "Laura? It's me, James. Open up." I thought I heard her on the other side, but she wasn't saying anything.

"Please, Laura. It's James." She pulled the door open as far as the chain would allow. She was wearing a bathrobe. Her hair was wet and pulled straight back.

"I'm not dressed," she said.

"I didn't come to take you dancing." She undid the chain and stepped back.

We went to her living room. She sat on the couch, her legs tucked under her robe. She had no makeup on. Her face was scrubbed pink, which made her look younger. It was easy to forget, with that cocky attitude of hers, that she was a young woman just a few years out of high school.

"Are you all right?" I asked. I wanted to find out what had happened, but I was already afraid of the answer.

She sat without answering.

"Is there anything I can do for you?" I asked. I stood in the middle of the living room, my hands dangling at my sides like decorations. I should have been doing something, anything.

"There's nothing to do," she said. "I should never have called. I was upset. It was nothing."

"It was something," I said.

She started to cry then. I stepped toward her, reaching out, but it was the wrong thing to do. She yelped, cowering against the couch, and I jumped back. The sick feeling came again, and this time it would stay with me. I *knew* what had happened.

"We'll call the police," I said.

"No!" She seemed horrified.

"We need to call," I whispered.

"There are good reasons not to call," she said. "Everyone knew he was my boyfriend. And he has that picture. Who would believe me?" She shook her head and wiped at her eyes. "Besides, they'd let him out, let him out of jail, and he'd come back. He'd come back here."

I felt like vomiting. "What can I do?"

"Nothing," she said. Somehow she managed a smile. "I'll be all right, really." She closed her eyes. "I'm so sorry I bothered you. Would you please go now?"

I did what she asked. On the way home, I considered going to the police anyway. They could issue a restraining order. Perhaps they could keep a squad car on guard. But that was all silliness. There was nothing I could do.

Back in my apartment, I gave thought to other ways of helping her. I could go talk to Leon. But how do you reason with a man who'd slit his head with a razor to keep up a lie? I could threaten him, but if it came to a fight, he would win. He was older, and he outweighed me. Besides, how would beating him up help? Who would he blame, and who would he take it out on?

That's when I saw him sitting at my desk, facing the wall like it was a television.

"Leon. How did you get in?"

"Nice to see you, James. Did you have a nice visit with Laura?"

He turned the chair a little to face me, but I circled around to stay out of his gaze. "You don't mind if I change, do you? I asked, stripping off my shirt.

He kept staring. "Why, look at you. You have no chest at all," he mused. "You need to lift weights or something."

"No time for that," I said, adding a nervous laugh.

We chatted for a moment. I think we may have even mentioned the weather. It was hot, even in the middle of the night, which accounted for the sweat that rode his upper lip like a mustache.

"Laura's very upset," he said finally.

"Yes, she is."

"You know, I think she's at a point where she'd say almost anything. I saw her tonight, you know. Did she tell you that? She was very upset. I think she'd say anything to get even with me. I broke up with her, you know."

I knew he was lying. And he knew that I knew he was lying. He turned back to the wall. "We're friends, aren't we James?"

"Sure, Leon." I sat at the foot of the bed, watching him from behind. His voice was calm, even cheerful, and the words were soothing, but he'd broken into my apartment. My hands knew the truth. They were shaking.

"I'd never do anything to hurt Laura. You know that. Just like I'd never do anything to hurt you." He rocked back on the chair. "Friends ought to stick together, don't you think?"

I glanced to the side, at my bookshelf, and that's when I saw it. In that one moment, I knew what I would do. I moved quickly, so I wouldn't change my mind.

I grabbed the bowling trophy that Leon and Laura had given me. It had a marble base, and when I hit Leon in the temple with it, the corner punched a hole in the side of his head. He toppled out of the chair and lay flat on the floor, blood pouring onto the carpet. I remember thinking, I'd better clean that up, or I'll lose my damage deposit.

V

I only saw Laura a few times after that. We went bowling once, and had dinner once. I guess we were dating.

Then one day, she told me she was leaving town for a job in Denver. I helped her move. The week after she left, I drove down to help her paint the new apartment. When I showed up, the front door was locked, and nobody answered my knock. I could hear the radio blaring Cher's *Gypsies, Tramps and Thieves*, so I knew she was home. I went around to the back. She'd already started painting. The glass doors were open to let in the fresh air. I stepped through the curtains without saying anything.

She stood, her back to me, pushing a roller across the wall. She was in shorts, those legs of hers running most of the way up to her neck. She must have felt me behind her, because she glanced back.

And she screamed.

I'd known for a while that we weren't going to make it as a couple. The way her gaze darted when we were together, her forced smiles. The flinch when I brushed up against her told me there would be no happy-ever-after. The scream was a formal ending. After that, there was no pretense. And it wasn't just what Leon had done to her. Laura knew what I was capable of. I was the kind of guy who'd sneak up behind a man and bash his skull in.

And to be honest, nothing in my life before or after gave me as much pleasure as punching a hole in Leon's temple.

Laura was safe in Denver—as safe as a woman could be in a world full of men. I'd made certain of that when I put Leon down. But her scream was the picture that crowded out her smile in my memories, a snap-shot of what she thought of me, marrow deep.

I carry that memory with me now, years later. I hope she healed enough to share her life with a good guy, someone who would treat her like she deserved. Then I remember that she was with me, and she was with Leon. She had lousy judgement. And the world is full of men like Leon. And the Photographer. And me. I think her chances were pretty poor.

I was never prosecuted for hitting Leon, though the police didn't believe my story. I told them that I'd been startled by an intruder at my desk, and had hit without looking to see who it was. There were bits of truth in there. Leon had broken in, after all.

Leon didn't die, but he did need head surgery, which I find pretty funny. I shouldn't, but I do. When he was able to talk to the police, he verified my story. What was he going to do? Tell them what he'd done to Laura? Tell them he was there to threaten me? In the end, the assault charges were dropped. I stayed in town. Years later, I saw Leon at a convenience store, buying doughnuts. He looked old, like a Halloween pumpkin in November, whittled down and rotting. He stayed away from me, shaking a little at the sight of me, and I was comfortable with that.

By then, I worked in construction. I had married twice, and divorced twice. I took up serious drinking as a hobby, something I could excel at without breaking the rhythm of underachievement that would mark my life. I suppose I could have been a Literature Professor, or the husband of some clever, beautiful woman. Instead, I pound nails. I pour concrete. And I try to do the right thing, which takes all my energy.

There is one final piece of the tale, one last domino left to drop. All will be revealed, but the moral is hidden, waiting to be extracted. Nothing so simple as, "everyone has an evil side," though it would be convenient to believe the evil we do comes from a separate part of us. As if we could segregate our darkest impulses geographically, and have them removed. Like a tumor.

I sat in a downtown bar last December, drinking scotch, which I used to think tasted like good whiskey poured through a dirty sock. Now I think it tastes like Circe's nectar, the wine that helped Odysseus forget that his men had been turned into swine. Naphtha for the soul.

The bar was a black rectangle with a television on the liquor shelf—a night-light for the bartender to pour by. I liked that bar. Dirty glasses look clean in the dark.

Images of children flickered across the television screen. The sound was down, but I knew enough about Christmas specials to know that someone was probably rhapsodizing about the innocence of youth, as if we were all born pure and led astray, not the other way around.

At first, I didn't recognize the guy sitting next to me. When he ordered me a drink, I thought he was trying to pick me up. Hell, I still look good, and it's a modern world. To each his own.

He was always a pretty-boy, so it took me a while to recognize Davy through the puffy face and the red eyes. "How have you been doing?" I asked when I realized who he was.

Davy sold life insurance, which explained the blank, stare-at-my-forehead zombie gaze he was giving me. I was afraid that I'd be paying for the drink by listening to a sales pitch. Not even the twelve-year old scotch in front of me was worth that.

Instead, he wanted to reminisce. I let him ramble on, while I sipped and nodded. I told him I worked in construction, and he shook his head. "You were always better than that," he said. "I could never figure out why good things didn't happen for you."

I laughed at that one.

Then he let that last domino fall.

"Remember the missing cash at the restaurant? They never found out who was stealing," Davy confided. "Who do you think did it?"

I shrugged. I couldn't care less, but he wanted an answer, some conversation, and I might get another scotch out of him. "Tom, I think. Maybe Leon."

"Nope," Davy grinned. "Guess again."

I started to get that sick feeling, the one I got when I found out what Leon did to Laura. The one that comes when I remember the human race is a virus. I didn't answer him.

"It was me. I did it. I took the money. And here's the kicker—*you* gave me the idea. I took the cash box and stuck it in the mop bucket, and wheeled it out the door when I dumped the water. I put the cash box in my car, and drove it home that night. No one knew." He chuckled. "I mean, screw Manager Tom, right? Am I right?"

He seemed pretty happy with himself. I laughed, and stood up. "I'll be right back," I said. "I'm going to the bathroom."

I left Davy Milford there on the stool and headed for the front door. He'd put on a few pounds over the years, but his neck was still slender. I'd been working construction for a decade. I could have reached out and snapped that neck, snapped it like a twig. I could have pissed down his throat until he fucking drowned in it. It would have been justice.

But I left him alone on the stool and headed down the icy street, my fists jammed in my pockets, thinking about good and evil, and wondering if I had a clue about either one.

ABOUT THE AUTHOR

Brian Kaufman is the author of three novels, three novellas and three textbooks, a perfect symmetry he intends to break soon.

Kaufman lives with his wife and dog in the mountains of Laporte, Colorado. The home is practically zombie-proof.

In alternate universes, Brian is a pro wrestler, a lead guitarist for a blues band and a late-night radio talk show host. In this universe, he lifts weights, drinks beer and writes—all wonderful choices.

You can reach Brian via e-mail at:

brian@nunntelwb.com

Manufactured by Amazon.ca
Bolton, ON